The Elemental Witch Series

Father Sky has had enough. He has watched as the humans, created to be the caretakers of Mother Earth, destroy the Elements – Air, Water, Earth, and Metal. As humanity moves toward selfishness and greed, the importance of rituals to maintain the balance are all but forgotten.

While Mother Earth is angry, it is Father Sky who is on a rampage. The weather is his weapon of destruction. Civilization is in ruins. The Elemental Witches of Haven are the Resistance.

The Witches have dedicated their lives to the restoration of peace and harmony that can only come with equilibrium on Earth. When the renewal of the old ways of honoring our makers and sustainers—Sky and Earth—are attained, then there will be amity.

Until then, the Witches of the Isle of Haven fight fire with Fire.

The battle blazes on.

Resistance

Fiona Angelica Quinn

Caste System of the Mundane

THE SIGNIFICANTS

Enforcers

Proprietors   Intelligentsia

Defenders

Seers   Artists & Musicians

Productors

The Untouchables

Prologue.

My mother named me Ember when she first took me into her arms. The small, sustained glow of Fire in her hearth had caught her attention as she rocked me to sleep. As she contemplated that element, she felt the Fire alive in me - the ability to warm and nurture, or rage into an inferno. And she was right on both counts.

I became a soldier in the Resistance when I returned to the Range, in the same wooden boat that carried me to the Isle of Haven when I was five years old. There I studied the ways of Haven Elemental Witches. I was part of the rhythm in the dance of my ancestors. Since the Inquisition, it had always been thus-an ebb and a flow.

A Haven Elemental Witch was born in the Range in the world of the Mundane, then sent to the island of Haven as a *Youngling* to be instructed in magic. Steeped in the traditions that our makers, Father Sky and Mother Earth, held dear, we returned to the world of the Mundane as young adults. Here, we'd use our skills to unravel the pain caused by humans toward each other, toward Earth, and toward Sky. These were our *Offling Years*. With success, Witches returned to Haven in their twilight as revered Elders. These Wise Men and Wise Women held the responsibility of training the next generation of Witches as they, small and trembling, stepped off the wooden boats, moving toward their destinies.

The Mundane called Witches "devil worshipers." Witches didn't believe in the devil. We didn't invoke the devil. We didn't revere or serve the devil.

But the world was in turmoil. Weather was an enemy that no weapon could thwart. No amount of plotting and planning and strength could foil the might and wrath of Nature. The Mundane needed a scapegoat, something tangible they could point to, and they decided to point to the Witches and our adoration of Satan. Witches thus became the enemy to be routed and removed.

The Mundane hunted us. They tried to destroy us.

What they didn't understand was that their violence and abuse of Mother Earth was at the root of the problem. Earth was devastated, her heart was broken. After all, in the very beginning, humanity had been conceived by our Mother and Father and given powers with which to bring about harmony. Everything from our intellect, to our compassion, to our opposable thumbs was given to us as gifts to help the greater whole. To caretake the Elements, the flora, and the fauna. To do ritual for Earth, and Sky.

As humans turned their back on their gifts, over time they became Mundane. The Mundane feared the power of those that held tight to their beliefs and rituals. And the Mundane far outnumbered the Witches who were left. The sheer number of the Mundane gave them their power, where the Witches' connection to the Elements gave us ours.

With fewer Witches to do ritual and greater numbers of Mundane to wreak havoc, Father Sky lashed out at the destruction that had been wrought against Earth—the pollution that choked the air, the strip mining that leveled her majestic mountains, the shifting temperatures that hurt our Mother's beloved animals. And while Earth would shake and spew her anger, Sky raged to see his love so mistreated.

As Sky continued to rage, human survival was on the cusp.

In their fear, the Mundane dredged up the dark times of the Inquisition, the balefires were lit. Witches were burned at the stake and thus driven underground. Sadly, and so horribly misguided, the Mundane had set about ridding the world of the very thing that would save them, save us all.

The Elemental Witches.

Chapter One

I sat in the back seat, staring out my window as the car rumbled over the debris strewn roads. I stretched my mind toward the sun. My lips formed the ancient invocation, pulling down the energy, the strength that I'd need. Soon, we'd reach our destination. Soon, I'd be trying to pull off a "magic act," in the Mundane sense of the word. My success would depend on my body and training more than my ability to manipulate the energies around me. But a little sun wouldn't hurt. A little sun almost never hurt.

Gareth broke into my thoughts. "Ember, is everything okay?" His voice was deep and resonant. His face chiseled, masculine, made moody by the scruff of whiskers painted over his jawline. He wore the whisper of bad-boy like a heady cologne. It made women sway their hips when they walked by him, blushing at their secret thoughts.

"I'm daydreaming." I offered him a smile. It didn't come easily to my lips. Perhaps he'd interpret my expression as wistful, or preoccupied. If I was going to pull this off, he couldn't be suspicious in the least. I reached out a hand and rubbed his arm, hoping the

1

contact would make him feel warm inside, relieving any apprehensions I might have sparked. I turned back to the window, using it as a mirror to watch his reaction. He seemed preoccupied, as well.

I reviewed my mission steps in my mind. Gareth's movements were as important to this dance as mine were. Perhaps more. He had to end up on the mark at the exact right time, or I would fail. That was my job. One of my jobs. Get him in place. The right place at the right time.

Our car swerved from the right side of the road to the left, down the center, over to the left again as our driver avoided the chunks of building that still lay in the roadway; the debris from the latest tornado that ripped through the city. The latest angry swat that Father Sky took at the humans who had made such a mess of things. "My turn," Father Sky seemed to say, as he made his humans scramble to survive his fury.

But today he was tranquil. Not a single puff of clouds marred the azure blue expanse overhead. Above, it was clean and pure. A stark contrast to the filth and destruction all around us.

Our driver turned the corner. The engine choked and sputtered but functioned well enough. The cars that did exist were held together with a wish and a prayer. Coddled and prodded into use. It had been about thirty years since the last car had rolled off an assembly line. Today, ours was the only car on the road. Most vehicles that could be powered by eco energy had been seized for emergency use by the defenders, as ambulances, or were used for transportation inside the part the city that was held by the Significants of the Proprietors-the haves in a world of have-nots.

We had use of this car and driver because Gareth was a liaison between the two largest Proprietors enclaves. Gareth threaded the needle that sewed the interior world populated by the consumers to the exterior, left to the *Productors*— those who produced the foods and other goods— and fought for survival outside the enclaves. Out here, without the right channels, without the right connections, it was a hard -scrabble existence.

There were others in the modern caste system, the Intelligencia, the Seers, the artists, and musicians. The outcasts suffered the greatest in this modern age of misery. The outcasts, or untouchables as some called them, had always borne the worst conditions in any age. As I thought this, we passed a skeletal man sitting naked and vacant-eyed with his begging bowl resting in his lap. He was probably hoping someone would drop him a crust of bread. But bread right now… This last storm had blown through just as the harvest was about to come in. The people had run into the fields saving what they could, until survival tomorrow was not as precarious as survival in the moment. They had sought shelter from the onslaught, mourning the loss of the food, terrified by what that would mean to their future. To weather this never-ending storm.

I shifted uneasily in my seat. I didn't like that there were so may eyes on us. I sensed them behind the curtained windows and blinds as we motored by. They hid in the shadows of the ruins that dappled either side of the road. This car made us stand out. It made people look at us with curiosity. I pulled my hood up over my auburn hair and hid my silhouette in its depths. I didn't want anyone to be able to describe me later.

There wasn't a choice but to take a car out on this mission, I reminded myself, trying to quell the apprehension that danced in my stomach like the flames of a bonfire.

Still, this scenario made me uneasy.

Those who sought an extra ration of rice or a pair of shoes might be documenting our movements. Writing down our license plate on a scrap of paper. Running the information into the police station. Finding a willing ear.

I breathed slowly in, expanding my lungs, imagining that I could gather my nervousness and release it with my exhale. I did it again. And again. On the fourth time, I felt more settled.

This step that Gareth and I were about to take should be over before the authorities could get here to ask questions. And should they ask, Gareth had the necessary papers in his coat pocket. But with Fortune's smile, we wouldn't need to produce them.

This morning when I pulled my card from the Tarot deck, I was offered the Chariot as my day's foretelling – it was the fastest card in the deck when it came to change and movement. I wondered, knowing what my task was to be, if Fortune hadn't offered it to me today in a bid at humor. I didn't find it very funny. Terrifying might be a better word.

Our car pulled up alongside an iron gate. A decrepit building dating back hundreds of years stood like an old man in a too-worn coat. Haphazardly patched and looking like it just didn't care anymore, this building was living out its life until the inevitable collapse into its foundation.

"We've stopped," I said, edging a question mark into my voice. I sent Gareth a confused glance.

Gareth patted my knee. "I have a quick business stop before we head to the meet up." He swept his fingers through his raven hair. It was cut close on the sides, leaving the top a little long and unruly. Soft. Touchable. The kind of hair that a woman liked to tangle her fingers into. He used his attributes to get what he wanted. He *thought* he wanted me, so he upped his subtle qualities of seduction.

And I pretended to succumb.

I slipped my hand into his, giving him a little squeeze. I sent a bit of warmth down my arm to ensure that he'd interpret the gesture as one of affection. His eyes told me he got the message.

Good.

"You don't mind waiting for me in the car, do you?" Gareth asked, stroking his finger across my cheek.

I offered him a little frown and a sad huff of air before I pulled my hand away, pulling all the warmth with me. I folded my hands and looked down at my lap. "No," I said, making sure it sounded like a lie. Letting him know that I most certainly did mind.

He smiled with the tolerance of an adult dealing with a child. Bemused, at their antics even if they were mildly irritating. He dragged my hand back into his, popped open his door and pulled me along with him. "You can come. This will only take a moment."

I sent the warmth back along my arm, over my hand, and into his fingers. A reward. I wondered if he knew what I was doing, manipulating him this way. I wondered if he felt it on a conscious level or whether it was information picked up on a deeper plane. I had never been without the power of the elements. I was hard pressed to understand how the Mundane functioned with the few senses they had. Not enough information. It must be awful. Those kinds of thoughts were for another time, I reprimanded myself. Now, I needed to be focused. Every little thing could make this mission a success, or could bring death.

Gareth and I held hands as we moved under the stone archway into the building. The stairs that we took to the first level were littered with random objects of human life. Battered, ripped, and useless, they were coated in the powdery filth that had been whipped up by the gusts, grinding their way into any little opening, and settling as the winds blew themselves out.

My gaze took in the whole of the space, as I plotted my future moves. It looked like whoever had lived here had abandoned the location. It was more likely, though, that they cringed in fear behind barricaded apartment doors. I could taste anxiety in the air, bitter and salty. It made saliva pool in my mouth.

"Wait here," Gareth said as we reached the landing.

The air here was damp and smelled of mildew. Particulates danced in a stream of light coming from a tall window. I sneezed violently. And that made Gareth chuckle with a "well you wanted to come" gleam in his eye.

I did as I was told and waited as he moved off, but I widened my aura, expanding at the same pace as Gareth's strides. He reached a door, letting a key scrape into the hole. I felt the temperature of the metal grow warmer as he wrapped the knob with his hand and twisted to the right. Sleeping hinges screeched their disapproval as they were wrenched open. Men's voices conferred. There was the hard sound of fist to flesh. A yelp and moan of pain. The door banged shut and hurried footsteps followed as Gareth moved his way back to me, sliding the door key into his pocket. A smile on his face. Victory in his eyes.

As he approached, I sent my awareness snaking along the opposite corridor, counting hotspots that indicated people. Two guards outside. No idea how many might be in that room that Gareth had locked behind him. I'd assume there were two. Two outside, two inside would make sense to me. "Good?" I asked, sliding my ring of keys down my leg, to my foot, to the ground, and leaving them there as I stepped forward.

"Excellent," he kissed me with an exuberant smack then wrapped his hand around my arm just above the elbow. Propelling me forward, skipping us lightly down the steps, he whistled a happy tune. Out the door, under the arch, and back beneath the glorious November-blue sky, we made our way toward the chauffer who stood at attention.

Gallantly, Gareth walked me to my door on the street-side of the car and opened it with a flourish. I laughed at his antics, because I knew he wanted me to, then my eyes lit with horror as the blur of a black vehicle took the corner at high velocity.

Gareth jerked toward the screech of tires rounding the curve.

I reached out and shoved him with all my strength. Gareth flew backwards, collapsing over a rock, swirling his arms through the air to regain balance.

In the split second I perceived he was clear of danger, I took another step forward into the path of the barreling car. I gathered my energy and bent my knees. The cage protecting the grill and lights was next to me. And just as we had practiced in the meadow, I grabbed the top and middle bars, and pushed as I vaulted upward. I uncurled my clamped fingers, letting my body touch down on the hood as my teammate kept his foot down on the gas pedal. Pulling my limbs into a tight ball, I slammed into the windshield, bounced up to the roof.

He kept driving at breakneck speed.

I had no time for thought. No time to register pain. I lengthened my body, yanked my arms in tight to my chest – a buffer of protection for my ribs—tucked my chin, and crossed my legs at the ankle as I rolled over the top, down over the trunk, then slammed onto the dirt-covered pavement. I fought against the scream that wanted to erupt from my throat, that wanted to give me away. I kept it caged behind my clenched teeth.

That hurt a lot more than in my practice runs.

I rolled a few more times to distribute the energy I had gathered in these theatrics but loosened my limbs, so I'd seem unconscious. And now that my forward momentum had stopped, I held myself perfectly still in the middle of the street.

It took immense concentration and trust not to flinch, as the rampaging car spun three-sixty and headed back my way. It took enormous self-discipline not to at least peek to see how Gareth was receiving this turn of events. I curled deep inside myself. Deep. Deep, into the meditative abyss where I didn't need air to circulate through my system, didn't need my heart to pump. I was barely aware of the fingers pressed to my neck, checking for signs of life. Gareth grabbed my collar and gave me a hurried and graceless tug, which at least moved me out of the path of the racing tires.

Gareth yelled to his driver. "Go. Go. Go!" Doors banged. And Gareth's car was chased down the street, leaving me behind like more rubble to accumulate amongst the destruction.

Still, I didn't move.

I did allow myself a breath.

My heart beat picked up its pace as it worked to disperse air through my system.

A siren advanced on my position. Thank the Fates, my team had staged so closely. Some part of me thought perhaps a benevolent soul from the Productors might rush into the street and try to save me, when saving was the very last thing I needed or wanted.

My friends from the Resistance, who had "borrowed" an ambulance for this event, weren't very gentle as they put me on the gurney and covered me with the sheet that served as a shroud. They shoved the stretcher into the back, slammed the door, and drove around the block. They pulled into the alleyway and along its length until they were positioned by the front door of Gareth's building for a quick getaway, yet still shielded from sight.

Piper yanked the sheet from my face and peered down at me. Her hair was a glittering shade of blond somewhere between platinum and grey that confused people about her age—though, she was nineteen, just like me. We had been in the same village school back home on Haven, even if we were in different classes—her elemental affinity was air, and mine was flame. Still, that confusion about her age had served the Resistance well. Piper was a true chameleon with her disguises. "Did you get it?" she whispered.

I held up the key that I had grabbed from Gareth's pocket as I pushed him away.

"Amazing," she said, clapping her hands together.

"Yes." I said, sarcasm dripping from my voice. "I'm doing perfectly fine after the gymnastics act with the runaway car. Thanks for asking."

She waved her hand in the air. "We'll have time for that later. How many guards are inside?"

"Four if I'm guessing correctly."

Her face set in a grim line.

"I can do it" I insisted.

Chapter Two

Kael, dressed in an emergency operator's uniform–a bright orange jumpsuit with stripes of reflective material to make him stand out amongst whatever horror was unfurling—popped the door open with a look of trepidation on his face. He heaved a great sigh, when he saw my eyes open. "You're alive. Unbelievable." He reached out and pinched me, and I yanked my leg away from him.

"I have enough bruises for now," I said, reaching for the hands he extended to help me. I lifted myself off the stretcher. Every muscle in my body screamed angrily that I should lie still. But there was no time for that. We had no idea how small our window would be. Surely, everyone inside Gareth's building knew that there was a drama unfolding outside. Would this make them curious? Or would they think it some minor tumult not worth inspection?

I stood at the back door as Piper rubbed a dampened cloth over my clothes and pulled a comb through my hair, making me presentable again. I swirled a blurring spell to soften the look on my face, hiding signs of pain and worry. Piper looked me over. "Better," she said. "I think you'll do, if you can hold that blur in place at least until you're past the initial contact."

I nodded and moved to the front of the building and under the arch. I took the now familiar steps two at a time as I sent my awareness down either side of the corridor. Two heat signatures, one approaching.

"Oh, hey," I said with an embarrassed smile and a tight wave. "I think I dropped my keys when I was in here with Gareth Cordrill." I continued up the stairs as if that name gave me a pass for being anywhere I liked. If this guy had been watching out the window when the tires screamed their warning sounds, then this charade was futile. I searched out the other heat source. Not far, but far enough. In my body's present state of tenderness, I only wanted to take on one guard at a time. And as quietly as possible.

"There they are." I pointed to the keys I had dropped earlier and waited for him to bend at my service. Surely, he would want me to tell Gareth he was courteous. As he reached out, I pushed his head down hard, using my body weight until I felt a resounding smack against the stone stairway. His arms flew out wide to catch his balance, stunned both by the impact and the improbability of what was happening. I gathered the cloth at the top of his shirt in one hand and his belt in the other, forcing him forward, and ramming his head against the carved balusters of the staircase, then yanking him back toward the wall. He flung his head up, searching for equilibrium.

That last hit to the back of his head put him out. With another push and with the help of gravity, he tumbled down the stairs.

The noise brought the sound of feet pounding heavily against the stone floor in the hallway. I reached a finger into the air and swirled a circle above my head, casting a glamour around me. It would hold best without movement, this veil of protection. The man was a beast. Huge. Daunting. I pulled the energy I had gathered earlier from the sun and sent it throughout my body, lifting my own strength with the power of its rays.

He leaned over the side of the banister, saw his colleague in a pile, and searched the area for the reason for this scene. He ran for the stairs and as he passed me, I merely stuck out my foot, tripping him. He reached out and grabbed the handrail as he plummeted forward. His feet went out from under him, and he dangled from his grip. I sidled up behind him. Taking advantage of the confusion, I reached out to cross my arms in front of him. I grabbed his chin in one hand and his shoulder in the other, I used the sun's strength and body weight to yank in opposition until I heard the crack of his vertebrae snapping.

Two down. Limited noise. I grabbed a stitch in my side that threatened to double me over. I had to take a few precious moments to scramble into the shadow and catch my breath.

Once again, I reached out my awareness. The only thing I found in the corridor was cold still air.

My back pressed to the wall, hugging the shadows, I moved silently toward the door. Thank you, Gareth, for showing us how to find the good Dr. Brighton right down to the room he was held in. I reached into my pocket and retrieved the key. I could get in without a key, but this was easier and a sure thing while lock tumbling magic most definitely was not. Attempting and failing an entry could mean noise. My magic techniques worked best on empty rooms. If the room was occupied, it would bring early detection and no surprise. Surprise was crucial to success. It was always one of my most useful weapons.

I assumed that the fight was about to get harder. There would certainly be at least two guards inside. And they'd be armed. As I slipped the key into the lock, I sent up my second prayer of gratitude to Gareth. He'd proved a very useful contact, and I was sad that I'd had to sever that relationship. But this was the only scenario my team had been able to come up with. My playing dead as necessary as anything else. If I had simply related this information to the Resistance and handed off the key, Gareth would have me killed. Play-dead was much happier than for-real dead. Besides, he spent most of his time at the Northern Enclave, so here in the south I should be able to stay in the background. *Should.*

Before I turned the key, I reached my hand up and placed it on each of the three hinges, sending warmth. I spoke to the metal, "Friend, please, allow me to pass unannounced." I waited until an affirmation tickled my fingers. With a twist of the key in the lock. I turned the knob. The door edged open without the screeches of dismay that had accompanied Gareth's entrance. Without that alarm of sorts sounding, the room's occupants went on about their business. A man stood at the window, a hunting knife on his belt. A second man sat on a sofa with his playing cards spread before him. A solitaire game held his attention. Neither spoke.

There, on a chair in the middle of the room sat the man I hoped was Dr. Brighton. Well, it was somebody that they wanted captive. The man was tied up. His face was bloodied and bruised. His eyes had swollen to mere slits, and his breath came in labored gurgles. Could he walk? What would I do if he couldn't walk?

I inhaled as if I were about to dive from the high boulder on the side of the cliff down, down, down into the sea below. It was a test of courage back on Haven. Every student was required to make that dive over the cliff daily in our last year of school. It built resistance to the inevitable anxiety – the fear of death or disability. Fear of inescapable pain that came with every plunge. It developed a mind that could quickly process and act after crashing through the surface of the icy waters. I inhaled a breath in exactly the same way to remind my system that I'd faced frightening things many times before, and I always walked away. I'd walk away today too, I told myself. I cast a spell:

Pele, Goddess of Power, I call to thee.

Fleet and strong,

I undo this wrong

So I speak it, so mote it be.

My prayer was quick; time was of the essence. I could imagine that once Gareth had dodged the chase car, he would come back for my remains. He was a spirit that danced between the dark and the light. Above and below. The night and the day. Up until this point, I had represented the things that brightened his soul. Warmth in a cold and austere world. Yes. He'd be back. And when he didn't find my body, he'd begin his search. He'd discover this scene I was creating. I needed to be long gone.

Throwing the door open, I burst into the room. I moved without hesitation, planting my foot on the coffee table where the stalled card game lay. I clipped the player under the chin with a hard kick from my metal-toed boot, before he could even register the intrusion.

The man at the window had the hilt of his knife wrapped in his hand. The glittering blade sliced the air. If my dear friend Gallium were here, she'd simply ask the metal to forgo its edge and round into something benign. I couldn't manipulate metal beyond offering warmth and gaining cooperation. I couldn't conjure a breeze to float dust and dirt into this man's eyes like Piper could. My affinity was the flame. And here, I saw nothing to manipulate to my advantage. Nothing to help me as the enforcer slashed the razor-sharp edge toward my face. I had nothing but my training standing between me and this blade.

I bent backward, allowing his thrust to carve the air in front of me. I twisted at the waist, using the momentum of the move to bring my leg around to smash into his ribs. The metal toe of my work boots broke the thin flexible ribs beneath the man's jacket. He gasped out, realizing this was a fighter's fight. The dainty young woman who'd barged through the door wasn't here for tea.

I yanked my knee to my chest and thrust out, planting my heel into his solar plexus, expelling any air that he had breathed in, confusing his diaphragm into convulsions that would not let him take up another breath. The blade hooked up over his head and slammed down toward my heart. I backflipped, feeling the impact of his swing on the heel of my boot. The power of my legs as they whipped around forced the knife from his hand. I heard the rip and twang as it stuck in the wall.

Purple faced, eyes bulging, mouth open, biting the air around him, the guard tried to find oxygen to fill his lungs. He reached out and snagged me in a bear hug. He lifted me from the ground. Compressing my ribs in his powerful grip, he placed me in the same dire straits that he was.

Sun, God of power and light.
Bring your strength to me, I pray,
I need your energy for this fight,
So I might live another day.

I closed my eyes and in the nanosecond of time I thought my prayer, I imagined the Sun surrounding me in golden warmth, I imagined myself as a sponge, sopping up the rays. I lifted my arms toward the light and popped the man's hold free.

He lowered his shoulder and rammed forward, trying to catch me in a tackle and drive me to the floor. But I was able to spin backward toward the wall, toward the hilt stuck in the plaster. I dragged the blade from its resting spot, twirled the weapon in my fingers until the knife-point faced the enforcer. My back to the wall, I braced my elbow and allowed him to impale himself on the blade with his own forward momentum.

Just now able to suck in his first sliver of air, he looked down at the gash across his stomach, and covered it protectively with his hands. His eyes rolled back in his head, and he slipped into death.

The smell of bowel filled the room.

I made my way quickly to the other guard. No one could be left alive who could describe me. I inspected him. My boot had crushed his trachea. He was no longer a problem.

Dr. Brighton's brows were in his hairline, his eyes stretched wide against the swollen flesh of his eye sockets. I tasted the fear he sent out in waves from his skin. It tasted like soured milk and made my stomach heave.

"I'm from the Resistance. I'm here to help you."

Dr. Brighton shook his head in disbelief as I cut the rags that bound him in place.

"Up we go." I pulled his arm over my shoulder, and he howled. "Sorry." I lowered the arm back down, wondering what they had done to him during his captivity. Beat the living daylights out of him was a given. But how badly? Could he walk? That was my most pressing question.

I got behind him and squatted with my hands under his armpits. I registered the moisture of his fear-sweat as I hoisted him up. "Sir, if you want to survive. You have to walk. You have to move."

My pep talk did nothing. He swayed on his feet, and I thought for sure he'd collapse. How much time did I have to get him down the stairs?

I rounded in front of Dr. Brighton and pulled his arms over my shoulders, wearing him like a backpack. "I can't do this alone, sir. Move your feet. Come on Dr. Brighton, freedom is just down the stairs. I have an ambulance waiting for you. One step. Good. Okay another. Come on!" My voice ratcheted up as I kept my awareness on the wind shifting with the forward movement of an approaching car. It was getting ever nearer. "Dr. Brighton, please. They're coming!"

Chapter Three

*K*ael stood at the bottom of the steps, the tension around his eyes made the dark coloring seem more pronounced, blacker and flinty. He saw that I was all but dragging the weight of a man much taller than me and ran up the flight taking three steps at a time with his long legs. "These two down here are dead."

"Good," I whispered on my exhale. I was using up my reserves quickly.

"I'll get the torso." Kael maneuvered behind the now almost unconscious Dr. Brighton. I pushed backward to lower Dr. Brighton into Kael's waiting arms then bent and scooped up the man's legs. Like that, we ran forward, under the arch and out to the ambulance.

Piper was waiting with an ink sponge and piece of paper. As we loaded him onto the gurney, she pressed three fingers into the black ink and made a print. Comparing the prints to what was in her file, she looked up and nodded her head. "We've got him."

"Not for long," I said, hefting the foot end of the gurney into the ambulance with Kael taking the head.

They both swung their faces toward me. Kael was Mundane and wouldn't have the ability to sense. But Piper... Her face lifted, and she turned in the direction of the wind swirl. "Black crows at night, he's coming. Gareth!"

Kael looked confused as we backed away from the interior, allowing Piper to slam the back of the ambulance shut.

"Women's intuition," Piper said, sending Kael a marked look of pity that he was born with XY chromosomes, then dashed toward the driver's door. Off they flew.

And I, I was left behind to determine what repercussions might come from our counter measures.

I jogged across the street with my hood covering my head and shadowing my face. I hoped that the noise of anguish had forced people to hide in their homes rather than watch and bear witness. It was safer for them if they saw nothing. Safer for us, too. I clawed my way up the broken edifice of the building sitting cattycorner to Dr. Brighton's recent prison. I hid amongst the gargoyles, shuffling about until I found a position where I was supported and could hold still for a while. There, I would wait for the car to come to a stop before I cast a glamour to help hide my presence.

Glamours were a dangerous business. All of us who grew up on the Isle of Haven were well practiced at this basic ability to mask our presence, or the presence of some object we wished to safeguard. But one never knew how effective it was. There were some amongst the Mundane who had natural talents. They even had

24

an ancient phrase, "I can see right through you." This phrase actually began as "I can see right through your glamour." It was shortened over time. But it remained ever true. A glamour was a good tool. A useful tool. But not a tool that one could depend on. Right now, it was the best I could do.

As the adrenaline and sunlight left my system, the great weight of fatigue burdened my ability to pay attention. Even though I could now see the car tracing its way toward me, I had trouble staying sharp and aware. A nap- what a luxury it would be just to close my eyes for a few minutes. To rest. To recuperate. My eyelids grew heavy…

The crunch of gravel punched a boost of adrenaline into my system. It woke me up, alright. I slipped a glamour into place and peered down to watch Gareth climb from the back of the car. The energy he gave off was a combination of grief and confusion. He stood with his hand on the door, his gaze scanned the environment- over the ground, up the buildings, along the roof tops.

My cells screamed to run, but my training was louder. A flinch, a bat of eyelashes could give me a way, even hidden as I was behind my spell. I mimicked the gargoyles around me and willed myself to be a statue.

Gareth called toward the edifice of his hidey-hole, then walked down the street to examine the place I had hit. He followed my roll, then his drag. He squatted for a long moment, fingers in the dirt, tracing the marks left by the gurney wheels, the number of footsteps.

25

He walked the tire tracks until they turned the corner. His gaze focused back on his building, he stalled. Then, he took off at a run, calling out to his men, using their names.

I wished he hadn't done that.

Over and over the names were called and each one was a hammer swing driving that name deeper into my conscious. I had killed four men with my own two hands. Four *more*. Four to save one. Four from the dark to save one of the light. Still, it seemed disproportionate, even if necessary.

This was the dark side of Gareth, playing out below me. The Gareth who was willing to saunter into a locked room, punch a man who was tied in place, and walk away whistling a happy tune.

Why Gareth had captured Dr. Brighton, I didn't know, exactly. But I did know that Dr. Brighton knew too much about the Resistance and its players to leave him in Gareth's hands. Dr. Brighton knew too many names. Too many faces. Too many locations, and routes, and goals.

My goal had been to save Brighton. To bring him back to further our work of breaking down the barriers to survival and allowing all the caste—not just the Proprietors—to have the necessities of life. Maybe even a little more than the necessities, maybe even a bit of hope and respite from worry.

To do that, the Resistance must be protected at all costs. If I had failed in my prioritized goal to retrieve Dr. Brighton, I was tasked with killing him. We couldn't afford the liability of allowing him to live. Killing a man of the light so he would not succumb to the dark was something I was loathe to do, no matter how essential. I had cast a spell last night so that wouldn't be necessary. Tonight, I'd perform a ritual of thanksgiving.

"The Gods be damned." Gareth's voice echoed as he emerged from the building throwing a punch at the air, then planting his hands on his head.

He should know how dangerous such a curse was to utter. Of course, he was Mundane and wouldn't put the words and what played out afterwards together. I bet he didn't hear the low rumble in the distance—Father Sky's reply.

Gareth was looking around as if for a direction. A next step. He moved to his car and climbed in. From the roof top where I perched, I had a long view. I followed his path as the car drove away from this part of town toward the university. I bet he was headed to my dorm. I bet he was going to talk to Piper. I hadn't thought of this. No one had. Would he try to take her hostage? Would he hurt her?

In this age, there was little we had in the form of communication systems. Those that existed, belonged to the Proprietors, and even they used them sparcely, as every syllable uttered was scrutinized by the defenders at the behest of those highest up amongst the Significants, the Noble and Highborn families. No one liked taking those kinds of risks.

But those from Haven had the means unavailable to the Mundane. I had read that in World War II there had been a group of indigenous peoples in the Americas who spoke their ancient tribal language to pass information, a language that was never decoded by their enemy. Ours was such a form of communication. Only by another Haven Witch could a message be received. I hid where other eyes would be thwarted and pulled a box of matches from my pocket. Striking the Sulphur-covered head against the rough surface of the roof, I waited for the fire to burn fat and strong before I told it the information I needed sent:

Flame, my friend, I call to thee,
By the power of three times three,
My beloved Piper must be warned,
A worrisome plan Gareth has formed
Heading North, he nears our home.
Beware.
Prepare.
My worries grown.
Piper, this protection I send to thee,
Thus I speak, thus you shall receive.

Now it was up to Piper to be paying attention and to pick up my prayer in the wind.

***

I waited until dusk to make my way home. As far as I could tell, as I wended my way through the tight pedestrian alleyways of the ancient hillside town, things were calm. No cars were in the area. No angry Gareth was screaming my name.

I had searched the air for a response from Piper and got none. That could mean so many things. My message hadn't been received, Piper was unable to contrive a way to while eyes watched her, or… No, I wasn't going there. I wouldn't think that someone had hurt Piper.

But as I stood and focused, I felt the vibration of anxiety around the idea. These feelings wouldn't let me hunker down the way I had planned to do, waiting until just before the curfew siren to make my way across the greenspace. My discomfort forced my feet back toward center-village just to the east of the ancient Capital Square. Now used as a university, this was where those who passed the rigorously competitive exams amongst the Producers studied. I had been one of them. And was no longer. Not after today. For now, I would slide into a shadowed life. More difficult. More dangerous. But it was the price I had decided to pay. I was the only one in the Resistance who had the connections to get to Dr. Brighton before Dr. Brighton gave us all away.

Looking at him, tied in his chair, with his defeated spirit, I wasn't quite sure that I'd gotten there in time. Dr. Brighton hadn't given my name up. Of that I was sure. Had he done so, Gareth would have killed me instead of kissing me that morning.

I moved out of the shadow toward the stairs to my dorm. Piper's dorm. I couldn't live here anymore. This was the most exposed spot in my effort to check on Piper. There were enough people in the area that the energies were too complicated for me to read. I pulled my hood over my head and tucked my bruised hands into my pockets. Before I moved into the greenspace, I stopped to taste the air. It had the pickled taste of frustration.

There, to the side of the building, I saw a black car, shiny beneath a coat of dust. It was the car that had driven Gareth and me to the apartment building. I filled my cheeks with air and blew it out. I was right; he had been heading for Piper.

I saw a friend from my engineering class and followed along behind her as she used her key to go into the south facing dorm across from Piper's. I smiled at her as she held the door and sent me a curious glance. I wondered what my face looked like. Was I covered in blood or sweat? Surely, dirt and filth. I looked down; my pants were ripped. I needed to get to a mirror and water. I needed to get straightened up before I called too much attention to myself.

I sidled past the woman and moved to the staircase. Jogging up the stairs, I counted the floors. I lived on the eleventh floor with Piper. I'd get eyes on the place. I'd make sure she was okay.

Stealthily approaching the door of the room that would be the opposite of Piper's dorm window, I knocked lightly. When no one answered, I rapped a little harder. Still nothing. I touched the knob, sending warmth.

Hello, I've come as a friend
There is no need to defend
Open, open, open for me,
So I speak it, so mote it be.

With a twist of the handle, the door swung open to a messy room. Clothes, papers and books were strewn across the floor and over an unmade bed. At first, I thought the room had been tossed by a defender team. But then, I saw a young woman asleep on a chair, a mathematics book over her head. She slept the sleep of a student who had too many late nights preparing for finals. I softly snicked the door closed and tiptoed to her window. Standing to the side, I peered out.

Our blinds were open, in our dorm room – well, in Piper's dorm room. The light was on. I could see her standing with her back to the glass French door that lead to our balcony. She worked behind her to unlock the door. Her raven, Socrates, paced over the slim balcony and tapped at the pane asking for crumbs.

Gareth moved into my view. He yanked Piper's arms from behind her and gave her a shake before he pushed her aside and thrust open the hinged window. He took a step out on the balcony and looked around. His face was painted with suspicion, and anger. The hard Gareth. The dark Gareth.

I twirled to put my back to the wall as I sucked in a gasp of air. Slapping a hand over my mouth, I cast my gaze over to the sleeping student. She didn't move.

31

I rounded toward the window and focused on Piper. She bent and whispered to Socrates, and then pretended to shoo him away. Gareth wrenched her around by her shoulder and slammed the window shut.

One thing for sure, Gareth was furious. He stalked back and forth in front of the window, his body rigid, his gestures tense. Piper was crying and wringing her hands. I wondered if he was telling her I'd died. I wondered if she was acting or if her body was telling me the truth of what was unfolding. Piper stood on one barefoot then the other. She was in the sleep shirt she wore when she was buckling down to a study session. Gareth had his hand wrapped around her arm, now, holding her in place, as if she were a wild animal who wanted to escape. Little did he know how silly that was – what she could conjure with a single spell. Of course, doing so would expose her, and she'd be on the run just like me.

I needed to get back outside so Socrates could wing over my head and pass me the message. I snagged up a pair of leather pants and a teal tank as I passed through the room, holding them up as I slid into the lavatory. They looked my size. I peed, then washed myself clean, combed my hair and changed my clothes. I slid aching arms into my coat, then hustled down the corridor to the sign for the incendiary where I shoved my old clothes down the chute. I jostled down the stairs and out the door.

As soon as I reached the sidewalk, Socrates was over me. *Run!* said the wind beneath his wings. *Run! Hide!* With a squawk, he flapped to perch on the flag pole.

I turned and tucked my chin, as I pulled my hood up over my hair and moved away from the dormitories.

Not four steps and, "There she is! Here she is! I've got her."

Chapter Four

I turned and quick-walked in the direction of the market, keeping the pace of someone in a hurry but not someone on the run. Vendors' Square would be busy with people loading their stock into boxes to protect them for the night. As soon as I was out of the greenspace and in the maze of narrow streets, I flew over the cobbled stones. The sound of my heels cracked and resounded in the air. To my ear they called to my pursuers, "This way!"

The men had mimicked my pace, slower in the greenspace but not at all self-conscious as they tore after me. Grunts and bangs, angry yells from those pushed out of their way were like a high tide lapping further up the shore toward my heels. Almost within arm's reach.

Now, I could hear the smack of leather slapping leather as the man behind me pumped his arms.

The alley stopped. I had to decide left or right. I had no idea what lay in either direction. If either route might lead me to a dead end or others on Gareth's team. I put my arms out in front of me to stop my forward momentum and to push me into another direction. Right. My body chose to head right.

Here, I was dodging hand-pushed carts and a swell of people. I slowed my pace, trying to blend. I pulled off my jacket as I approached a woman sitting with her back to me, her leather jacket draped on the back of her chair. With a deft hand, I switched my coat for hers, pulling it on as I moved forward. It fit well enough. It was thin but warm. Too warm after my long run. I reached into the pockets and found a collection of things, including a piece of ribbed rope. I worked my long red hair into a high ponytail since the men would be searching for a woman with flowing red hair. I pulled the collar of the jacket up to conceal the shape of my face, and I walked like those around me as if I was preoccupied with getting home to my chores and not running for my life.

I'm safe.

I'm safe.

I'm safe.

No, no matter how many times I chanted it, something told me this wasn't true. Not in the least. I remembered my Tarot card this morning. The quickest card in the deck when it came to change. I thought I had understood; but surely, I had not. It wasn't a tongue-in-cheek joke from the Fates about the cars involved in this morning's ruse. It was a true foretelling. The change? I was no longer the hunter, I was the hunted. Me. I was the prey.

"There she is. I see her! She's in a black coat."

I ran up this alley and down that one. They were ever just behind me. No matter how hard I pushed myself, I couldn't seem to put distance between us. I side stepped as I forced my way around a group of people and used their bulk to hide my dive into an open doorway. I put my back to the wall, my chest heaving as much with exertion as with fright.

The heavy running steps faltered. "Get out of my way," the man growled. The group must have complied because there were no more commands.

A woman walked into the room. A towel in her hands. Dark circles under eyes pinched with hunger. She stood, staring at me.

"A strange man was trying to touch me. Forgive me. I was hiding from him." I lowered my eyelashes as if I felt shame.

She nodded and went to her door. When she swung around she said, "I believe you're safe now."

I wish that were true. I got what she was telling me. She wouldn't hide anyone in her home. I understood that. These were dangerous times. Times when one didn't take even small actions that might get you on some list, under someone's scrutiny. People formed tribes for safety, made pacts of defense, and she had no alliance with me. She lifted her chin toward the door, and I knew if I didn't leave, she'd call out for a defender.

As I walked past her, I reached out, snagged a scarf, and slid it into my jacket pocket. "Thank you," I said with a tremulous smile, meaning to keep the charade going so she wouldn't make that call and point out my direction as soon as I was out of sight.

Rounding a corner, I tied the scarf over my hair. I walked with the hung head and slack shoulders of someone making their way home after a difficult day.

This had, indeed, been a massively hard day—hard ground, hard fists, hard decisions.

I found, the farther I moved away from the market, the sparser the population, the more battered the landscape, the more ragged and desperate the conditions. I needed somewhere to sleep tonight. I needed it to be safe both for me and for whomever I took shelter from. My mind was so occupied in trying to find a plan that I didn't sense the man sneaking up behind me until he wrapped his arm around my neck and squeezed. "She's here. I've caught her," he called out.

Hunter to hunted to captured. Yes, Tarot, I'd say that was a fast-moving change in the energies. I couldn't believe I'd made such a novice mistake. Stupidity had put me in this choke hold with my heels dangling off the ground. But desperation would set me free.

I tucked my chin and bit him. Hard. My teeth sank into a huge chunk of muscle and hair-covered flesh until they clicked together, and the chunk came free in my mouth with a gush of salty blood. I hawked it out where he could see it. He shrieked with surprise and pain. His grip lost its power. I pried myself loose and took off running for the trees in the distance. Running. Weaving. Dodging.

Turning my routes. Trying to find hard surfaces where it would prove difficult for trackers to do their job. This was exhausting.

I was exhausted.

I couldn't get the taste of flesh out of my mouth, no matter how many times I gathered saliva and spat. That was something I hadn't imagined I'd ever do. It was nothing I imagined I could do. But I had pulled enough people away from the torturers to know a few things. The men inflicting the pain were merciless. The agony was unimaginable and unending. The words they wanted to pry loose would eventually leave my mouth whether I wanted them to or not. And lastly, and most importantly, even though I was an Elemental Witch, and even though I pledged my oath to the Goddess in all her forms, that would *not* help me.

I thought about the man whom I had bit. He knew who I was, and he would want his revenge. I'd imagine he'd need to go to the hospital and have things sewn back in place. Had he spoken to Gareth yet?

Would they suspect that I was with the Resistance?

My tactics in my escape could be credited to any child who was street savvy, except that Dr. Brighton had been taken from them, and I was in that mix. I slunk into a shadow and lifted my hands above my head, my thumbs and index fingers pressed together to form the triangle of trinity – maiden, maid, and crone.

On the run, I have not time,

By my will his thoughts to bind.
The circumstances mist and fogged,
The memories stopped and clogged.
By the Fates, this I pray,
Encroaching danger dost allay.

I couldn't count on that working; I didn't know how susceptible he was to magic. I needed to get word to Piper what was happening. Socrates would tell her I'd received the warning. He wouldn't be able to tell her what I planned to do about it. I was not of the wind element; I didn't have Piper's skills. I couldn't call a bird to deliver the air from my words.

But right now, communication was essential.

I needed the Resistance to give me the name of a secured location to hide in before curfew. At curfew, the defenders would shoot to kill. No questions asked. No chance to talk my way out of things. I patted my pockets and remembered I had some other woman's coat. She had my matches. I stripped off the leather jacket and searched it thoroughly. Finding nothing useful, I quickly disposed of the woman's belongings. Surely, she had reported her loss. If the defenders found me, and she could identify anything about this jacket, I'd be put into hard labor – or worse.

Maybe I should ditch the jacket. That was my thought when I saw in the distance the razor wire fencing that separated the

Proprietors and the Productors regions. I had run a lot farther than I had speculated. Adrenaline can do that to the brain.

This was an option I hadn't considered. Gareth and his men would be looking for me in the Productors' Range. They'd never think to search within the Enclave.

Gareth probably had no right to search within the Enclave…

As I left the tree line, I belly crawled over the open ground to the wires. Both thankful and sad that the Sun had set for the day. Mother Moon was on the rise. But she was cold in her femininity, I wouldn't be able to gather strength from the Sun's reflection of light against her surface, no matter that her face was full tonight.

Lying beside the razor wires that separated the two regions, I lifted my hands and warmed the bottom rows. "Hello," I said. "I offer this warmth as a gift. I wish for safe passage, if you would be so kind. I would like to stretch you upward, crawl under, and then have you return to your form."

Stress met my fingertips. The impression I picked up was that if they stretched the way I had asked, returning to their original form would not be possible.

I let my hands continue to send warmth to the metal. "Would that be allowed? Would you permit me to pass through and return to what shape you are able to hide my path?"

A tingle of assent was offered, but also a warning image, the metal, even while heated, could only stretch but so far.

"Thank you, my friend." I gently lifted the ropes of wire with their life-threatening edges. My fingers were positioned carefully between the razors.

The wires rounded and a small hollow formed.

Too small.

I had reached the limits of the wires willingness to flex. I pulled off the jacket and draped it over my head and back. My body hugged the packed earth as I slid my arms under the fence just like I did when I was surface diving into the ocean. My breath was ragged with fear. This was a high crime. There was no defense. If I were caught breaking through the barriers, I would be executed. If I stayed here in the Range, I'd be caught by the defenders and shot for curfew violations. If I returned home, I would face Gareth's wrath and all that it would entail.

Wow, today was full of hideous ways for me to die. I thought as I scooted another few centimeters forward, pushing with my toes. Including, the possibility of the wires changing their mind about their permission and snapping back into place before I was through. Getting caught, the wires would slice into my flesh, and I'd bleed to death out here on my own, without a single chance of being saved. Even without the change of mind and return to their original form, I knew I was going to get cut. There just wasn't enough room to accommodate my size, thin as I was.

I swallowed my fear. Paused my action. My arms and head were in the Enclave, my torso and legs were in the Range Productori. I held.

Something. Something in the air. Something I needed to read. To know. Some wisdom. I lay my cheek against the ground to relax my muscles and free my thoughts. I reached out with my mind, but the vibration was strange to me. I didn't understand. This was like a foreign language.

Mother Earth and Father Sky
I cast this spell both close and wide
The next step is not clear to me.
So you wish it, so mote it be.

I waited. Dangerous as it was, I waited. I didn't want to pull back to the Range if I needed to be in the Enclave. I didn't want to push into the Enclave if I needed to be in the Range. And most of all, I didn't want to anger the metal who was graciously allowing passage.

An owl hooted in the tree line. I couldn't tell on which side of the barricade.

I waited, but after hearing nothing more. Sent out another spell.

Goddess Athena, I heard your call.
I'll do your bidding big or small
Tell me what you want from me
So you wish it, so mote it be!

Almost instantaneously the night hunter on his silent wings dropped low in the sky, flying just over my head. With a down beat of his wings the owl soared back into the inky darkness. The air shimmered from the power of his wings' flap. "Save her," it said.

Save her.

Chapter Five

The directive to go save someone gave me no route forward. But the blast of the curfew siren did.

Under it was, into the Enclave where, as far as I knew, there were no curfews but plenty of defenders and private enforcers.

I cast my aura wide and felt no mammals nearby, no humans, no dogs. *Okay, so...keep moving,* I told myself. I wriggled forward, reaching around me, searching out a means to get myself through the narrow opening the metal had allowed me.

I grabbed a thin root. "Hold fast, my friend," I pleaded, then pulled. My shoulders slid under, my back. I heard the ripping sounds of the leather. I felt the bright sharpness of the blades slicing into my flesh. I reached my hands up the root and pulled again, panting at the pain blazing across my back. Once my hips were through, the rest of my legs and feet slid without difficulty.

I sat up, trying to catch my breath. I pulled the jacket around and examined it. It had been transformed into a fringe of leather. I thanked the Fates for what protection it had afforded me. The leather had taken the worst of the damage. Though, my shirt became damp with blood. Droplets trickled and tickled past the red-hot slices of my skin and pooled along the top of the leather pants. The leather on these pants was thick enough that I was protected from the razor slashes below the waistband.

My eyes scanned the expanse around me. I had nowhere to go. I was at a loss for my next move. I needed to find a flame, so I could gather answers. I needed to know where I could seek help. What I should do. Whom it was I needed to save.

I pushed to my feet, gasping at the pain. I closed my eyes and painted a salve charm over my body. It was a kitchen Witch's spell, a mothering spell, something that one did to sooth a child when they'd tumbled down and gotten a booboo that couldn't be healed with a kiss alone. It was enough to take the edge off. It quieted the disruption to my awareness. Earlier, I had gained first-hand experience with what could happen when I allowed myself to be distracted. Unbidden, the taste of the Enforcer's blood and flesh was in my mouth, again. I would need to do a ritual cleansing to rid myself of this cellular memory. For now, all I could do was gather some saliva and spit.

I looked about me. The moon was so bright tonight, it was as good as having a torch. The cloudless sky so clear that I could read a book. I stood in the open space of the borderland that allowed the defenders to see if there was a breech. I wondered about an alarm, but the metal wires didn't give me any kind of warning that one was in play. Besides, it would use up precious energy to have an alarm running continually over such a great distance.

I turned to look where I had shimmied through. There was an obvious area where the straight lines were now displaced. There were blots where I had rolled, streaks where my blood pooled, unabsorbed by the hardened clay. If someone were the least bit observant, it was obvious there had been a violation of the perimeter. How long would I have? Where should I go?

I sent my aura wide—as wide as I could stretch myself. Who and what was around me?

My choice to do that left me thin and vulnerable. It was at that moment that a shock of vibration exploded through my system dropping me to my hands and knees. The air shuddered with the energy of forward movement that had slammed to a sudden halt. It formed a tsunami-sized current, blowing outward. It swelled above my head as it expanded and disseminated, leaving an eerie quiet in its wake. It was a split second. And then there was peace.

Gripping at the weeds, I listened to the tinkling of glass and the low moans at the far distance of my auric perceptions. With a deep inhale, I brought my head up to scan the horizon. A sob. A forlorn cry for help. Had the Resistance set off another bomb? No, that made no sense. Socrates from his perch on the flag pole would have seen the direction I was running. The Resistance would know the general area I would be. They wouldn't put me in that kind of danger, either of being caught in the blast or being caught by the Proprietors and charged with the crime.

"No!" a man's voice gasped out. I turned my head searching for a clear route.

"Grab her!" called another voice, a younger, angrier voice.

I pulled the thin fabric of my aura back to me, then took off running in the direction I had registered the tumult, toward the sounds of bodies grunting as they were impacted. When I arrived on the scene, two men were in a clinch, each getting off a blow where they could. I couldn't tell who was the bad guy and who was the good guy, or if there even was a bad guy and a good guy. Save her, had been my order. But as I took in the unfolding event, there was no *her* to save.

Two cars were involved. It didn't look like an accident—the one car looked just fine. The second car though had hit a rock and rolled. The glass was broken out as the frame bent and squashed with the weight and speed. The shards were like hail, shimmering and translucent under the scrambling men's feet. I focused on one of the men, fighting in a uniform suit, the other was in pedestrian clothing. I shifted my gaze to the car. The uniform must be the driver. I imagined he had crawled out of the window only to be set upon. Though, even in the dark, I could see that both men's faces were set in fierce determination. But who was attacking, and who was defending? What should I do?

I glanced around me, realizing how exposed I was, and that this event had been staged where there would be no interference. Here, there was nowhere to hide. And no one to call to for help. I painted a quick glamour over myself. It might hold, even as exposed as I was, since no one was expecting a lone woman to be out in the middle of nowhere. I stood still, waiting to understand. It could well be that I had no purpose here, and I shouldn't intervene. "Choosing one's battles is half the battle," was a Haven saying that we were taught early in life.

The men were growling now, pulling up the last of their reserves in this fight. I saw movement over at the wrecked car. A man wheeled around the back with a crowbar in his hand, slamming it into the back of the uniformed man's head. That man dropped like a stone.

"What were you thinking?" the other guy asked, hands on his knees, catching his breath. "If you missed you'd have cracked my bloody skull instead of his."

"He was about to get the best of you. I had to do something." The man was laughing.

Some big joke.

Killing was never a joke. A necessity at times? Absolutely. It was part and parcel to my job with the Resistance, but it was always for a reason. And every single time it packed another cold shard into my heart, stabbing at me. I could feel the pain in my chest from this morning's mission. I'd have to warm that space to defrost and stay sane. I needed to perform a cleansing ritual, and a thanksgiving ritual for my successful flight. At least I was away from Gareth's enforcers and out of the reaches of the Range defenders.

The man stood and rubbed his knuckles. "Is she okay?" He focused over on the crunch of steel and aluminum. "That wasn't supposed to happen."

She?

"She's alive for now if that's what you're asking. Let's haul her out, throw her in the trunk, and get the hell out of here before a defender happens by."

Okay, those were the words I needed. This was the mission I was called to take on.

I couldn't separate them, one from the other to fight them one on one.

I couldn't sneak up on them.

I had no weapon.

As I thought that, the man with the crowbar took out a rag and swiped it up and down the shaft to remove his prints, then whipped it like a boomerang in my direction.

Thank you, Goddess. Metal, I call you to me.

Without enough oomph from the throw, it didn't land in my hand, but it was near enough to my feet that, with a twirl and a crouch, I swooped it up, continued the spin and focused on my target's head, choosing the man who had delivered the blow to the driver. The other was still fresh from his fight and probably as exhausted as I was. A more even fighting field.

Ogun, Fire God of the metal tool,
Your power I require as I unspool,
Cast this weapon far from me,
Take down my target is my plea,
By the power of three times three,
So I speak it, so mote it be.

It was a graceless spell, awkwardly woven. I held my breath to see if it was good enough. If not, I'd just thrown my weapon away and brought attention to my presence.

The man with the smirk jerked as his peripheral vision picked up the black object whirling toward him with velocity. With a thunk and a twang, he slipped to the ground, his partner's jaw dropped in astonished shock. His eyes scanned for information. And just as quickly, I was there in the kill zone.

Surprise!

I grabbed the inside of his collar with one hand, crossed my arms and reached into the opposite side, then yanked. As my elbows spread wide, the cloth tourniqueted the man's throat, choking him. I had been sure to catch him on the exhale. He gripped my wrists, trying to pry himself free.

"Who are you?" I hissed.

His eyes bulged. His face turned red.

"Who sent you here?"

His mouth opened, searching for oxygen. His thick tongue lolled out, no longer fitting in the open space. I held tight, I needed to weaken him before I released him. But it was a fine line. If I crushed his windpipe, he wouldn't be able to tell me. If I let him go too soon, he'd fight me. Honestly, I didn't have much fight left in me. I released him with a push. He staggered backward, fell to a knee, rose again, slamming an uppercut under my chin. My head whipped back to its fullest extent.

The power of the blow was stunning. I could taste my own blood as I bit my tongue. My arms swung wide for balance. As I fell, I kicked him in the soft place between his legs. A hard-enough kick to the groin could kill a man. Or make him wish he were dead. We were on the ground, both of us, each in a tangle. Each scrambling to get the upper hand as we defended ourselves. The ground was always a dangerous place to fight, no matter the level of training.

The man got a foot underneath him. He looked over at his dead partner, the dead driver, the crowbar. We both scrambled for it. Our fingers wrapped on either end. *Metal, hear me! Help me!* I sent heat down the crowbar.

I call to fire, within me burn,
This evil man I wish to spurn,
Power now blaze within me.
So I speak it, so mote it be!

The metal heated to glowing. He dropped his end, his fingers spread wide, shaking them in the wind to relieve the pain. I brought the crowbar down across his skull. My stomach heaved at the crack and thump. His lifeless body crumpled into a heap.

I was stunned, as I always was.

Stunned that I had the power and the will to do such a thing.

A soft voice from the car cried out, "Help me!"

Chapter Six

I moved toward the flipped car, assessing the situation. It must have been travelling at breakneck speed for the wheel to have hit this stone and flipped the way it did. From the place it lay, it looked like it rolled three times. The space the driver crawled from wasn't much bigger than the space that the razor wire had allowed me to scuttle under.

I stalked the car that was parked right there beside the wreck, with its dark-tinted windows. Was there anyone inside?

With the crow bar ready to swing, I slowly opened the door. An interior light popped on.

Empty.

A fob sat on the driver's seat. My safety, more or less assured, I went to check on the voice. I moved slowly, my senses wide. If I got into trouble, I couldn't help anyone. Better slow and steady than leaping forward.

My hand on the car's frame, I tried to sway the bulk. It seemed to hold. All the same, I went to the small boulder and sitting down, propped my feet against it, my legs bent up to my chest like a frog's.

I need the help of Earth and rock,

To this wreckage, I need a lock.

Keep the metal from rolling on me,

So I speak it, so mote it be.

I imagined the rock moving and wedging itself under the roll cage-a design developed by engineers long ago to protect their passengers from being crushed. From my unpracticed eye, that frame seemed undamaged. But in the dark of night, with only the illumination of a full moon, it was hard to tell. I focused on the rock—too big for me to move without divine help—I focused on the place I wished it to land. I imagined myself straightening my legs and the boulder sliding into place. When the vision was clear and strong in my imagination, I visualized the Sun and the power it could give my words, then I pushed. The rock complied.

Thank you, friend.

I crawled to the car then laid on my back skootching into the tight space between the window frame tilting toward the ground. The engine was still running, I reached in past the shards of glass still clinging to the frame and pushed the off button. Quiet blanketed the night.

"Help, please." This time it was much softer. The call lacked hope. But searching the interior of the car I saw no one. Floundering around, even with the stone in place seemed a dangerous idea both for me and whoever it was who was speaking.

"I'm here. I'm helping you." It was dark inside the car. Too dark to see, tilted as it was at such an angle that even the moon's light couldn't reach the interior. No one seemed to be in the seats. I rolled out to see the sky. Not a cloud in the expanse.

Goddess, if it is your will that I save her. If this is the "her", I was sent to help, I need your aid. I decided to try a spell of necessity. I'd seen it cast by an Elder, but I had never been in a situation tenuous enough for it to be needed. Without the need, without the fear-driven energy of a life or death event, my plea would not be granted. I pointed at the sky with my right index finger and at the interior with my left one. With my mind I called, *Illuminate!*

With a crack and a swiftly following boom, electricity shot through the air. A brief moment of light filled the sky. And there, I saw her, wedged at the far side, dangling above the ground. She was but a crumple of clothing and long brown hair. That was it. It was enough.

I crawled back out, calling as I did, "I'm not leaving you. I'm coming up with a plan to rescue you."

Mewling like that of an injured animal answered me.

My heart stuttered.

Goddess be with me. Fates advise me. This was going to test me to the core. This was me facing my dragon. I had a horror of being trapped in a small space. Far back in my childhood. I had gone exploring in a small cave when the tide came in. It came in at such a speed that I couldn't swim against it to get out. I was stuck in the cave to drown. I found one small pocket of air where the rock had a fissure on the ceiling. For what seemed an eternity, I pressed my lips to that space, I sipped the air as if from a straw – my face underwater as I tilted up, clinging to the crags of rock for stability. Dark and cold, I thought of the cave as my tomb. If I lost my footing, I would lose that tiny spot of hope, and I would die. Hours. It took hours for the tide to reverse.

Confined spaces ignited panic attacks that no amount of spell work and healings had fixed.

Just thinking about the trapped woman, my heart beat too fast, my palms sweat. I gasped at the air, trying to fill unwilling lungs.

What I needed was to be in my rational mind and to come up with a plan. I went to the attacker's car and took a moment to expand my aura and search for any movement headed to this area. I found none. I'd stop and wonder why later, when I had more time. Why would a woman be here along the barricade at this time of night where there was no road?

I took the fob and popped the trunk. They had mentioned tying her up. Perhaps they had rope and maybe something else, an electric torch would help. I should have thought of that before. Opening the trunk, a light popped on. No torch. No matches so I could ask advice or send a message. But yes, to the rope. Nothing else helpful, I left the car doors and trunk open to increase the ambient light.

I tied the rope to the axel and threw it over the hood, running it out to a nearby tree. The tree's trunk was thick enough, and it was alive. *Hold fast, my friend.* I said, giving the bark a pat. I walked around the trunk three times then tied the rope off with a figure eight knot. I twanged the rope testing the taut line, traveling from car to tree. Between the wedge of the small boulder and this rope, the car shouldn't tumble forward. There was always the chance it could tumble backward. But this would be the most I could do to secure the vehicle.

As I worked, I'd formulated a plan. Near as I could tell, she had been thrown from the seat when the car rolled and crushed. The space she'd been pressed into held her fast. There wasn't enough room to work in the interior, maneuvering the crowbar. And inside, I couldn't trust myself to stay in my head. To think rationally. No, the best laid plan was to work from above.

If I couldn't get her free by opening the space wide enough for her to slip through, then she'd have to drop. It wasn't far, a meter and a half at most. But if she were injured, as she must be, that drop could be dangerous.

There was nothing I could use to cushion the impact.

Out was better than in, though.

"I'm still here. I'm still working to get you free."

"Please," she moaned.

"I am. I'm coming." I grabbed the crow bar and scaled the bad guy's car to get to the roof. From there I could climb to the improbably angled side of the damaged car. Slowly, carefully, not fully trusting my rigging, I pulled my way along until I came to the rear door of the vehicle.

"Can you hear me?" I asked.

"Yes."

"I can see the problem. I'm going to work at it. But for sure, at some point you're going to drop."

"Oh," she squeaked. That didn't sound like a woman, that sounded much younger.

"While I work up here, is there any way that you can try to move so that your feet face the ground. When you fall if your feet hit first, it's better than your head or your shoulder."

Her answer was a puff of air.

I had other options, I thought, as I stuck the claw into a crack. I could try to go get help. I leaned my weight onto the bar. And the metal screeched with outrage. *Oops. Sorry!* I hadn't asked for permission or help. That told me I was off my game. I put my hand on the spot and sent a bit of warmth and contrition.

Then, I stopped to consider.

They had rescue crews that came out. I didn't know how far help may lay, or in which direction. Even if the woman in the car could direct me, I didn't know if I'd be killed on sight or taken into custody by the defenders of the Realm and held without anyone allowing me to speak. Held away from the possibility of the Resistance finding and rescuing me, or perhaps just putting me out of my misery. It was also possible that I'd come across someone's enforcer. If I crossed private lands, the enforcers could do whatever they wanted to me. None of these options seemed quick and easy, or painless. And if I was going to be perfectly frank with myself, I was running on reserves since I pushed Gareth out of the way of the racing car.

Possibly, I could drive the car, but without the girl with me, what would people think? That I had caused the accident? That I had killed everyone and stolen the car?

I could jog. I shook my head. That wasn't a viable option. I really was very close to burning out.

Fates, I need to know what's best, I need your help, again. Please. I tried to release my inner resistance, the doubt-thoughts that would prevent any magic, no matter how eloquent the spell.

"Help," the girl cried softly. I was sure now she must be a teen, someone younger than me.

I felt a charge of adrenaline when I heard the fragility of her voice. I was her hope.

I pointed at the distance, my other finger to the sky and with the sheer determination to follow the Goddesses' will and save the girl, I called with my mind, *Illuminate!*

Flash! The sky lit with a sheet of light. The thunder rumbled, low and angry. I quickly spun three-sixty, searching out even the smallest bump in the darkness that would mean buildings were nearby.

Nothing.

I was on my own, and this was a predicament that I knew little about. I had only been in a car on a few rare occasions and that had been with Gareth and his driver.

I reached out my aura and felt the dizziness and confusion of the girl inside. Darkness and greyness swirled about her. She must be in and out of consciousness. Head injuries could be fatal. And that's how it felt to me. Her breathing felt thin. I'd seen no blood. Well, I'd seen very little in the flash of lightning. But there wasn't a pool of blood. She wasn't bleeding out. And that, at least, was a positive sign.

I placed the crowbar, again. This time, before I pressed, I drew a pentagram in the air and whispered:

Metal, my friend, I regret your plight,
I ask permission, if I might
To further bend this door askew
And save the girl trapped in you.
I call to the Goddess who has instructed me,
To bring me power, three by three
To do her will, and bring no harm,
I set in place this magic charm.

The metal refused me. Granted, I was exhausted and using little force. Still, it felt like a blow, a personal rejection. I sat down in frustration.

Goddess? I searched but got no answer.

I knew the answer.

I'd have to climb inside where I'd face the possibility of the wreck falling and trapping me with no one the wiser. I was called to put myself at risk for a girl when all I knew of her was that her hair was brown, and she needed me.

My reluctant feet traced my path back to the ground. I bit my lip as I looked at what I needed to do.

For both our sakes, I took a moment to close my eyes and envision a grounding cord travelling deep, deep into Mother Earth, down through soil, rock and metal to the very center of the planet and there, I attached it. I imagined the tether as a chute and sent my terror energy down the length to be received, absorbed, and cleansed by Earth. I let go of my ego, as much as I could, imagining myself as star dust, a tool of the Goddess. Once I had my shaking under control, and I no longer hyperventilated at the thought of where I was heading, I lay down on the ground and pushed with my feet.

I had to turn my head to fit my nose under the door. I wondered how the driver, who was much larger than I, was able to make it out, and thought about just a short time prior when I had raked razor blades down my back to get into the Realm. I'm sure he was equally impelled to face pain and damage in order to get to safety. I looked over to where his body lay. It turned out badly for him, anyway.

Fear licked the taste of my thoughts and lapped at them hungrily. I took another moment to try to dispel that monster. Fear could grow to a dragon's breadth and consume good intentions, destroying a mission.

I had taken a vow to serve the Goddess, retreat was not an option.

I curled as I pushed farther into the car's interior, trying to keep my face away from the sharp edges. I got myself into a squat and reached to the back of the car.

"I'm here. I'm helping you," I said, if only for my sake. The girl, I realized as I pushed the strands of her hair from her face, was no longer conscious.

The back of this car was larger than a normal car. It had two sets of seats. One had faced the other. I'd never seen a car like this before. It was good that it was so large. I had space to maneuver. I felt along the wreckage, along her body. I reached up behind and bid my fingers to paint a picture for me. To find the problem.

It might have been my imagination, but it seemed to me that the metal was protecting this girl. It was almost as if the metal, as it rolled and bent, embraced her and was holding her safe against being tossed about. The screeches and the obstinance, when I stood at the top and was using the crowbar, I now perceived as an animal protecting its young, and batting a clawed paw at the person approaching, no matter their intention. I touched the metal as I formed those thoughts. The metal sent a vibration in response.

She needs help, my friend. Let me get her free.

I wish I knew her name. I wish she were able to tell me her story. Who was she? Why was she here? And why would two evil men want to tie her up and put her in their trunk?

It took time, but slowly and as gently as I could, I tugged this piece of her and that until gravity pulled her down. My hands did little to protect her from the tumble, though I tried.

Now for the next step. How could I get her out? The back area could not be accessed. The windows were either against the ground or smashed closed.

I'd have to crawl over the front seat to get in the back with her, assess her, and somehow maneuver her over the seat to the front, out of the wreckage, and to the attackers' vehicle. Then, I'd find a way to get to someone who could help her. And I'd somehow explain my illegal presence in the Realm without being killed on sight.

"That sounds easy enough," I said aloud as I lifted my leg over the seat and wriggled myself around.

Chapter Seven

As my eyes blinked open, it took me a moment to remember where I was. The smells that assailed my nostrils were unnatural and had a nasty bite to them. I tried to reach up and scratch at my nose, but my hand could move only inches. I pulled again and realized—with the clang of metal against metal—I was restrained. I pulled my other hand, that one too was handcuffed to the roll bars of my hospital bed.

The feeling of being trapped and endangered drove my thoughts to dark and terrifying places. I thrashed and gasped as the pain precipitated by my movements shot through my system.

There was a snick as a door opened.

"Nurse." It was a man's voice that I didn't recognize. It had the gravelly sound of disdain. Someone of authority.

The call came from above my head out to the hallway. I shuffled and squirmed around to see who was in the room with me. The bite and pull at my back stopped me instantly as my skin screamed.

A woman dressed in blue rushed to my bedside. "Don't move," she said, pressing down on my shoulders to hold me still. Under her breath I heard, "Why they have you on your back, in the state you're in is beyond me, the idiots."

I'm sure she read the trapped animal look in my eyes. She moved away; there was a rush of water. When she came back, she smoothed a cool rag down my arms. Angry bruises and bandaged cuts made the track difficult. "Look here. Look at me." She waited for my gaze to focus on hers. "You're safe. You're in the hospital. Remember?" she asked.

Flashes of last night, came back to me. I was dragging the girl to the functioning car, pressing the motor button, figuring out what the pedals did, how the wheel worked. I remembered driving a distance over the barren ground then standing on the roof and calling for another flash of light when I couldn't figure out my direction and was afraid that the girl was slipping into the beyond. I remembered driving to the Defenders' Station to beg them for help. The buzz of terror made me unable to speak, I merely pointed at the girl passed out on the back seat.

That terror confused me.

Yes, I could be killed on sight but that was part and parcel with my job and my vows. Death was part of my everyday world. I didn't know this girl. Why was I so invested in her survival? I did my duty by the Fates. I saved her. I knew that this predicament was the best-case scenario. But why did I feel so uncharacteristically afraid for her? Attached to her?

The defender had shoved me from the driver's seat and had raced the car to the hospital. The girl was wheeled off in one direction, and I was wheeled in another. I was stripped, examined and given a shot, so they could debride my wounds and sew parts of me back together. Too many for a local anesthesia, they'd said.

I pulled at my restraints.

They knew I was trespassing into the Realm.

Why would they keep me alive? My mind battled through a fog of medicine to figure it out. Then, I remembered the bodies. I remembered telling the defender the direction I'd come from and the vague story of what I'd arrived upon, and how I'd gotten the girl into the car. They'd want to keep me alive long enough to answer their questions.

Okay, that made sense.

"Might I have a sip of water?" I tried my voice. It was raspy, from yelling. I had done a lot of yelling last night at the accident scene. I yelled at my claustrophobia, at my fatigue, at the Goddess for asking me to sacrifice myself. Yelling had bolstered my fortitude to power on. But it left my throat raw and painful. There wasn't a lot of my body that wasn't painful. But the pain was muffled under the soft fluff of their medications. A blessing and a fear. I needed my brain to be sharp.

I tried to conjure a spell, but nothing came to me. I wasn't sure what would help this situation.

As the nurse moved away, I gave another half-hearted yank on my restraints. My nose still itched. I had momentarily forgotten about it.

"You are not Significant." The voice was too loud for the stark furnishings of the room. There was nothing to absorb or soften the sound. It bounced off the walls and ricocheted around the space.

I tipped my head back to see if I could find a face to go with the voice. "No, sir, I'm not."

Hard-soled shoes strutted into my line of view. "And what is your lineage?" The man who stepped forward sported a well-tailored business suit. A thin ring of grey hair encircled his head from ear to ear like a Grecian victory wreath, leaving a bald crown dappled with age spots. Slack folds of skin did nothing to soften the sharp angles of his face. The man focused hard eyes on me.

My interrogation had begun.

Stay bright, Ember! Every word could turn into a nail in my coffin, unless of course they discovered I was a witch, then they wouldn't bother with a burial. They'd just roast me in a bon fire. "My father was a defender, and my mother was a musician."

"Was?"

"They died during the famine… at the time of the last famine," I explained. Not of hunger. My parents were too smart and too strong. They'd always found a way to survive by cunning, brawn, or spell—my father was a Metal Witch and my mother had an affinity with air. During the famine, they'd sent me to Haven to be with my mom's family. It was my time to go, anyway. All of those with magical lineage sent their children "home" to be educated and trained. The adults stayed in the Mundane world until it was their time to return to Haven and take on the cloak of Wisdom, educating the next generation of Witches for the Resistance.

That was our way of life and had been since the beginning of the Inquisition, when the ancestors sought refuge on an island hidden in the wide expanse of the Atlantic. They cast a glamour that had been preserved and fortified with each generation of witches ever since. It was our task at the completion of our training, before we left for our Offling Years, to add our prayers of protection and obfuscation. And no matter what technology the Mundane developed, they never showed an inkling that we existed then and persisted today.

As the famine worsened through the lands, and people died by droves, my parents decided it was time for me to go. They put me on a ship with other young Hereditary Witches, and we were sent off to be trained. I never saw them again in the flesh, my parents, only in the ether when we spoke each day. They had stayed back and fought in the name of the Fates to return the lands to the safety and freedom that had once existed.

There was a time when one could express one's spiritual convictions without reprisal. But then, those in power made us

Witches the focus of enmity just as it had been in the Inquisition. They returned to burning us, which forced those with power underground. We were not just disrespected and reviled, but hunted and killed. The truth was, Witches were all that stood in the way of humans being erased from the Earth all together. Father Sky and Mother Earth were utterly dismayed by humanities' actions and just about done putting up with the irreverence.

My parents were both killed doing the work of the Resistance. Martyrs. Heroes.

The man snapped his fingers in my face, startling me.

Blasted medicines. *Focus, Ember!*

He reached out and tapped a finger on my university bracelet which allowed us students into the library and laboratories. "You were tested. Apparently, you are of an intellectual caliber that allows you a path to the intelligencia caste. That's a rare and mighty capacity. Kudos to you."

I nodded. He didn't mean to congratulate me at all, he was laying a trap. A little ego stroking, a feeling of sympathy—as if this man could muster sympathy—and down comes one's guard. He was so smug. So self-certain. Old men often looked at me and thought they had the power. They had the overt power, granted. But their putting me into a box that said I was a sheep easily led and maneuvered, it almost always served me well. I liked how obvious this man was. The look of cunning superiority in his eye would be his downfall. I pulled my hand against the restraint. That was, if I got free.

"And yet, with as smart as you were deemed, you don't seem to understand the laws enough to know that no matter your intellectual capacity, those of the Productors may not pass into the Enclave without the proper papers and chaperones. It means death."

I looked over to the slim window, searching out a beam of Sun. The sky seemed oddly green. An ominous sign. Weren't these men paying attention? Father Sky was angry today. "Yes," I said, letting my voice sound defeated, letting the man think he held all the keys. He didn't hold all of them. He held some of them. I thought about gathering the Sun and sending him warmth. But when I turned back and saw his stony face, I knew that it would do nothing to improve our relationship. "I knew that as I crawled under the razor wires. I knew that there very well would be consequences."

"Why did you do it?" That was another man's voice. Warmer, sincere. Curious.

I licked my lips. 'Because death at the hands of the curfew defenders was the closest threat,' seemed like a poor choice of explanations. "There was a terrible noise, a girl's scream, a call for help. There was so much pain in her voice, I just acted, sir. There was no calculation involved."

"You got under the wires? That's impossible." This was a third man. He stepped forward as he spoke. Enough so, that I could see him a little. Also a suit. Also the smugness. Younger. A full head of hair and no jowls. He didn't seem to be an enforcer, though I didn't doubt that he had *enforced* mightily along the way. No, I read him as a right-hand man. A confidant. Less than an equal but esteemed, and therefore privileged by his position.

I shook my head. "I don't know. There was a bit of a bend in the wires there. My jacket gave me some protection. I was wearing a leather jacket."

"The trackers found the area where you entered. The fencing is misshapen. We found the trail of you sliding under, your blood, your jacket, your stepping forward and then hesitation. Why the hesitation if you went under to save someone without thinking?" The right-hand man asked. At the same time the old man was saying, "You waited until after you were wounded to plan? Not very smart for a future member of the intelligencia." The tone of his voice said, *what is wrong with the testers that they let this imbecile through.*

Yes, please, keep thinking that way.

I closed my eyes picturing myself standing beside the root that I had used to pull me under the fencing. Truth, as much as possible, was always the way to go in an interrogation, I was taught. "It was dark. The noise came from all around me. I wasn't sure, once under the fence, in which direction to go. I had a hundred and eighty-degree arch to consider, and I knew the cry had come from some distance. Then, there was a crack of lightning that lit up the landscape, and I saw the tree and something that looked dark. I decided to try in that direction."

"It was a cloudless night. Odd for there to be a sudden lightning strike." The old-guy said under his breath.

Here lay danger. Would he consider that I was the one who had pulled down the heat from the sky? Would they realize I was an Elemental Witch?

"Yes, sir, if you say so, sir." Right-hand responded.

The old man stepped back and conferred with the men who were with him. I wished they'd all come into view without me stretching my eyes so far to catch them in my peripheral vision. I wished they'd introduce themselves. Of course, I knew that keeping me in the dark about their names and the roles they played was all part of the game. The old man was toying with me. He was the cat and I was the mouse, in his view. He was wrong, I reminded myself. For the moment, he had an upper hand. But eventually they would untether me, and then I could bring my own powers to bear.

I pulled the heat of the air they exhaled as they whispered to each other closer to me, so I could hear their words.

"Do you remember lightning? Is she telling the truth?"

"There were three strikes, and they were on the southern border and about the right time."

"It seems odd that there were lightning strikes on a clear night. Could that light have been something else? Could it have been an explosion?" The other man asked. This one didn't sound like an enforcer to me. He felt like an elite, pampered and privileged. He actually seemed angry that Father Sky would have the audacity to strike out with lightning whenever he chose. No…that wasn't quite right. He was angry, but not about the lightning, and there was fear there, too, deeply rooted fear with an overlay of emotional pain. *Interesting.*

"Why are there tornadoes on otherwise calm days?" The old man asked as if this was all too imbecilic to wonder about. "Why do the hurricane winds wait until harvest to sweep the food away? Those are the questions that our intelligencia are supposed to answer." He took three steps back to me. "A lightning strike didn't cause the accident?" he demanded.

I widened my eyes at the idea that I would have the answers he was looking for. "I wouldn't know, sir, about the events prior to my getting there."

The side of his nose wriggled as if he smelled something foul. "You would know if you were the cause of the accident. If a Productor, such as yourself, was to suddenly pop out of nowhere, the driver might have swerved to miss you, mistaking you for a Significant."

Flames licked through my system, as my eyes flashed with sparks, I closed my lids. He was suggesting if the driver didn't think I was a Significant that he wouldn't have tried to avoid me and would have run me over without a qualm.

I had to imagine the ripple of a brook along the forest edge on Haven, cool and serene. I held that image until my scorn was quelled, and I was in control again. Only then did I attempt an answer – a misplaced word would get me killed. "Sir, is that what the girl is saying?" I paused, then whispered, "Is she okay? Did she…" I hesitated. I did care. My concern was genuine. Both for the girl and also for the accomplishment of my directive. The wind from the owl's wing had carried this mission to me, *save her.* I hoped I had. "Please, did she survive?" My voice was plaintive. "I'm sorry. I don't know her name. Can you tell me her name?" I laced warmth around each syllable, I sent out pictures of sunlight and sisters holding hands, skipping in circles, their heads back as they lifted their giggles to the Sky.

"Answer my question," the old man growled. And when he did, the right-hand man took a muscle-bound step forward, but so did the other man, the elite—the one with the anger and the fear. He was much younger, than the other two.

With a sniff, I pulled back my images and warmth, leaving the room cold and empty. I allowed my tears to accumulate on my lashes. I felt the sudden shift in atmosphere as much as anyone else, the shift was so stark that it left me feeling bereft. I let a few tears dribble miserably down my cheeks. I could see the younger two men were affected. They felt it. They were moved by it. The old man was stone.

The elite stepped to the end of my bed. "Tera is her name. She's my sister. The doctors are working on her now. They feel she will recover very well, but they say that without your intervention, I would be in mourning now." He searched out my gaze. I rewarded him with the warmth of sunlight and the image of giggling siblings again. I watched surprise cross his face. Curiosity. Apprehension. Decision. And there, purposefully hiding from me was the seed of affection. I sent a shy and hopeful smile toward that specific feeling.

One thing I remarked was no one had asked me about the three dead men. I had a story all ready for them. I arrived on the scene, they were battling it out. Two were down, one man was standing and when he fell, I rushed in. But no, not a single question. And that was very good. It meant that they hadn't considered that I had taken part in that fight and that I was capable of killing.

A knock sounded, then the door opened. I expected it was the nurse returning.

"Is she awake now?" a man asked.

I recognized that voice, instantly.

Gareth.

Chapter Eight

"Gareth, come in," the old man invited him into my room as if it were his own living room. "She's awake. And I have a meeting. I'll let you handle this, and I'll catch up with you later. Swing by the house for dinner."

"Yes, sir."

Gareth. By the Fates, he's going to expose me and kill me. How did they make a connection between us?

Gareth moved to the foot of my bed next to the elite. I reached out my aura to take his measure. Despite the stoicism and indifference of his outward demeaner, he was confused and scared. Anger was a low burning flame, and it wasn't sure that it should connect itself to me. That anger energy reached out to see if there was guilt on my part. The Mundane did this like Witches did, but they seemed genuinely unaware that they had this skill and equally uncaring about the answer in any real, conscious way. No matter, I had put a demarcation spell about me as I came awake, a well ingrained habit taught to us on Haven. As I opened my eyes, I called my spirit back from wherever it had travelled in my dreams, and set up my energetic protection so that no one could sense anything about me that I didn't intend.

I felt Gareth's energy lapping like a wave on the shore at the outer edge of my aura, and it found nothing. No contrition, no fear, no guilt. Oh, I felt those things. But my feelings were mine and not for him to discern.

Gareth cleared his throat and shuffled. "Crispin, would it be alright with you if I spoke with Ember McGraw alone?"

"Why?" Crispin asked Gareth. His guard was up. Some kind of vibe sizzled back and forth behind a curtain of camaraderie.

This was interesting.

Crispin, I let his name tumble around in my memory to see if Gareth had ever mentioned that name before, checking to see if I had any information about who and what he was. *Crispin,* it was an unusual name. He was a handsome man, with green eyes and rusty blond hair. He reminded me of the Viking warriors I'd studied in books. I could envision him wearing furs, long hair braided against the winds on the ocean, anvil raised to the sky calling in his sacred circle, "Hammer to the North!" Poetic. Heroic.

His energy seemed oddly ensconced in the tailored clothes of the elite.

Crispin. A very unusual name. Something about that name shimmered. I'd have to tuck that information away and think about it later. The thing I remarked now was Crispin was checking the temperature between Gareth and me. He wanted to know if we had coupled. Sure, we had. Many times. It was both enjoyable, and it served my work. How else would I have gotten to the building to save Dr. Brighton?

Here was a dilemma to be weighed. Gareth, who wielded immense power in the Range, seemed to have less authority here. Though he had some level of authority here, it seemed slightly dimmer to what Crispin held. If I aligned myself with power in the Realm would that hurt me with Gareth if...*when* I was back on the Range? Would I need Crispin's power here in the Realm to stay safe? Did Crispin even exercise that much power? It seemed he had little authority when his father was around. But on that, I could be mistaken. How to play this...

I'd play it smart and wait. This was not a good time for decision making and line drawing.

I closed my eyes and let out a soft moan. In a charade designed to elicit a conversation about my being held prisoner, I moved my hands to grab my head only to rediscover that I was chained. Through my lashes I watched both men step forward to help me, and both men come to the conclusion that they didn't know how to help.

"Ember, what have you done to yourself?" Gareth exhaled. "Look at you, you're beaten black and blue."

I slit my eyes and sent my thoughts his way. *No kidding. You watched me bounce off the top of a speeding car and left me in the road to die.* I added pictures to the silent communication. His fingers on my neck checking for a pulse, his grabbing my collar and dragging me to the gutter, his speeding away. *I saved you.* Pictures of me thrusting him out of the car's path, putting myself in danger. *You left me.* Pictures of the back of his black car, racing away.

Gareth was not clairvoyant. But he had lived a hard-scrabble life. An orphan in the streets, he'd pulled himself up to the position he had now. Not an easy task. Not a probable outcome. I knew he had some sense of etheric understanding. If he didn't, he would be long dead.

I wasn't sure how much of my communication he got, but he got something. His face flamed red. Good. That showed me that some inner part of his consciousness, the part that could not be controlled by will, recognized the situation and interpreted his behavior as shameful. It also reminded me that no matter what Gareth had done, he hadn't sold his soul in his fight for survival. No matter that he played with both the dark and the light.

I batted my eyelids open, dropped my jaw just a bit and panted in a play for sympathy for my injuries and pain. It wasn't that much of an act. I'm sure it read as sincere.

"The hospital had your identification from your student bracelet, and they contacted me in my capacity as liaison to get in touch with the university," Gareth was explaining. I was sure he was feeding me information, so I'd understand the circumstances that had brought him here. "Imagine my surprise when they gave me the student's name to take to the dean, and I discovered that I recognized it from your scientific work on the battery project your class took on for my client."

Ah, that was the story he told them.

"What happened that you're here and banged up like this?" he asked.

"She saved Tera. Crawled under the blasted razor wire and *saved* her."

Gareth recognized the name and his brow creased with confusion.

Crispin slid his hand over mine. "Ember my father didn't say it. But I will. Thank you."

I stammered, "Anyone would have—"

"No, you are absolutely wrong. In fact, no one would have." Crispin was emphatic.

I shifted my arms to remind him I was restrained, rattling the chains against the metal guardrail of my hospital bed.

Crispin turned and asked Gareth, "Are the restraints necessary?"

Gareth caught his eye and passed him a yes without using words.

"Are *both* restraints necessary?" Crispin worked his jaw. Grinding his back teeth to make his face look aggressive. A holdover means of communicating threat from the ancient days when men fought tooth and nail, clawing and biting their enemies. He set hard eyes on Gareth.

Gareth came to my bedside and pulled out a key to unlock my shackle. Okay, another question. Why did Gareth hold the key and why could he make that decision?

He leaned over to better see the lock. "Your life is on the line," he murmured, then pursed his lips. There was a tick under his right eye.

"I'm aware," I mouthed back.

As, Gareth worked the lock to release me, I noticed that the seed of Crispin's interest in me as a woman was sprouting now that Gareth was in the room to add fertilizer to the soil. And by fertilizer, I meant crap. A deep pile of donkey dung. My problems were expanding exponentially. If asked my druthers, and now in hindsight, the truth was that I'd probably rather have been shot at curfew than get caught in this net with the high potential for advanced interrogation methods. Of course, I had been compelled into this situation by the mission to *save her*.

And that's when I got a shudder of foreboding. The car rescue was not my end task, it was a first step. Tera had not yet been saved. I hadn't completed my task.

I stilled as I sought those thoughts and checked them for veracity. Using my clairvoyant skills, I looked at a picture of the mission. It did not have the golden corona one received as a victory trophy, displaying accomplishment. It sat there, dull and incomplete. By the Fates, I was still mission activated.

That changed things. I'd have to juggle these two men—their egos and their feelings for and about me—over a longer period, not just to secure my own freedom but to save Tera. I was under no illusion. My looks and my personality gave my energy entrée, but it was my spell work that manipulated them into thinking thoughts of emotional entanglement. A tool in my tool box. A weapon in my arsenal. Could that still work for me here?

Gareth stood there, his mood on a low boil. "They said you drove a car. *A car,*" he stood tall, his voice ratcheted up with each syllable until he was bellowing. Crispin puffed up in response. He would have no bellowing at me, his stature said.

Gareth dropped his level of anger. His rage seemed to be borne of fear rather than fury. I didn't think he was reacting to the fact that I killed four of his enforcers and kidnapped his hostage. I think he'd talked himself out of believing that I was capable of such a series of actions. And since he was the one who brought me to the site, he'd have to question his own ability to read character. And he'd have to ask himself if I had cared for him in our relationship or if I had just been using him. The answer was yes. Both. I cared for and enjoyed him. And that didn't get in the way of my doing my duty. And never would.

"Crispin and I want to help you." Gareth looked over to affirm that Crispin was on board.

As he nodded his affirmation, Crispin sent out a subtle claiming flavor to the energy he directed toward me. It tasted of dark chocolate. Bitter more than sweet.

Interesting.

Gareth was picking up on none of this. He seemed okay with what he saw in Crispin's demeaner because he proceeded. "I have to understand, so I can intervene on your behalf. You are from the Range. How in the world would you understand how to drive a car?"

Okay, Gareth needed me to keep quiet about the fact that I had driven with him on several occasions. Maybe the fear I picked up from him was part self-preservation. I could play along. "I studied them at the university, cars. I've read about them in old novels. I didn't find it difficult to figure out." I pulled my brow together. "Though, to be honest, I was very bad at it." I looked from Gareth to Crispin with a little self-deprecating frown. "My whole body was shaking and that made it hard for me to work the pedals and maneuver the steering device, the steering wheel."

"You were shaking because you knew you'd be caught," Gareth said, "and you knew the repercussions."

"I was shaking because of the girl," I sought out Crispin's gaze but was careful not to send him any warmth, lest Gareth get jealous. Besides, by pulling the warmth from the room, it made them cold and uncomfortable. They should be. What happened was terrifying. Life threatening. No, this wasn't a time for warmth. This was the time for the cold hard truth. "Her name is Tera?"

Crispin nodded.

"Tera was unconscious, and I was afraid my inability to drive would put her life on the cusp. I was terrified that I wouldn't be able to do what needed to be done to save her. I did my best." I pursed my lips and whispered loudly enough that I knew they'd hear, "Thank all that is good that she survived."

A low rumble stopped our conversation. I glanced back at the window and the sky looked bruised, streaked as it was with purple and green. Hail clattered against the panes.

Crispin was at the window, searching the sky. "Tornado," he yelled.

"Gareth, unlock me," I cried out.

Gareth turned toward me with a look of indecision. I wondered what role he played and why he felt he needed to keep me trapped.

"Please, Gareth, I'm not running away, but if I'm tethered here—"

The windows rattled violently in their frame. A branch hit and cracked the glass, as Crispin ducked to the side.

"Gareth," I screeched, yanking at the cuff. I couldn't release the lock with magic in front of them.

Gareth whipped the key from his pocket and worked at my second shackle as another branch flew through the panes. Glass shards glittered the air. The wind wolf-called its way into the room, churning up everything in its path.

Crispin threw his torso over my head to protect me.

Screams filled the hallways, echoing off the stone walls as the roar of the wind picked up its volume and the power flickered.

Father Sky and his battle against humanity.

Our most skilled Wise Women on Haven told us that Father Sky would rage until the believers—the Witches and Heathen—were allowed to worship the makers of all, our creators Father Sky and Mother Earth, openly and lovingly, again. That was the task Haven's Hereditary Witches in their Offling Years were supposed to bring about. Our directive was to bring down the new hierarchy and restore peace, so Father Sky would stop raging. Simple, in theory. Generations of Witches had fought for the reality.

"Can you walk?" Crispin asked as he pulled me from the bed into his arms and set me gently down on my feet. His arms still held and steadied me.

I took a step to test out the idea. It wasn't my injuries that would keep me down, but the fuzzy attention-wandering medications that made linear and focused thought so hard. "I'm woozy," I replied, letting myself sway. I wanted Crispin to have the opportunity to play hero and protect me. To make an investment in my wellbeing.

A crash, more screaming.

Crispin lifted his voice over the tumult. "Go," he yelled toward Gareth, "see how you can help. I'll keep Ember safe."

Gareth looked at me as he did a side shuffle then took off into the hall to do as he was bid.

Crispin bent his knees and scooped me into his arms. "Hold on around my neck. I'll get you to the stairwell."

Everyone from the hospital who could possibly maneuver themselves to the stairs was packed in tightly. The power gave way in an explosion. Pitch black. Moaning and sobs. Crispin maneuvered me into a corner before he lowered my feet to the ground. With his arms on either side of me, posted on the wall, he made a protective cage for me with his body. "Hold on to me, Ember. You'll get crushed if you slip to the ground."

I cinched my arms around his waist. Through the thin fabric of my hospital gown I could feel the hard-chiseled ridges of his abdomen. My cheek rested on his strong chest. I swirled energy through my solar plexus and let it radiate into him. Gentle heat. I didn't want him to think this was sexual energy, *yet*. I wanted him to softly warm to the thought of me. I sent the energy up under his rib cage to envelop his heart. I knew he felt it when the beat grew stronger and quicker under my cheek. And I knew I had affected him the way I wanted when Crispin bent his head and breathed in the scent of my hair.

Chapter Nine

"Magnetoelectric multiferroic materials," I said with a smile that let Crispin know I didn't expect him to have any idea what I was saying, and also because I was slurring a bit.

"Alright, you've got me." He laughed. "Wow is that a mouthful. Say it again."

"Magnet-o-electric multi-fer-roic." I broke down the words and tried to annunciate them clearly. "I want to apply my research to batteries." I was resettled in my hospital bed. The tornado had ripped through the area and was gone as quickly as it had come. They had restored the power, boarded my window, and swept up the glass while Crispin ran down to the underground levels where his sister was being tended, to check on her. He came right back announcing that she had slept through the storm and was none the wiser. He'd left her to her dreams and had returned to sit with me.

A nurse followed him in and checked my vital signs, had seen that I had not been returned to my restraints, glanced toward Crispin, then cranked the head of my bed up so I was lounging instead of lying flat. She left without a word.

Now, untethered and upright, I felt less vulnerable as we spoke. "It's a means of capturing the Sun's power and making it useful for months on end. Such a development would help us get through the darkened days when the rain fall seems never-ending. We could grow crops inside buildings, so they didn't die deprived of light or from being flooded or ripped up by the winds. If we can get the batteries functioning, those in the Range would have heat in the cold and cool in the heat. With better energy, there would be less suffering."

Crispin blinked. His thoughts were visibly whirring.

He probably only knew suffering as a concept and not a daily nagging pain. Here in the Enclave he'd probably not been a child who took the food their parents offered them knowing their parents would do without. I didn't fault him. Truly. I understood this. I had a magical childhood in all the meanings of the word. I wanted for nothing in my life on Haven.

I tugged at my sheets. This conversation was headed toward a place of conflict; I needed to change the direction. "Tera is an unusual name for someone who is not a Seer." I had met members of the Seer caste, and they were charlatans. There was no power surrounding them. They didn't even recognize the power that I carried with me. I knew when I was in the presence of an Elemental Witch of Haven. To me the energy around them sparkled and snapped.

The Seers, what a joke. No, not a joke, a problem. They took the message of the Significants and Proprietors, offering up their snake oil to the desperate citizens on the Range. The Seers worshipped the false gods of money and greed and led the Mundane to feel that nature was meant to serve them, that Earth's blessings were there to be exploited. How wrong this mindset was. How dangerous.

The Seers were weapons wielded by the Elites, against free will and free religion. And this is what set Father Sky off on his warpath of destruction. It would lead to everyone's ruin.

The Seers were the enemy of the people as far as I was concerned. Even when they made a good gesture, a soup kitchen, or shelter in the storms for instance, it came at a high price – a sermon on the benevolence of the Elites and prayers for their success. I would rather starve.

That wasn't true.

I'd never been in a place of going hungry for long stretches. I thought back to yesterday morning, driving by the naked man with his begging bowl. Yes, if he could make his way to a charity soup kitchen, he'd be willing to listen and pray to get to nourishment. It was ridiculous to hold others to standards I had never personally experienced.

Still, the thought of Seers riled me in ways that few others could. As a fire element, I tended to be a bit of a hot head, passionate, and effusive. I had to balance my fire energy with a cool pragmatism, making wise and calculated decisions. Somedays it was harder than others. Years of training usually stood me well. *Usually.*

Crispin stepped closer. "Are you okay?" He rested his hand on the blanket over my ankle.

His touched snapped me back to here and now, to my hospital room. I didn't like these Mundane medicines. "Oh." I laughed. "I'm… the medicinal patch they put on me. It makes it hard for me to concentrate. My thoughts are meandering around like children lost in the woods. But, we were talking about Tera."

That was it.

This was too dangerous.

I reached my fingers down to my thigh, playing with the edges of the patch. The risk of a reprimand was far better than my inability to concentrate. I ripped off the patch as surreptitiously as I could.

There was no chair in the room, and Crispin indicated the corner of my bed. When I smiled and opened my hand invitingly, he slid a hip onto the mattress. "Tera is short for Terabithia." The corner of his mouth tweaked up, and I read it as embarrassment. No not embarrassment, more like sentimental, no…huh, complex. There was a complexity that surrounded her name, but certainly not his feelings for her. She was his little sister by, I would guess, a good ten years or so. But there was a parental feel to his energetic field, and I imagined with the stone-faced father, and no mention of a mother, yet, that Crispin had stepped forward to fill a void.

"From the novel?" I asked. "No, that couldn't be right, that ended so sadly. I cried for hours when I read it."

"Ah." He tapped his index finger on his nose. "But you are focusing on the wrong part of the story. You're focusing on how the girl, Leslie, drowned and the sorrow she left in her wake. My mother, when she named my sister wanted her to embody the qualities of the place the two friends had created, a place of imagination and wonder."

"She was an artist your mother?" It was the explanation that made the most sense, the art that the young boy from the book so desperately wanted to make, the drawing of an alternative reality.

Crispin squinted his eyes and tilted his head, looking at me curiously. "She was," he said, then paused. "She applied her skills as a clothing designer before she married my father."

"Are there other siblings? Are you the eldest? Were you the first to get a whimsical name?" I asked.

He threw back his head and laughed heartily and for some reason I was both exhilarated with pride and at the same time confused. The longer he laughed, the more uncomfortable I became. I was glad when he finally sobered. "I'm sorry, yes. The answer to your question is yes. I have a whimsical sounding name. I'm the eldest of two, no other heir, just me and Tera." He reached out his hand to shake mine. I was surprised by how gently he slid his hand into mine, how lightly he gripped me. Normally, I disliked handshakes that weren't earnest and strong, but I realized he was cautious of my bruised hand.

"We weren't properly introduced," he said. "I'm Crispin Noble."

I froze. He was a Noble. A *Noble*. The ruling family of the Significants in the Southern Enclave. He spoke, and others did what was bid of them. Whatever he wanted. Whenever he wanted. He was powerful in ways that I couldn't imagine. Of course, I too had powers in ways he couldn't imagine, so we should be on a level playing field, I worked to convince myself that was true. But, no. It just wasn't the case. With a thought, a whim, he could have me lauded. He could have me killed. Or anything in between. Any whim at all. I felt like a wild animal that had been backed into a corner, not sure if the form that approached me would pet or strike at me. Not sure what posture to affect so I had the best shot at survival. I looked at the restraints still attached to my bed, realizing my options were slim.

My distress either went unnoticed or was something he chose to ignore. I would guess the latter. He was keenly intelligent and aware, that was evident. I imagined that he was used to my reaction and his way of handling it was to move the conversation along as if his station was a non-issue. Until, of course, it wasn't. Gareth was right, here lay a great danger. I sent warmth down my arm over my hand and into his grasp.

He changed his grip relaxing his handshake to simply hold my hand. Our hands resting on the mattress, he slid a little closer toward me. "My mother loved to read the ancient books. Loved the classics. She had a crush, I believe, on Shakespeare's King Henry V."

"St. Crispin's Day speech?" I managed after swallowing hard.

"Yes, well, I was born on St. Crispin's Day, you see. And Mother thought it was poetic and wonderful that it was my birthdate, so she gave me the name. My father was away during both Tera's and my births, so he didn't have a moderating say." His eyes dropped and a sentimental smile rested with no small amount of sadness on his lips. I wondered if he realized he was stroking his thumb over the pulse in my wrist. "I think she chose those names purposefully to prove some point to my father."

"What do you think your father would have called you, had he had the choice?"

Crispin tilted his head. "You know, I can't even imagine that. I have no idea what he thinks a good name would be."

"And your children? What kinds of names will you call them? Or do you already have children?"

"No children, no wife. I had a fiancée but she..." his voice trailed off. He pursed his lips and shook his head, then visibly swallowed.

Okay, that was interesting. Something significant had happened, and he had used the past tense in referring to her. I needed to find out what happened to the fiancée. I wondered if this had anything at all to do with Tera's safety. Yes, somehow those two energies felt connected.

"I'm so sorry," I whispered, and I meant it. I changed the rays of warmth to become a comforting spell, hoping to add balm to the wounds our conversation had exposed.

"Yes, well…"

I reached for a lighter subject. "Crispin," I said. "Crispin Noble." I tipped my chin up with a frown "Did the kids beat you up over your name?"

He laughed again, this time I could tell he was charmed. It was ridiculous that anyone would lay a finger against a Noble.

"No," he said. "I was always a big kid, and so I could hold my own. But they did come up with some rather obnoxious nicknames."

I found myself smiling back at him. As far as enemies went, he was very affable. "Like what?"

"Crispy, Burned to a Crisp, Cinder Ash, then Ash sometimes Coal."

"That's rather silly isn't it? Not even clever as far as name calling goes."

He rubbed his chin. "No, I guess not. Ember is an unusual name."

"My mother was an artist too, a musician, she played string instruments and sang. She told me that she was practicing the harp late into the night, and when she looked up there was a single ember burning in the fireplace, and she knew she was pregnant with a red-headed girl, and that she would name me Ember." I looked Crispin in the eye. "I don't believe her though. She was always trying to turn the everyday into the extraordinary. I think the true story was that she had a case of heartburn," I quirked my brow, "realized she was pregnant and somehow she wove that into a new narrative." I brought a wave of warmth through me and stilled to let the energy flow to him. This time it had a taste of seduction to the warmth. A picture of our bodies, naked and tangled together. Of our hair damp with sweat. I was trying it on for size, looking for a reaction.

Crispin seemed stunned. Not quite taken aback, but…flustered. "She lived in the Productor Range?" His voice caught as he said it, and he had to stop and clear his throat. He was receptive to the idea. That was good to know.

"We aren't from this area. I came here when I passed the exams and earned a place in the university."

"Ah, so where are you from?"

The door opened with a bang, and Crispin withdrew his hand as he stood and turned to see Gareth had come in. "There you are," Crispin said. It sounded like he was annoyed that Gareth had taken so long, but I knew Crispin had been enjoying the sensations and was ticked that the spell had been broken. And there was also the impropriety of a man from a Noble family consorting with a university student. It might be okay once I was part of the Intelligencia, but right now I was considered a subpar part of society as a Productor.

"I have to finish my interrogation," Gareth tried to bite back the snarl in his voice but wasn't very effective.

I'm pretty sure Gareth had pushed through the door the way he did because he had some suspicions about Crispin's feelings.

Gareth had seen what he thought he would.

"Exactly. What kept you?" Crispin asked evenly.

"A wall collapsed in the office wing, we had to get the people out. No one died. A few broken bones," he said then turned to me. "You made it through that storm just fine." Now his words held jealousy and were accusatory.

Mundanes didn't seem to understand that thoughts are energy. The thoughts are transformed into words that are expressed, increasing that energy. If one is dexterous with energy, as every trained Witch from Haven was, then the words have more meaning than the vocabulary that was chosen. The seed of the thought – the emotion of the thought is evident. And that can be very useful information, indeed.

Right now, the tone and choice of his words told me that Gareth would love to be alone in a room, so he could yell at me. Fear and anger over my situation, jealousy that I had created a connection with Crispin, were parts. There was more though. I'd like to talk to him about it and work things through. But right now, Gareth wanted nothing more than for my temperature to heat up to the level that his was. I didn't rise to his bait. *Honestly, if you want to see an inferno, keep taunting the red-headed Elemental Fire*

Witch and see if you like the price of her ire. I pushed a breath through pursed lips. I let those thoughts flow away from me.

I still didn't know what I was going to do to get myself out of this situation, and I couldn't get myself out of this situation until I was sure that I had saved Tera from whatever situation put me into play.

Crispin and Gareth were a big problem. Right now, both had life or death control over me. And if I were to be honest, Gareth might be leaning toward death. I knew too much about him. He confided way too much to me. It wasn't consciously his fault; he wasn't indiscrete. I had charmed him into sharing. Only a Witch would have the ability to soften his constraints. He didn't know I was a Witch, but I hoped he knew that his secrets were safe with me. My life depended on it. And my aligning with Crispin would read as dangerous in Gareth's eyes. I hoped we'd find a moment to talk, then I could explain to Gareth that for his sake, as well as mine, it was best if Crispin was a tightly-held ally. Gareth would understand that, even if it would make him leery in our relationship. Gareth thought we were a couple, and he, like most men, would be none too pleased to think his place was being usurped. Gareth could be a volatile man. And his mood had already been dark.

This wasn't good.

Gareth found a position against the wall and folded his arms over his chest. "We were talking about your driving the car when the storm hit."

"Yes."

"I'm still not clear about how you got to the point of having Tera in the car. You heard her scream, you said you thoughtlessly went to her rescue…fill me in. What's the story?"

"Thoughtlessly connotes insensitivity and selfishness. I don't believe I was thoughtless. I acted without thinking. I believe there's a big difference."

He glowered at me, dark and stormy. The mood suited him somehow.

I pulled the sheet off the bed and wrapped it around my shoulders. The best way to handle this was to tell the truth and let my emotions flow. All of it. Everything I had masked over and pushed down. All the barriers I'd thrown up to get the job done, to live up to my vows. Vulnerability, that's what needed to surface. "I arrived on the scene," I began. "There were three men. But I had heard a girl scream. I was confused. I lay on the ground." I pulled my legs up to crisscross them and knotted my hands in my lap. I gathered the horror I had felt at seeing the crowbar impact skulls and brain matter slide out onto the ground. I let the horror ride my breath out into the room and fill it. Horror felt sticky - like you'd never be able to wash yourself clean from it. People worked to avoid horror. And I wanted to avoid this subject. So, yes, this seemed like the right tac to take. "They were yelling. They were fighting. A man went down." I moved my eyes across the wall, reliving the scene in my mind's eye. Making sure that I didn't look at either Crispin or

Gareth. "They, the two men left, were talking about taking the girl, tying her up, and putting her in their trunk. I... it was... it happened so fast." I scrunched my eyes and shook my head. "The fighting was awful." I scrambled from the bed and moved to stand with my back in the corner, pulling my limbs in tight. I had seen victims of violence do this time and again while recounting their experiences. As I mimicked their actions, I found that there was some level of comfort, feeling that two walls of strength helped to support and protect me.

With the medication patch off me, I revisited my idea that the men could have killed each other, and I rejected it. There was no way that the crime scene would reflect that story line. I'd have to tell them something close to the truth, a watered-down version. I paused and took in a shaking breath.

Athena, I answered the call of your owl,
Into the dark I did prowl,
To do your bidding I fought and won,
Now the damage must be undone,
Guidance and wisdom, I need from thee,
So I seek it, so mote it be.

My eyes searched over the floor as if I could find the words I needed there. "I ... I couldn't let someone put a girl in a trunk. We all know what happens after a girl goes in a trunk." I stopped talking. Silence swelled in the room. From under my lashes I could see both Gareth and Crispin had expanded their poses, legs wide, fists bunched. I lifted my head up, so they could see the torment in my eyes. "I don't really remember all that happened." I paused to find that faraway look of someone travelling back to the moment. "I was running to help. They hit the man. The girl was crying. They said to put her in the trunk. I grabbed the bar. Then they were fighting with me, and I was fighting back." More silence. "I was terrified. I didn't recognize myself in that moment. It was like I was a wild thing. A mouse caught within the clutches of a lion, and I knew that if I didn't fight hard, I would die. And the driving force beneath that was that if I died, the girl would be captured. And then…" My voice caught, and I choked, then pushed myself to continue. "I remember thinking that she probably wouldn't die right away that these men meant to hurt her, torture her. I remember thinking…" I cut myself off, letting a deep sob of anguish, truly and deeply felt, move up from my gut, over the icy death shards in my heart, and release into the atmosphere.

I put a shaking hand to my mouth to stifle the sounds. I just let my body react. Swaying on my feet, I began to sink. Crispin was beside me in a single stride. His hands wrapped my arms as he lowered me to the safety of the floor. He moved to the ground with me using his body to support mine.

I brought both of my hands over my face as I cried. I let my vibrations slide into Crispin's unprotected aura, so he could feel what I felt. He hugged me tight against him and rocked me. "Thank you. Thank you," he chanted, pressing kisses into my hair. "Thank you."

After a moment in this position, I realized that the room had a cold spot.

There stood Crispin's father, unmoved and unconvinced. In my dive into the bowels of emotion, I hadn't heard him come in. He walked to the door. "Nurse, your patient needs medicating."

Chapter Ten

There was electrical current available here at the hospital twenty-four hours a day. This was unique even for the Realm. The hospital and other emergency services had the eco batteries that kept their vital functions going day and night. First the Significants then the Proprietors electrified their homes and offices with eco panels. Once they had their needs met, the next use of the panels went to energizing the non-urgent transportation.

Few in the Range had energy, the government did, the emergency stations, the university–to run our labs—and a few factories. But those panels only worked when the Sun shone. And there were times when Father Sky grew grumpy and vindictive. He'd cover the Sun's rays leaving the world dim of both natural light and the ability to restore the batteries for stockpiled energy. Father Sky would bring rain for weeks on end, until it seemed all of humanity was waterlogged and depressed.

The thing I thought about was that because of the consistent electricity and health needs, here at the hospital, I was told that they had the luxury of hot water that came from a tank instead of being heated over a fire.

Instant and copious hot water.

It would be wonderful to take a deep hot soak. It would make my muscles feel so good. The nurse gave me an emphatic no to my request. Instead, she sponge-bathed me, anointed me with antibacterial salve and rebandaged my cuts. She wanted to replace my pain patch, especially since Daddy Noble had been so harsh about it. But I was able to convince her that it made me feel worse. She offered me some pills instead, and I hid them under my tongue until I could spit them out and flush them down the drain.

Here, alone in my bed, sleep evading me, I revisited the strange dynamic that had unfolded with the Noble patriarch—"Noble, Sr." was what he said I might call him. I was surprised it wasn't "His Majesty". I was lying in Crispin's arms, having relived the horrendous fight, where truly and without hyperbole, I could very easily have been killed. And more, his sister would have suffered. Crispin's father walked in and growled for the nurse. Crispin moved as if to block me from his father's sight and tightened his grip. So, Crispin must perceive danger there that he wanted to protect me from.

Hmmm, interesting.

Gareth, whom I was sure was reacting to some unspoken order given by Noble Sr. moved over to crouch beside us. He gave Crispin a significant look that read as though they had a lot of history, maybe even something like friendship but with a hard edge to it. Their communication, instant and silent, took place, and Crispin released his hold. Gareth scooped me into his arms and laid me back in the bed.

I needed to know more about who they were to each other. And if their comradery would decrease my danger or make everything worse.

One thing I knew for sure was that my sudden appearance shifted the dynamic considerably. I was a variable they hadn't calculated into their equation. And it wasn't about the fact that I was manipulating their emotions for my own ends – well, the ends needed by the Resistance. It was my presence. My actions. Yes, I'd need to keep a finger on that pulse.

Once I was set down, both men stalked out the door to confer with the father. What conversation I was able to sip from under the door as they moved away had been about Tera's wellbeing.

Now, clean and alone, I lay there staring at the ceiling. Wondering what would come next. The restraints hung from my safety bars, but I remained uncuffed. I didn't know if they were forgotten or were left there as a threat.

All of the unknowns made me feel antsy and agitated. I was a Fire Witch, lying still was antithetical to my nature. I wanted to leave, but truth be told there was nowhere to go.

If I went back to the Range, I couldn't help Tera.

I sat up cross-legged and sent a surreptitious glance toward the door. I expanded my aura to taste the environment. Outside it all tasted bland, like boiled potatoes without salt. Convinced that I would have the time and space, I pulled my energy back in the room with me and closed my eyes. With the ease of years of study, I moved my breath to take me into a trance state. A flame, of course, was my direct link to the Haven Council with clear information and directives. Barring that, I could at least get a *sense* of what was happening. I could call to the Fates and asked for their communication.

I began by imagining myself as a light being, merely energy within the space I sat.

Sending a grounding cord deep into the Earth, I asked that any peripheral energies that had glommed on since I'd last done ritual be released.

In my mind's eye, I used a besom, a broom made of twigs, to sweep the space free of interference from any malevolence – the kind of negative energy that filled one's thoughts with disapproval and self-doubt. Misdirection. Inaccurate interpretations. All of these things lead to dis-ease, upping the potential for danger by not seeing clearly.

When I felt that the space was clean, I cast my circle.

In the absence of actual salt, I had to rely on white light to form my boundary. White light was not my favorite tool to work with. It had a power of its own and was sticky. It could quickly fill a space and be difficult to rid oneself of. I considered it advanced magic to be able to work with white light. I could do it—we were trained—it was just that... I let that thought fade. There were pros and cons to using each of the magical tools. White light was strong, and often difficult to direct. But I thought I could rationalize my choice; with everything going on, I needed strong magic.

I drew a pentagram in the air with my index finger and imagined myself out in the ritual field on Haven. In this vision, I turned my face to the North and pulled from my imaginary pocket four gifts.

Earth to the North! I call to you, and I placed a moss agate on the altar at the top of my circle. I chose that gem stone as it aids courage by releasing trauma and anxiety. It is the stone of relief.

I walked eastward and placed the feather of a bluebird on that altar. This feather represented my dedication to protecting my family at all costs. "My family" I defined in this meditation as the traditions and the ancestry of Haven Witches. *Air, I call to you*

Now, I moved to face the south. *Fire my heart!* I called in my vision. I imagined myself placing a sprig of sage, for wisdom, on the pyre. I struck a match and held it to the small balefire that the acolytes of this glade always had laid and waiting for a need.

I moved to the altar in the direction of the setting sun. *Water to the West, I call to you.* I pulled the cork from a small cobalt bottle and added more rainwater to the that which was collected in the great cast iron cauldron. I dipped my fingers in and felt the coolness and purity. As always, water was the contrary to my spirit and this could either work well in containing my fire spirit, or it could make a mess of things. Sometimes it's just better to let a fire burn itself out.

In my meditation, I was skyclad. We always went to the sacred circle without clothing during ritual on Haven. My nakedness was my being willing to experience vulnerability and to trust. It was a sign that I had nothing to hide from the great divine. I walked to the center of my circle and raised my arms to embrace the ether.

Elements, each fierce in your own right, destructive and devastating. And each a blessing-a life-giving, life-sustaining miracle. It is in the sense of destruction and creation that I call on you today.

This circle is cast, blessed be!

I let my image find a place to sit in the center of the protected circle. I pulled a necklace over the tangle of my hair. In my meditative state, I chose citrine—the stone of the sun—to be my pendulum. It was a stone of clarity that cleared fear and emotions from a question, allowing the true answer to be understood with precision of thought.

I held the pendulum before me. "Permission to play?" I asked.

It swept back and forth in a strong line.

"Any reason not to learn the truth?"

The stone swirled in a wide circle, the way I had trained my physical pendulum, the one I had left back on the island, to say no.

"Fates be with me. Goddess that I serve be with me. My higher self, I call you in. I don't know what's going on, and I need answers. My first question—when Athena sent the owl, was Tera the one I was supposed to save?"

The pendulum swung back and forth in a smooth arc, *yes*.

"Have I finished the task of saving Tera?"

The pendulum swung widdershins, a lefthanded circle. *No*.

"I should stay here with her in the Realm for her protection?"

Yes.

Hmm. "I should trust Gareth?"

A deosil circle to the right. Undefined.

"I should trust Crispin?"

A deosil circle to the right. Undefined.

"Besides my connection to the ether, have I any allies on this task?"

Circle to the left, *no*.

This always proved tedious, trying to get the answers I needed by playing the children's game of twenty questions. And to be honest, I wasn't sure how long I had behind the Veil before someone would pop into my room. Being jerked from the ether to the mundane was confusing and physically painful. It left a broken sacred circle in its wake and uprooted the magic. None of that was good. This was not the time to be disrespectful to the powers that be. I needed to focus and close as quickly as possible.

"I will have to stay somewhere in the Realm to be close to Tera, shall I stay with the Noble family?"

Yes.

Okay, I had a destination, I had a quasi-goal, I had no allies. I wished I could speak to someone on the Council. They would have these answers. Who or what did Tera need saving from? Why did she need magical intervention? And why would the Fates care enough to send me? I needed a flame. Some way to communicate. I wondered if Socrates couldn't come and pay me a visit, carry a message back to the Resistance, and at least let them know I was alive.

"Is Piper okay?"

The *yes*, was glitchy, not a smooth sway.

"Is she in danger?"

Left-handed circle, *no*.

"Does she think I'm in danger?"

Smooth arc, *yes*.

"That's the problem? She's worried?"

Yes.

"Am I? Endangered, I mean."

My pendulum swung and jumped, swung and jumped, an emphatic yes.

Okay, enough of this. I vanished the pendulum and my image came to standing. I spread my arms in a wide circle taking in Earth and Sky; I spread them wide in supplication, then used my whole body to add physical action to my mental plea.

Fates hear me, this I pray,
Tera's lived another day.
A family of means, a place of wealth,
Tera's life and Tera's health,
A protection spell, I doth lay.

Here come I, by fire and sword,
Standing fierce, my focus forward,
Open a space in Tera's home.
This spell I cast from witch's tome.
Repay my service with food and board.

There, I'll watch, wait, and spy,
To do the service of finding why,
To then answer the question of who and when,
The evil, I swear to unbend.
The will of the Fates is my cry.

And so, I end this spell, this plea,
To do the will of Air and Sea,
To honour the Earth in all her guise,
A blaze of Fire, fierce, and wise.

Fiona Angelica Quinn

By the power of three times three.

So I speak it, so mote it be!

I could feel my name on someone's tongue. They were speaking about me somewhere nearby. Would they burst through the hospital room door? I decided to quickly close my circle. I thanked each direction, each element.

Mother Earth for your love and support, I thank you
Father Sky for the light of the Sun and the air I breathe, I thank
you.
Water you cool my agitation and impatience, I thank you.
Fire, my heart, we are always one, I thank you.
The circle is open, but never broken.
Hoozah!

I took a deep lungful of air in. I exhaled a cleansing breath out. My eyes popped open in time to see the door push wide.

"Ember! I thought that I had only dreamed about you, but there you are."

Chapter Eleven

Crispin chuckled and tapped her shoulder, so the girl would move forward. Long chestnut brown hair, plaited into a braid and tied with a blue ribbon, hung over her shoulder. She was slender and wore a nightgown and robe of beautifully embroidered satin material, lined to make it thick. It looked warm and comfortable, and I wanted to pet my fingers over the luxurious fabric to see how it felt under my fingertips. On her feet she had fur-lined slippers. My guess—now that I was seeing her in the light—was that this girl was about thirteen years old.

"This is Tera," Crispin said, with a doting smile. "She wouldn't lie still. She had to meet you."

"I had to thank you." She bounded over like a puppy. It was quite jarring. Not only did the regal quality of her clothing seem odd on someone of her age and exuberance, but she looked nothing like she had last night. If I had been asked if I'd ever seen this girl before, I would truthfully have said no. I needed a moment to adjust.

Luckily, Crispin provided a commotion as he pulled two chairs through the door. They were the kind that could be stacked and stored. I guessed that he planned to stay for a conversation. *Good.*

"I hope you don't mind the company," Crispin said. "If you need quiet or privacy, you'll let us know?"

"I'm happy for a distraction." I wanted to make sure they both felt welcome, so I filled the room with warmth and painted the air with the color of the rose quartz, the gemstone of calm and peace. It seemed to work on Tera, but Crispin seemed...edgy. Anxious. Nothing overt but an underrunning current. I wished I understood where those feeling were stemming from, but he held the vibration tight against him, and it held no pictures for me to decipher. He seemed to be a man who had had to be on his guard. Funny, with the life of a privileged Noble, it would seem to me that all the worries would be taken care of for you.

But that wasn't true.

If it weren't for my getting "lost in my thoughts" and straying too close to the border, his sister would have been captured, tied up, and thrown in a trunk. Three men had died in the event. Crispin's driver amongst them. If I were Crispin, I'd be anxious, too.

Tera came to stand near my bed and scrutinized my face. She was slurping up the energy I was putting out like a thirsty puppy lapped at her water bowl. And then I thought how odd that thought was and stored it away as noteworthy.

"I recognize you. I truly do. I dreamed about you." It popped out of her mouth with no hesitation. She hadn't weighed the consequences at all. Were Significants allowed to have prophetic dreams? Seers, possibly, but she wasn't wearing that mantle of distinction, and Seers were older. If she were a novice, she'd have her head shorn. No, I think this was just an ebullient indiscretion. That was a dangerous thing to say in this day and age.

I looked over to find Crispin's startled reaction. His sister's outburst obviously disturbed him.

Tera saw his expression, too. "Oh stop. Ember doesn't care if I have dreams or not. I wouldn't have said that around anyone who is going to throw me on a bonfire." Then she laughed as if it were a joke.

It most certainly was not.

If she had ever heard the death screams of a human being tied to a stake with the fire flickering up their bodies, she would not be able to laugh.

Tera plopped into the chair her brother pushed toward her. "I have an invitation," Tera announced lacing her fingers and pulling her hands up under her chin. "I was talking to Crispin as we came up the stairs to visit when it suddenly occurred to me that you're injured."

I blinked.

"Well, obviously you're injured, you're here." Her face flamed red. "I mean I realized, as I came up the stairs, that you're injured because of me. And thank you for that." She dropped her chin, and her voice softened to a whisper.

"I'm not here because of you," I challenged. "You're every bit the victim as I am."

The atmosphere suddenly chilled around Crispin, like a blast of arctic air. He was concerned about what I was about to say. More than concerned, agitated. I reached out and tried to interpret the warning he was giving off, but all I got was an emphatic no. No what? No information about the event? No discussion of victimhood versus perpetrators? Had they not told her what had happened while she was unconscious? As that thought came to mind it felt smooth— a key that slides easily into its lock. I'd couch my words carefully. "You had nothing to do with landing me in this hospital. The car accident is the reason I'm injured."

"Our family is in your debt," Crispin said.

Hold those thoughts, Crispin, until the mission is over, and she's safe. "No," I shook my head. "Not at all."

"You can't go back to the university dormitory," Tera said. "They don't have enough hours of electricity. You will get an infection. I've decided, and convinced Crispin, that until your new term begins at the university, you shall live with us. I've sent a runner to tell Maid that she's to have the room across from mine prepared for you. And you can tell Cook what it is that you like to eat, and we'll have that."

Cook? Maid? She addressed these people by the name of their job?

I wasn't at all surprised at the invitation. I thought my spell had been well crafted and well received. I had projected an invitation, though I thought it would be Crispin who'd insist. So, Tera had some spunk. I turned to Crispin to see what he thought about Tera's invitation. And as always, I wondered at the Mundanes and their inability to feel the course of energy that moved their thoughts and actions, that they didn't fathom my spell work… That was probably because they weren't trained to spot magic and believed that they had rid the world of Witches, or near enough. Of course, the day the last Witch dies, is the day that Earth and Sky would remove all of humanity. With no Witches to do ritual, there would be no reason to put up with human destruction. Humanity would be considered an experiment that went very wrong. And this mistake would be erased, down to the very last human.

Crispin seemed earnest enough as he said, "I hope you'll accept our care and hospitality. The very least we can do is restore you to your previous good health before we send you back to saving the world with high tech batteries." He smiled.

The pendulum had said his role had not yet been defined.

Crispin was a wielder of power. He could very well appease his sister by letting me come to the house, but as soon as the time was up, and the new university term was beginning, he could have me disappear, either by death or imprisonment. And Tera would be none the wiser.

Still, this was good. *Thank you, Fates, for intervening and bringing about this turn of events.* I had time. A very short time between the terms, but I would take this step by step. This opened a door for opportunity. "Your invitation is very kind." I hesitated, I couldn't be too eager, they needed to persuade me. I needed to be in their home as a favor to them not a favor to me. "But, I must decline."

Shock was evident on both Crispin and Tera's faces. They assumed I would say yes and that it was all a done deal.

"I must insist." Crispin's brow drew in as he edged forward in his seat.

I smiled at how effective my gambit had worked. "Please let me finish, your invitation is very kind. But, really, I can't accept. You see, it's exam week and if I don't sit for my exams, I will fail the term and be released from my program. I can't let anything interfere with getting my Diploma Intelligencia. This is not life-threatening as was the case last night, but it is life-style and livelihood threatening."

"That's simply arranged." Crispin waved his hand through the air. "Gareth will speak to the university, and he can proctor your exams. He'll go to your dorm and gather what you need to prepare and bring the items to my home."

Gareth. I would like to talk to him and see what light he could shed on this situation. Of course, my asking him would have to be done with great care. He could be a foe or a friend. I needed to know more about his connection to the Noble family and to Crispin specifically. I wondered how Gareth was seeing me now versus how he perceived me yesterday when we were sitting in the car side by side, holding hands. "That's so generous." I let my voice become unsure and a little shaky. "Still, I have to decline."

"But why?" Crispin was truly looking at me as if I were a puzzle to be solved. I understood this; a Producer would normally jump at the chance to luxuriate in the Realm with food and heat. I reveled in the power of his confusion. "What else is standing in your way?" he asked. "Surely, you'll put your health first. As my sister said, it's dangerous for you to return to an environment without hot water and electricity and the help of a nurse to attend to you. You can't even reach your wounds."

I licked my lips then pulled them in, I tried to look both embarrassed and vulnerable.

"Please, you can tell us," Tera pushed.

Ducking my head so my hair fell across my face, I said, "I'm afraid that your father would be disinclined to my being under his roof."

"Ember." Crispin waited until I looked at him. "He can be abrasive." Crispin laid his hand on his chest, letting me know his words were heartfelt. "I'm sorry for his behavior earlier. He is

123

fiercely protective and rather paranoid at times. With good reason."
He let that sentence fade. It tasted of sadness. My thoughts got stuck
on the cottony dryness of it. I had to shake my head to focus in on
what he was saying.

"My father's disposition comes with our standing. But the truth
is." He smiled and cocked his head to the side. "It's my roof. I have
my own home. Tera and my father are living with me while my
father's house is being rebuilt. His roof was dislodged in a recent
hurricane. While Father is a curmudgeon, and dislikes people as a
whole, he is not in a position to have a say about my guests."

Backbone. How attractive. Crispin just sailed up in my
estimation. Noble Sr. was not a man easily stood up to, of that I was
sure.

Tera sent him a look that told me how tightly these two were
connected. I wondered if this was what had put her in danger,
Crispin's devotion. Did a group feel that they could take Tera and
manipulate Crispin or their father into money or some other gain?

Silence filled the room to overflowing. Crispin added, "I'm not
inviting. I insist you come home with us."

I sent him warmth as he held my gaze and little by little I
upped the heat from friendly to sexual. To stay safe, I needed to
appeal to Crispin's male nature, to have him claim me, and then
protect what was his, harkening back to the biology of our ancestors.
Playing with this kind of energy could go very wrong. Jealousy and
patriarchy were formidable energies to manipulate. But I thought

this was the quickest and safest route. Up. Up, I moved the temperature between us. As I saw his face blush a rosy pink, I said, "Thank you, then. I would really appreciate a safe place to heal."

He slapped his hands down on his thighs and stood. "Good. Now that that's been decided, I need to check with the hospital about getting you released. Tera's already been signed off with instructions to stay calm and rest for a fortnight." He placed a hand on her shoulder. "Though, that's a little like telling a brook to be still." He moved toward the door. "If you can't go now, we'll keep a close eye and bring you home once your doctors have confidence that you're well enough to make the change." He said that last part with his hand on the door knob, looking back at me.

"Thank you," I said. "While you're asking them about that, would you please inquire after my ring?"

Crispin wrinkled his brow.

"It was a ring passed down in my family for generations, a small fire opal in a gold setting. It is very dear to me, and I believe they took it off my finger when I was medicated."

"I'll check on it." He pointed a finger at Tera. "You'll stay put and get to know Ember?"

"Of course, I will."

Crispin pulled the door open and as he walked out of the room, he shot a glance over his shoulder toward me, telegraphing a message. A very clear warning, perhaps "plea" would be a better word. But that was all that I got from his look. He hadn't been trained in how to send thoughts through the ether. In the void, I was left with a feeling of caution as he left the two of us alone.

Chapter Twelve

"It will feel good for you to be back in a familiar bed," I started. I wasn't sure once we were at Crispin's home, how often we would have privacy. I wanted to extract what information I could from her, now. "Do you mind if I ask how old you are?"

"Twelve," she said. "I'll turn thirteen in a week."

The thirteenth year was very important one in the life of a Witch on Haven. Thirteen was a deeply spiritual number. There were thirteen full moons in a calendar year, thirteen weeks between each of the four seasons: Spring Equinox, Summer Solstice, Autumnal Equinox, and the Winter Solstice. Thirteen was the number in the Major Arcana of the Tarot that stood for death. Death on this card could make students who were new to the Tarot feel frightened. But this kind of death didn't signify slipping into the beyond. It was death to an old way and the birth of a new one.

On Haven, in the thirteenth year, a student performed special meditations to find their life's calling.

I was called to wield the sword of Fire. To rebel. To fight. To resist.

And not to be caught and burned.

If Tera was an ancestral Witch of Haven, this was the year she would change. Gone would be her childhood, now she would enter into her preparation for adulthood. She'd pledge her duty to the Fates, the Gods and Goddesses. But here as a Mundane, living in the Noble family in the Southern Realm of Significants, I had no idea if this year meant anything more to her than another candle to blow out on her birthday cake.

Looking at Tera, I thought how bubbly she was, how playful even at this fearful time when someone was out to hurt her. With that thought, I felt sure that Tera didn't know what had happened last night. That was the cold that froze my words when I was talking about being a victim. That was the warning Crispin hoped to impart. I was almost certain of it. "Tera, what did they tell you about the circumstances of my helping you?"

"Oh, that you were out walking and heard the accident and were moved to come to my rescue. I can't remember the accident, but they said that Crispin's car was crushed, and that Driver died in the event. Had it not been for your bravery and cunning, I would have died, too."

She was a girl telling me a story about her day. Nothing deeply concerning about the "event" as if she'd washed the life and death struggle away like dirty water down the drain. But I guessed if you weren't hurt, and you had no recollection, then it might just be like listening to a fable from a book. I'd imagine that was what was going on here. That and her age. And her naturally optimistic character.

Though, to be honest, it almost seemed like she'd been charmed.

I expanded my aura and sure enough, I sensed magic swirling about her. This didn't have the accent or signature of my spell work. Sure, I could be hasty and graceless at times with my spells, but this one seemed chunky. Like a toddler with a fat crayon, trying to stay in the lines. Here was another mystery to solve. For the time being, I'd keep on with the mystery at hand, why was Tera's car off the road in the far reaches of the Realm?

"Do you remember any of the circumstances of the accident?"

She sighed. "Others have asked me, as well. The last I remember is the point where we left the road. We were at the barricade being warned, then there is a blank place that the doctor said was typical trauma amnesia. When I woke up here in the hospital, I was so glad that Father and Crispin were with me to explain why."

"You're okay though?"

"I'm bruised and sore. It's been enough hours that I'm no longer here for observation. They said the blow to my skull had no lasting effect. Crispin says that's because I'm hard-headed."

"No doubt." I smiled. "I hope you are. It will serve you well."

"Not around my father it won't, he likes to be the one with the hardest head." Her laughter was a sprinkle of sunlight on clear water. It was so naïve and wholesome.

"You know," I said, "I got to drive a car for the very first time that night. It was kind of scary to do. There's a trick to working the pedals just right. I'm not sure if I was glad that I was driving on dirt or if I would have done better if I were driving on a road. For sure, I was confused because I've never been in the Realm before and didn't know where I was or how to find help for you." I tipped my head. "How is it that you were so far away from buildings and so far from the roadway? I didn't even know there was such a desolate place in the Realm."

"I was visiting a friend's cottage by the lake. I love the water. Don't you?" She moved from her chair to perch at the foot of my bed like we were old friends, and she was completely at ease. She curled her arms around her knees. "It makes me feel happy to be at the lake." She looked toward the boarded-up window. "Of course, this time of year, it's much too cold to even stick a toe in." She focused back on me, lifting her braid and playing with the bow. "When I'm a woman with my own home, I'll insist that I live on the water's edge year-round. If I'm in the city where my father's house is, away from nature for long, Father says I get unbearably mopey."

"It's nice that you had friends to visit," I said, trying to picture a map and where she could have been driving in from.

"It got so bad this fall that Father had had quite enough of my attitude, so he sent me off to visit our friends."

"You were coming home when you had the accident?"

"Yes, the family was closing the cottage for the winter season, and Driver had come to fetch me."

"Did your driver become lost?"

"No there was a barricade across the road, they said there had been an isolated storm that caused the roadway to collapse. The men had a map and showed Driver how to navigate toward the barricade fence and follow it along until we reached a secondary road that would take us in the right direction for Crispin's house."

"Is that usual? Driving where there are no roads, I mean."

"Usual? No. But it has happened before. Once when Crispin was with me, he had to steer the car, and Driver had to walk in front finding a path forward, moving tree limbs and debris as he went. The storms, you know, can make a real mess of things."

"Your driver, he was okay with that last night? Driving in the dark over the ground?"

"He seemed so. Perhaps he thought it would be an easier drive than it turned out to be. After all, I'm told that he hit a rock and the car rolled. And he died at the scene, unable to get me free." She sighed and looked at her hands.

"That's such a frightening story," I said. "I'm glad I heard you call out and was able to come help." I held out my hand, and she slipped hers into my grasp. I sent her warmth. "And I'm glad to meet you. I want to learn everything about you, so we can be great friends."

I understood why Crispin would try to shield Tera from knowing that someone had orchestrated and manipulated the circumstances to get the car off by itself. I was sure the kidnappers had not intended an accident. There were too many variables to what the outcome of that would be. I bet they meant to isolate the car and get it stopped. Probably, the Driver was evading, and the speed and quick maneuvering along with the dark of night led to the crash. Hadn't the kidnappers thought that through? The driver would have been held accountable if he survived and Tera was taken. He would have been executed for failure to keep his charge safe. The driver would have also known that it wasn't likely they'd keep him alive if he could identify them or tell anything about the circumstance. As much for Tera's sake as his own, the man was driving for his life.

As we sat quietly together, and I mulled the scenario over. The kidnappers would have succeeded had it not been for the accident and for, well, me. I was something they hadn't planned for. I imagined how things would have played out. Once the men backed off the barricade and cars traveled freely again, no one would have thought to look in the desolate place they had directed Crispin's driver. No one would know that the car was stopped, and that Tera had been taken. When a search party went looking, they wouldn't search out in the middle of nowhere. This would have given the bad guys a chance to take Tera wherever they had wanted to, get themselves organized and situated, and reached for what they wanted with a ransom note.

What did they want? And from whom did they want it? Crispin? Noble Sr.? Was there anyone else who held Tera dear and would be manipulated by her disappearance?

"Let's speak of other things. Thinking about your accident is very unpleasant." I squeezed her hand, so she'd know that I wasn't meaning anything negative about her. "My room is to be across the hall from yours. Is your brother's house very big?"

"Big? No, it's about the same size as the house I grew up in. Regular size."

Close quarters then. That would make my getting away to investigate much more difficult.

"Do you live near anything interesting? Will we be able to take walks and look around?"

"Yes, oh yes! There are many interesting things. While we're on the outskirts of the city, where Crispin could have a little land around his house, he still lives within walking distance of things to do. There are lovely shops, and there is the Culture Center where the musicians perform, and the artists make beautiful things. There's the aqueduct, and, up the street from there is the Temple. You can go in and ask an Oracle to look into your future and give you their counsel."

"Have you been to the Temple often?"

"My school goes once a year to gather our words of caution and wisdom for the year. I don't like it there very much. I feel funny around Seers, not in a good way but in a sick to my stomach kind of way. I haven't been there since I was seven. I've always found an excuse."

"Wow," was the only thing I could think to say to that. Yearly school pilgrimages to the Seers? Now that was interesting. Since they weren't magical, and not truly offering information but were snake oil selling charlatans who dealt in quackery, there must be a different reason for the students' going. People of power must have wanted something that they could get from such an event. "Did something in particular happen when you were seven to make you feel uncomfortable?"

"The Seers told me that I would be punished for stealing if I continued to take Johnathan's treats at lunch; they "saw" me do it. And it was sending me down an irreparable path to be removed from the Realm and cast out to the Productors."

I frowned. The way she said it sounded like she would be cast to the vultures and shredded in their beaks. The Productors was indeed a hard life, but it wasn't a death sentence, necessarily.

"Have you been to a Seer?" she asked.

"No." I shook my head. "Never."

"I didn't take Johnathan's treats it was Sarah who was taking his treats. It was Rudolphia Sarah's friend who spread rumors about me to protect Sarah from getting caught. And Rudolphia had been

134

three people ahead of me when the students came for their prognostications that year. So I knew the Oracles were phony; they couldn't see a thing. Not only that, but the Seer I spoke with was asking me all kinds of questions about who came to visit my father and what they were talking about."

And now my question was answered. They were spies, using their robes to gain power through information. "Did you tell them?"

She blushed. "Well, I told them about Baker, and Vet, and Clothier. I decided I wouldn't tell them about who came to visit my father about other things."

"Like business? Or does someone from the Noble family even need to do business?"

"Oh, yes, people are in and out—"

The door swung open with a bang, and Tera gripped my hand tighter. I winced at the pain, but she didn't let go until I petted her hand and sent her a smile.

The right-hand man walked into the room with a travel bag. He set it on the end of my bed beside Tera.

"What are you two talking about?" he demanded.

"My name is Ember McGraw," I replied.

"I know that already." He stood with his feet spread wide and his arms folded across his chest. A thug stance, but since he was in a business suit, it came off as odd rather than threatening.

I could tell from the tip of his jaw he thought he was doing a good job intimidating me. Wow, was he going to be surprised when we rumbled. It occurred to me that that thought was in the future tense not the conditional. Somehow, I'd concluded that I was going to end up fighting this guy. I'd bet he was a good fighter. Aggressive and without the constraints of rules. I'd have to watch him and find his Achilles heel. Everyone had one. *Thetis, Goddess of water, make his weakness clear to me. So I ask it, so mote it be.* "You know my name, but we haven't been introduced. What shall I call you?"

"Ember, this is Edgar Marsal, he works closely with my father." Tera turned back to Edgar. "These are the things I asked for from Clothier?"

"I haven't opened it. Runner just handed them to me for you."

It was jarring to hear these people refer to others as if their name and their station was the same. It was dehumanizing, I thought. I wasn't sure I could do that. It seemed so robotic and plastic.

"How are they getting you back to the dorms?" Edgar asked. "Is Gareth going to convey you?"

"I haven't been told, and that's a while in the future, yet," I said.

"My understanding was that you'd be released from the hospital today," He inched his jaw forward.

"Ember isn't going home until she's well. She'll be staying in Crispin's home until her semester starts again."

His harsh gaze raked over me. "How did you fenagle that?"

"I said yes to the invitation that was extended to me." I had to work to keep my voice cool and calm, my anger wanted to blaze up

136

against this man. His aura was jagged and menacing. He was working hard to make me cower and to gain power over me. What that would serve I didn't know, but being here with him, I knew he was a dangerous man – not to be feared but to be dealt with one way or another. I didn't doubt for a second that he wanted to put his fingers around my throat and choke me until I spilled my secrets. I also knew he thought that I was chock full of those secrets and my story of arriving to save the day was absurd to him. That's okay, it was absurd to me too. I just needed to tell what truths I could and be quiet about the rest.

"And your Father is alright with this arrangement?" Edgar asked Tera.

"I haven't seen my father since the decision was made, so I can't speak to his opinion. However, it's Crispin's home. My father and I are his guests. Crispin is free to invite whomever he wishes, whenever he wishes."

Spunk. Very nicely played! I wondered if it was because she sat in a seat of privilege that made her think she could speak to an adult with that tone of voice, or if it was a natural aspect of her personality to feel of equal footing with those who were so obviously capable of violence.

On Haven, we spoke to all the Wise Generation—who served as our teachers, mentors, and surrogate parents—with the utmost respect and deference. But they deserved our admiration. It was unsettling, to be honest, to listen to a girl speak to power with her

137

own level of power. My background made me different from the Mundane who were raised and lived in the Productor Range, but those in the Range seemed closer to my understanding than this situation. Did all the young people in the Noble family act this way?

Tera turned to me and said with a grin, "Shall we see what Clothier sent?" She popped the clasp on the bag, dragging it onto her lap. She pulled out a new pair of black leather pants, a lovely cotton turquoise tunic, a pair of leather boots, a pair of wool socks, and a jacket, then she tipped the bag to show me that there was a set of underclothes there as well. They looked like they were made of silk and lace. I'd seen lace in books on Haven, and there some of the elders would crochet something they called lace, but it wasn't the kind one would want to wear under one's clothes. This was delicate looking and very pretty. And most important, it all looked like it was made of natural fibers. Artificial fibers played havoc on magical work. It sent static into the communication between the Witch and the ether.

"If they fit, then this is perfect."

"It's just for wearing home. Clothier will talk to you about your requirements once we get there. I asked her to wait until we do."

Crispin came in with a nurse. He sent a curious glance toward Edgar, then saw the bag and that seemed to clear up his question. "You're all set. This is Nurse." He gestured toward the young woman in her blue uniform. "Nurse will help you get dressed,

Ember. She'll be accompanying us to my house where she'll look after both you and Tera until you're both right as rain."

"Thank you," I said. I wondered how closely she'd be paying attention to me. How much freedom I'd have from her scrutiny.

Edgar said to the room, "You'll excuse me then, I have a task to perform for Noble, Sr." When Tera turned to ask Crispin about my ring, Edgar leaned close to me, "You don't fool me for a second, gutter urchin. I will uncover your plot. And you will pay a dear price."

Chapter Thirteen

What in the world was Tera thinking? She said Crispin's house was a normal-sized home. I'd imagined a townhouse with perhaps three stories, two bedrooms and a bath where Crispin and his father on one level, another level with two more bedrooms that Tera and I would occupy, and then a ground floor with a living space and an eating space.

I was so wrong.

I peered through the window as we approached. Tera was chattering about her time with her friends at the lake, and I let her words wash over me while I considered the layout from a tactical point of view.

I'd never seen a house this enormous. House wasn't the right word. Mansion wasn't even the right word. Castle was a better term. It wasn't grand like Buckingham Palace of Old England or Versailles of Ancient France. This was more like the castles found in Ireland and Scotland, the ruins of which, I was told, still dappled the countryside. Large enough to protect the Noble's serfs but not large enough to be monstrosities. This castle still looked like it could be a home. Well, a home-like fortress, if such a thing were possible, somehow this one threaded that needle.

It was built at the top of a steep incline, which was smart. The sheer height of the hill would protect the compound when Father Sky decided to create a flood despite Mother Earth's protestations. Like any mother, soft-hearted Earth still saw the good in her children and wanted to protect them. It was Father Sky who was the disciplinarian. He was becoming more and more aggressive and indiscriminate; his wrath was evolving into abuse. And the only thing we had to placate him – the only thing that worked— was the soothing rituals performed by the Witches.

Hiding our true nature made our work difficult; it would be life-threatening to expose ourselves. There were times that we've been unable to come out of the shadows and weave our magic to pacify him. Father Sky would bake the soil into a hard rock with the heat of his sun, then he'd send a deluge. The thirsty ground couldn't drink fast enough through the crust, so the waters would rise, run, and destroy. If the waters rose up Crispin's hill, the massive stone walls would keep it at bay. I assumed safety, more than aesthetics, was the reason for both the house's placement and barrier's design.

The driver gunned the engine to move us up the steep incline. At the gate the ground evened out and the car powered through the opening. This brought us to a parking circle with a massive water fountain trickling in the center surrounded by winter flower blooms. Behind us, two enforcers clanged the gate shut, sliding a heavy security beam into place. It would be prison-like except for the beauty. The stone castle, the turrets, the slate roof, the window boxes of bright pansies and long strands of English ivy. It was as picturesque as it was formidable.

Four stories stood above ground. And by the long thin windows that ran along the pavement, there must be full basements, as well.

A servant opened the back door of the car. Crispin climbed out first and walked forward to speak to a man in a black suit and mirrored sunglasses. An enforcer proffered his hand to help Tera and then me from the car. He reached for the case that had contained my new clothes and stepped back to let the nurse exit, unassisted.

I watched as the mirrored glasses guy panned toward me, held, and panned away. Maybe he thought that his rigid facial muscles would mean that I couldn't read him. He was so wrong. I knew he had been told I was a rat come to nibble at their cheese. He did his own assessment of the situation, ascertaining what level of concern to apply to me. I knew it was coming and had painted myself with a blur charm of fatigue, pain, and confusion. As his head swiveled left, he had decided I wasn't a risk at all.

Ha!

I scanned the surfaces around the exterior, and they all seemed impervious to flame, which, in the scope of natural disaster, was a blessing. To a Witch with a Fire affinity, it made me feel very unwelcome. As I thought that, my gaze caught at the window where a man sent thought daggers my way. Daddy Noble. Wow was that some hostile energy he was dumping out.

I turned away from him, searching for exits. There seemed to be only one, the barricaded metal gates – though a secondary egress must exist for safety's sake. Over the walls, I could see the tips of bare-branched trees and evergreens. They didn't crowd up to the wall. This would mean no one could spy from the trees, or worse, breach the barrier. It would also make it harder for me to get over and out if need be. As I contemplated this, I thought about the ring of gravel that surrounded the exterior wall and why it would be there. It seemed to me that was a step to secure them from the fires, but it would also give excellent line of sight for anyone trying to move from the estate to woods or woods to perimeter. A clear shot for the enforcers' weapons. But practically, the enemy thwarted by this design was fire.

Father Sky was big into lightning strike fires. But a set up like this? Very well thought out. It would hold off the sparks until, in the safety of the night, the Witches would emerge and, skyclad beneath the moon, perform the rituals to abate Father Sky's wrath. They would call down the rain to extinguish the flames and save humanity from further devastation. Sometimes Father Sky would listen to us Witches and sometimes he was so riled up that we couldn't placate his fury right away. We worked our rituals until we succeeded. Each year, we Witches were fewer in number and each year Father Sky was more violently angry about that fact.

My head swiveled back to the house when a servant ran out and took hold of the carry case that the enforcer handed off. I followed along behind as Crispin made his way to the enormous double-wide front doors. The wood was a good three inches thick. Crispin's thoughtfulness in keeping himself and his family safe might just be the thing that thwarted me in saving Tera if events heated up.

Tera grabbed my elbow with both hands and was bobbling next to me. "Shall I show you around?"

"Tera, the doctor wants you to be calm for two weeks," Crispin said. "Try. If not for your sake, then for Ember's, to follow orders. Ember is cut and bruised from head to toe. You're hurting her with your antics." Crispin reproofed her.

That stilled Tera, and I can't say that I wasn't glad. Crispin was right, I was banged up pretty badly. Most of it came, of course, from my tumble over the hood of the car to feed the narrative we'd given Gareth to ingest.

Sedately, Tera tucked her hand in my arm and steered me inside for the tour. As we moved through the house, I mapped the interior in my mind, counting steps, counting doors, so I could make my way about the place in the dark of night if need be.

As we walked I spun a charm. I let the words swirl about us in a dance of pink and star glisten. I added the warmth of yellow. I added a touch of red, so we could be grounded and pragmatic. I added a sprinkle of orange to bring energy to the situation. I didn't

145

have time for things to slowly unfold. I knew that if things were meant to unfold slowly and gently, the Fates would have sent a Witch with a different nature – Air, or Earth, maybe. But they'd sent Fire.

Open your mind, open your heart,
Be bold, be brave, be strong, and smart.
Here I am your bosom friend,
I'll fight for you 'til mission's end.
Your help is vital; our time is dear.
I've come to learn what danger's near.
Why to you have the Fates laid way?
What makes you special? Why are you prey?
Work with me to untangle this web,
To secure your safety, the dangers ebb.
And so in weaving with Fates this charm,
I cast protection against all harm,
By the powers of three times three,
So I speak it, so mote it be!

I'd watch and see if Tera accepted the energy I'd put out. I crossed my fingers, a powerful symbol that both called in the good spirits but also anchored them to me until my spell came to fruition.

So far, all I learned from Tera were the times I could expect to have my meals and that Cook had a room off the kitchen, so he was available at any hour should I wish something to eat outside of meal time.

The thing that struck me as we walked through the house was the number of men. Everywhere I looked, men. Those I was introduced to Cook, to tell him what tastes I preferred, Runner, Driver, Groundskeep, Chamberkeep. Men. It was odd. Very odd. I could imagine that a female nurse was hired because Tera and I were females and would probably feel more comfortable being so personally tended by a woman but…

"There are only men," I whispered.

Tera laughed and laced her fingers in mine as she skipped toward the glass doors of the conservatory toward the outdoors. "Of course, there are. Women don't work."

I stopped dead in my tracks. "What?"

"Women don't work, you know that. Well, no that's not right. Some women do. They can be in the Intelligencia like you will be and my mother and Seraphina were, and they can be medical personnel – nurses, surrogates, lactators and such. But jobs must go to the men who are the leaders and providers." She stopped and looked at me for a long moment. "You look completely dumbfounded." And she giggled as if my expression was a good joke.

Dumbfounded was a vast understatement. On Haven, Witches had roles based on proclivity and calling not on outward appearance. "Everyone works in the Range, no one can be idle and survive."

She reached out her other hand to touch my arm, and with great sincerity said, "I'm so sorry."

What that sorry was for, I wasn't sure I understood. What I did understand was that her value system and her norms were constructed by her family and her position at the top of the food chain. The last name Noble gave her experiences that set us worlds apart. Mundane and Witch, Significant and Resistor. My job wasn't to point out our differences but to forge a friendship, so I could figure out the secret of why she was in danger. My only reason to be here now was to save her.

We were walking over a mosaic terrace, and I wondered how long it had taken the artist to lay each piece of miniscule tile in its place. A raven called, catching my attention. I moved towards it, hoping it was Socrates. The raven swooped low over my head, which made Tera gasp. I turned and laughed, to show her that this was nothing to fear. It was indeed Socrates. He was checking on me for Piper. If he came back, I didn't want Tera to whack at him and possibly hurt his wings.

Socrates swooped over me again. "I'm fine, thank you. I wish I had a means to talk to you," I said as if playing with the raven. He climbed to the sky. If he took that message back to Piper, she might be able to send him with a candle and some flint. I could surely find steel somewhere around the house.

"You talk to birds?" Tera asked.

I sent her a bashful smile. "He seemed like he might want to be friends."

Socrates flew away, came back, then flew out again. He was showing me something. I danced down the stairs, and there off in the distance was a clearing with a round firepit. "Oh!" I exclaimed as I moved a few steps forward. I mimicked the way I had seen Tera hold her body when she was excited. I used her facial expressions and her tone of voice as I clapped my hands and bounced. "A fire circle, how lovely."

I took her hand and headed us in that direction. "Do you come here often?" I gestured toward the configuration out in the middle of the field. "Do you enjoy a fire at night?"

"We haven't had one in ages. Not since..." and her voice trailed off. Her face grew ashen and sad.

I couldn't allow that. The field fire had to be joyous. I needed her to want to sit around the hearth more than I did. I absolutely needed a flame to do a cleansing ritual. The pain of the six deaths that I had wrought were stabbing me, and I desperately needed respite. I sent warmth from my hand to hers. I sent her pictures of a black velvet night, sprinkled with stars. I sent her the picture of rest and recuperation, of reading books together as a family. Each person wrapped in a bright wool blanket beside the dancing flames, each alone with their thoughts and yet together and happy.

I worked on sharing these images as we approached.

And then that name niggled its way back into my thoughts. "Who is Seraphina?" I asked.

Tera stopped and blinked.

"You mentioned she was with the Intelligencia, and she worked."

"Yes, she did. She was an architect. Her specialty was creating designs to protect people from the weather. She was working with some new materials, lightweight, fireproof, waterproof, and very inexpensive. She wanted to develop housing for the people in the Range, so they could be safe and comfortable."

Well that would be helpful. Why hadn't I heard of this work? "Something happened to her?"

Tera nodded.

"I'm so sorry." I pulled my hand to my heart. "Did she die? Was she close to you?"

"She was close to Crispin. He was engaged to her. This was her favorite place to be." Tera stretched her arm wide to encompass the hearth and seating area. "She loved the fire. Loved to watch it, just like I love to be near water. This wasn't in her design. Crispin built this fire ring before he even built his house. We'd come of an evening and have a lovely time." Tera looked back at Crispin's fort. "But of course, she never even saw any of this built."

I frowned. This didn't bode well. I was thinking entirely selfishly. Crispin build the fire ring for Seraphina. Something happened to her or to their relationship. He might think of this as a sacred space and not want to be here or have anyone else here encroaching on its sanctity.

More, Tera, I need more. Tell me so I can understand. I sent the thought and crossed my fingers again to rejuvenate the spell I had cast earlier in our tour.

"She didn't die," Tera said. "She disappeared."

Chapter Fourteen

Well, now, wasn't *that* interesting. Seraphina, Crispin's fiancée disappeared. Why? How? When? Could it be that Seraphina's disappearance and the attempt to kidnap Tera were connected? That would be a long game of chess. If the person didn't get what they wanted from Seraphina's disappearance, why would they be successful with Tera's? If nothing else, it gave me more information about the anxiety and anger that swirled around Crispin in the hospital. It was more than his sister; something had happened before. "Tera, how in the world can someone just disappear?"

"They don't believe she was kidnapped because no one asked for anything. Crispin and Father sat with the enforcers and the defenders for days on end waiting for word of what the kidnappers wanted. Crispin would give anything. But they never heard a word. She was here then *poof* she was gone. Like magic." She snapped her finger. Then she sent me a wide-eyed gaze. "I told Crispin I didn't need to watch my words around you. Please tell me, if I say something like 'magic' and 'poof', does it distress you? I talked that way around Seraphina, but I know it's dangerous to use those kinds of words. My father has a fit about it. He won't let me read novels any more. He's afraid it will get me into trouble with the defenders."

"It's true, though. He's right," I said. "Those kinds of words can be dangerous. I would never betray you." I stopped to catch her eye, forging a bond, working to be her confidant so she'd spill all the secrets. I felt the pressure of time heavy on my shoulders. "But there are others who would, for their own evil reasons use those words to get you in trouble with the Seers. I counsel caution." I looked around. "But out here where there are no other ears, I think it's safe enough."

We circled around the hearth to a brick box where I found wood neatly separated and stacked. It was nicely-aged hard wood that would burn beautifully with little smoke. Without permission, I simply gathered what kindling and tinder I needed to be the base for a small balefire. I moved toward the round fire pit and began to shape the sticks into the magical pattern I used when I did a cleansing. If Tera didn't stop me, I'd prepare this for a ritual.

I moved back to get some logs. "Was Seraphina here in the Enclave when she disappeared? I didn't think things like that ever happened here. I thought crime only happened in the Range. That's what we're told."

"We have crime here in the Enclave. Just look at the fortress Crispin built." She gestured with a graceful hand toward the walls that surrounded us. "It's just that our crimes usually have to do with gaining power. Assassinations are as bad as it gets, mostly it's spying on each other's business dealings, and blackmail. I don't know, nothing to worry about like kidnapping usually. But if Seraphina wasn't kidnapped, why would she disappear?" Tera was looking up as if she were asking the sky.

I stacked the first three logs into a pyramid. "Did Seraphina's going missing make anyone more powerful, or conversely, did it make someone weaker? Your brother, was he able to do his job at the same level?"

"He is devastated. But no, he throws himself deeper into his work and has grown much more wealthy, by and by."

"That must feel like an empty hole." I walked back to the stack and gathered three logs. "Not knowing what to do—to mourn, to move forward, to wait, to search..."

"He still has enforcers investigating. He hasn't given up. Between you and me—and I say this only because I think you would understand—he feels like she's alive and is waiting for a chance to get back to him."

"Do you agree with him?" I reached out and added the wood one piece at a time, the spell I wove was done silently.

"I didn't love her." She was focused on her foot as she drew a circle in the dirt with her toe. The direction was deosil – a positive turn. "Oh, I liked her very much. We got along nicely when I saw her, but I didn't see her that often, because Crispin didn't live with us." Her gaze popped up to catch mine. "I guess what I'm saying is that she was someone I knew and liked, but I can't imagine that she's okay and just off somewhere hoping to be reunited with my brother. I wish he'd move on. But he's not had a relationship with anyone since Seraphina went missing. As a matter of fact, in the three years, you're the only woman he's looked at the way he's looking at you."

I stood and brushed the dirt from my hands. I blurred my face with a pink blush. "Like what exactly?"

"You know, all moony." Tera laced her fingers and brought them up to her cheek then rocked back and forth, teasing me. "Like he wants to kiss you, hold your hand, and have long talks staring at you and worrying about you." Her eyes were dancing with delight, and she put a finger to her lips. "Shhh, he'd be absolutely horrified that I told you that." She giggled. "But we're friends, and I thought you should know that he likes you. Do you like him?"

"Very much so." I was on my third and last trip to gather and place a set of three logs. Tera was trailing along behind me.

She sat on the brick edge of the fire pit as I lay the last of them. She bit her nail while I made my magical signs as surreptitiously as I could.

By the power of three times three,
the healing flames will set me free
Of others' pain,
my dragons' slain
So I speak it, so mote it be.

I capped the spell with holding power, so when I was able to get here and light the bale, the flame would remember it had a magical job to do and give me respite.

I tuned in late to what Tera was saying, "I want him to be happy again. It's so hard to watch him angry." She stood and sent me a smile that told me she was embarrassed she had said so much and maybe messed things up. I pretended not to notice. Instead, I went to sit on one of the lounges. "May I ask what Crispin does for work? It's probably naïve, but I thought Nobles didn't work."

"He's a builder—homes, infrastructure. That's how he and Seraphina met. Working on a project."

"She designed this home?"

Tera chuckled. "She thought Crispin should be in a castle fit for Henry V. It was a joke between them. It was only a design when she vanished. He had the workers stop everything they were doing around the Enclave and come and build this. He had them working all day and all night until it was done." Her eyes moved over the façade. "She did a good job. The weather has thrown everything at this house, and it's withstood it well. No problems at all. Where the last hurricane took the roof right off my father's home."

I followed her eye and saw Gareth standing over by the mosaic terrace. When he caught my eye, he waved his arm, signaling me to come in.

I raised my hand in return and stood to make my way over to talk to him.

Tera's gaze followed my focus. "You know Gareth?"

"I do," I said as we walked back to the house. "My class worked on an engineering problem for one of his clients among the elite in the Northern Realm. Gareth's interested in my work with batteries and storing energy. How do you happen to know him?"

"He's here a lot talking to Crispin about building things. He introduced Seraphina and Crispin when he thought Seraphina's designs might be interesting to Crispin."

"Was Crispin interested in her designs?"

"He was more interested in her. They talked a lot about the designs, but they were never built."

"Why was that?"

She shrugged and danced toward Gareth. "Did you bring me something?" she asked.

Gareth reached into his pocket and pulled something out, and held it up for her. As she reached for it, he pulled away, leaned in, and whispered to her.

Tera looked back my way, "Shall I make us some tea?" she asked as I approached much slower that she did, feigning pain with my movements.

Feigning… no, I felt pain. I guess, I wasn't hiding it the way I normally might. Perhaps I was even being a little hyperbolic. It was always good when someone underestimated your physical abilities. "Yes, thank you, tea would be lovely."

Tera looked back at Gareth, who handed her the thing, which she unwrapped and popped in her mouth as she headed toward the house.

"Candy?"

"It pays to have an inside friend," he said. The smile dropped from his face as Tera shut the door behind her. "You're alive."

"Surprise." I let my voice drip with poison.

"Don't be that way. I checked, I couldn't find a heartbeat. I pulled you out of the road. I had seconds in which to act."

"You left me to die."

He scrubbed his hands over his face and leaned backwards. He shook his head. "How did you survive that? I can't imagine how you could have survived being hit like that."

"I know how you survived the attack. I pushed you out of the way."

He blanched.

"Why did they want to kill you? Who were they?" Turn the tables, it was one of our first lessons preparing us for our work in the Resistance.

He shook his head.

"Was it something to do with that building we were in? There were other people in there. Did it have something to do with them?"

He let out a heavy breath. "I can't wrap my brain around this string of events." He looked up at the windows, scanning, then focused back on me. "I want to hold you. I want you in my arms, but it's too dangerous."

"You had your goons *chase* me."

Again silence.

I wanted him to be well on his back foot. "I dragged myself all the way back to my dorm after saving you, and then getting hit by a speeding car, and as I crossed the greenspace, your enforcers *chased* me. Do you know how painful it was to run? I thought they were going to kill me."

He closed his eyes tightly.

"I was so scared. So scared. Why did you want to hurt me, Gareth? What have I ever done to you?" My voice was sharp with agitation.

When he shook his head, I turned to walk away. I could feel his energy—bristly, confused, hopeful, shamed, and yes there was a base line of belief that we sincerely cared for each other. Though, his caring was more fixed, and he was less sure that mine would remain.

"Stop," he hissed to turn me back around. "Play nice or Noble Sr. will feed you to the pigs."

"For what reason? What have I done?"

"You were there when the men were killed."

"I killed them. The Nobles know that. It was a fight to the death, them or me."

"Not the men who tried to take Tera." He scowled, his nails bit into my arm. "What did you do with Dr. Brighton?"

160

I blinked and made my face as blank as possible.

"Dr. Brighton," Gareth insisted, "where is he?"

I reached out and swept his hand from my arm. "You're hurting me. And there was no Dr. Brighton with Tera in the car. There was a driver who died when the men killed him, and there were the two men that wanted to kidnap Tera. If Dr. Brighton was there, he escaped."

It was Gareth's turn to blink at me. Well, played, I congratulated myself.

Movement at the door caught my eye. Crispin was making his way toward us.

"You have no idea what you've landed in." Gareth said under his breath. "You have no idea how much danger you're in. I need to know how you're going to play this."

I kept my gaze on Crispin.

Gareth looked back and raised his hand in salute. "I suggest you get as close as you can to Crispin while you're here. He wasn't able to keep Seraphina safe. But he's still your best shot at getting back to the Range alive."

Crispin was in hearing range now.

Gareth changed his tone from life-and-death to conversational. "I have your books from Piper. She's beside herself with worry. I told her I saw you, and that you were bruised but there was nothing that wouldn't heal. I was told your personal needs were attended to, so I didn't bring clothing. Hi Crispin."

"You're back already, good."

"Yes, and the good news is that my friend in the president's office at the university was able to arrange for Ember to take her exams on schedule." He turned to me. "After I told them of your heroic actions and your recovery here at Crispin's home, they told me I'd be allowed proctor your exams." He stopped to smile. "They feel fairly sure that I couldn't help you pass."

"No." The smile I sent back was lackluster. "The subject matter is rather technical in nature." I was tired, and my heart ached with the pain of the deaths. I needed to manipulate a way to light the fire as soon as possible, maybe even now, and have some relief. As I thought that, thunder boomed overhead.

Gareth didn't seem to notice my fatigue, but Crispin did. Concern shined in his eyes. He slid his hand down my arm, caught up my hand, and tucked it in the crook of his elbow, gesturing toward the door, and we all set off to go inside. I rewarded his gesture with warmth, this time it was familial warmth. I wanted to establish a sense of my belonging.

"It was agreed that you would be off your pain medications and thinking clearly, but they would like an approximate date you could take your exam." Gareth was saying as he followed us in.

"I'm not taking the medications," I said over my shoulder.

Crispin stopped and turned to me with his brows knit together. "But you must need them. You looked—forgive me—you looked… Personally, I would want to be heavily sedated."

Somehow, I doubted that.

"I prefer the ache to the feeling of floating about." I turned my answer to Gareth. "I would like a little time to recover."

Thunder boomed again and from the window. A bank of black clouds flexed its muscles. The look on my face must have been one of utter dismay. Crispin tucked me under his arm. "Don't worry, the house is secure. The storm won't bother us."

Yes, perhaps his roof was on safe and sound, but my balefire would have to be abandoned and my mission pain would continue to make me suffer.

"Tea is ready," Tera moved into the hallway with Cook pushing a tea cart behind her.

Gareth stood in the foyer. "It seems the storm is only getting worse. I need to get home." He turned to me. "I have your books in my car, and some instructions."

When I took a step forward, Crispin took a step forward, too. I wondered if he was going to go out and chaperone my interaction with Gareth. That would be a problem. Gareth was trying for another opportunity to hand me information. I held a surreptitious mudra behind my back. A magical gesture to increase the power of my little charm.

Crispin, I need time and space.
You must go a different place.
Feel secure, let me be.

By the power of three times three.

Crispin looked between Gareth and me, again checking the temperature of our relationship. I had made sure that the energy between Gareth and I was cool but not chilly. The temperature of colleagues and nothing more.

"I'll follow you out then." I shifted toward Gareth.

"When you get back, enjoy your tea," Crispin said. "I have some work that needs my attention."

The servant held the door as Gareth, then I moved through.

I glanced up at the sky. *Truly Father, I'm in so much pain. I was doing the Fates' biding. I need a fire to do my cleansing ritual and to pay you the respects that you so deserve. Thank you. Thank you. Thank you for intervening with your light last night. Can you not find peace, so I can ignite the balefire?*

A magnificent wave of thunder washed across the sky and with it came an etheric message. The impression I got was that my pain would have to wait. Tonight, I was needed for other things.

Chapter Fifteen

Gareth's car was parked on the far side of the parking circle.

Through the tinted windows I could see his driver sitting behind the wheel, ready for his boss's instructions.

"When are you coming back?" I asked as I took his arm and made my way down the steps.

"It depends on the weather, as usual."

Socrates flew overhead. The beat of his wings held the message. *Please, help Kael.* I watched him land at the top of the water fountain in the center of the parking circle.

Help Kael?

From inside these fortress-like walls? Did Piper not understand where I was?

Socrates dropped something from his beak into the water and flew off. I turned my head to see if the enforcers had paid attention to the raven. Would they go and search the basin? They seemed intent on standing rigidly by the gate, looking forward like the pictures I'd seen of the olden days when there was a Queen in England and her guard stood at attention.

Alright, I needed to figure out a way to walk to the center circle and find what Piper had sent me with the enforcers all around. That was a task to think about later. Now, I needed to be smart about what information I could extract from Gareth.

Tera told me Gareth had introduced Seraphina to Crispin. I wondered if that were the reason Crispin kept monitoring Gareth's and my relationship. I thought perhaps Crispin was watching us through the window. I felt eyes on me, but I didn't turn to learn who was doing the watching.

I decided as we aimed for the car that I would try to get a clearer picture from Gareth about what happened to Seraphina. I thought Tera had told me all she knew. "Tera said Crispin's fiancée is missing, and that you were the one who introduced them. The way Tera mentioned you, I got the impression that before Seraphina decided to marry Crispin that you and Seraphina were a couple."

"Yes."

Well that was simple enough. "You met her at the university before she took the exams for Intelligencia and moved to the Realm?"

"Yes."

Loquaciousness was not normally Gareth's strong suit, but he was being irritatingly terse. I raised an eyebrow.

He answered in a low tone that wouldn't carry. "Yes, Seraphina and I were a couple. Yes, she preferred Crispin to me. No, I don't think it had to do with his wealth or position. They were, as

166

they say, two peas in a pod." He popped open the side door, dragged a bookbag out, and shut the door again, so the driver couldn't hear us. "I care for you, Ember. Heed my warning. You're swimming in shark infested waters. You're in *serious* danger. I can tell you that for certain because I know just what Noble Sr. thinks of you. He has told me in no uncertain terms. As long as you're healing and in this house under Crispin's watch, you're safe. The moment you leave...You can't just get into Crispin's car and think you'll ever make it back to the Range. Noble Sr. knows you were at the building when Dr. Brighton escaped. I think you should consider how you can disappear."

I held on to a couple of those words. I started with "Like Seraphina?"

"I'm afraid she didn't listen to me. I don't want to see the same thing happen to you."

"You think she was murdered and disposed of?"

"That was the plan. After Noble Sr and his goons interrogated her, of course."

"You knew about it and did nothing?"

"I warned her the way I'm warning you. Get as close as you need to to Crispin for the time being. We'll figure a way to get you out of here. Then we can talk about where we stand, you and I. Until then, I know you're making decisions based on this life and death situation. I won't hold anything you do against you, I promise."

"If you help me, it will put you in danger."

"Only if they know I helped." He dug in the bookbag and pulled out an engineering textbook. He dropped the bag to the ground at his feet.

"Would you?" I asked. "Help me, that is?"

He opened the book as if he were looking for a specific page. "Ember – you mean something deeply to me. You are the warmth in an otherwise very cold world." His voice was gruff with more emotion than I'd ever experienced from him before. I didn't think this was an act. But I couldn't let him lead. I lined myself up with him to look at the page he was showing me. It was blank. "And yet you're pragmatic. I know you. You're a survivor."

He pressed his lips together.

"I feel I can only trust you but so far," I pushed. "Even if you think you're being magnanimous by suggesting I play Crispin."

"From what I see, it wouldn't be playing."

"Stop." I reached out and took the book and fanned it to find another blank page. "Go back to this Dr. Brighton person. He wasn't at Tera's car accident? He was at mine, when I was run over? You said Noble Sr. knew I was at the building. Was Dr. Brighton in the building yesterday morning before I was hit?"

Gareth's eyes were hard on my face, searching out the tiniest grain of untruth. People who had lived traumatic lives, like Gareth had, developed a survival instinct similar, but less refined than a Witch's. I knew he could read energies, and I had prepared for that on our silent walk to the car, with a blur spell. Again, I'd painted myself with pain, confusion, innocence, and this time I added fear. Not of him, but of the circumstances in which I found myself.

"Dr. Brighton was brilliant. He'd developed an energy source that would help the Range. Just like Seraphina developed the housing to help the Range. Just like you are developing the batteries to help the Range. Seraphina disappeared. Dr. Brighton also disappeared. If your experiments are successful, you will disappear too. The elite, the Nobles, they cannot let anything mess with the present power structure."

"But…"

"We live in an authoritarian age. Power is everything. The haves wield that control with a mighty fist. They will do whatever is necessary to keep the Range desperate. If someone is searching for their next meal, they aren't fighting the politics. 'Keep them hungry' is a motto."

"You help the elite maintain this authoritarian power." I pointed to the blank page I found. "It seems from what you've said that you were helping them take Dr. Brighton hostage."

"While I was seeming to help the Significants, I was looking for a way to save Dr. Brighton. The Resistance found a means before I did."

"The Resistance was there? Were they the one's that hit me with their car?"

"I believe so."

"And you've accused me of helping Dr. Brighton. Are you suggesting that I let someone from the Resistance hit me with their car, so they could get to Dr. Brighton? Why wouldn't I just let them hit you? You make no sense."

He shook his head. I guessed when I put it that way, he realized how improbable the scenario was. Gareth pretended to read down the page and nodded. "This is war," he growled. "Bad things happen. I know it's hard to believe, but someone has to play both sides. Someone has to be the Grey Man. Otherwise, how would the Resistance know what was going on? How would they gather information? If I give the Proprietors information, I get information. I try to choose the information I give in the least harmful way possible and still make the Proprietors grateful. At the building, I checked on Brighton, I was planning to help him escape, I played a part, so others would trust me. I do what is necessary. In a fight for survival, everything is fair game." He snapped the book closed. "I would like to see the Resistance win. There are too many kids growing up in the streets like I did."

He was testing me. Seeing if I fell in with the Resistance. I let my feelings and expressions hide behind the blur spell. He reached down and gathered the bag then handed it off to me. "We'll talk later." Opening the back door, he said, "home," to his driver. He climbed in and slammed the door shut.

He either trusted me with that bit of information or he was handing me a load of malarkey to some other end. The pendulum said his behavior and the outcome was an unknown. I couldn't read our interaction at face value. Gareth was a chess player. I slid my fingers over my scalp, scraping my hair back out of my eyes as I looked up to scan the sky.

The clouds were closer, the thunder was picking up its tempo. It looked like we had a wicked night in front of us. I had a lot to think about. A lot of puzzle pieces to move around. I just wasn't sure that they all belonged to the same final picture.

As I walked past the fountain, I glanced over at the enforcers to see if I couldn't just go grab the gift Socrates had brought me. But both of them had their gaze hard on me.

The servant opened the door as soon as my foot touched the stair.

I moved through the foyer and back to the salon to go sit next to Tera.

"Oh good," I was afraid the tea would grow cold. "Can I see what Gareth brought you?" she asked as she poured a watery colored tea into a cup. She saw me looking. "This is herbal not regular tea. Regular tea is rather difficult to get right now. The last shipment sank in a storm."

I picked up the bookbag and laid it next to her. Then accepted my cup resting, on a saucer both of delicate eggshell china.

As she unclasped the flap, I took a sip. My mouth was instantly filled with a story. Images of the soldiers of the Inquisition on huge war stallions thundered through the gates. I swallowed. I took another sip. The soldiers yanked a wise woman from her home and was dragging her down the street by her hair.

The story carried by the tea water was so vivid that I could smell the drying horse dung in the streets, feel the rounded cobblestones under my feet.

Tera, opened my text book and was turning the pages, stopping when she came to an illustration.

I took a sip, my hand trembling as I brought the cup to my lips. The woman was balled up on the ground in the middle of the square. A soldier would ask a question and when the woman didn't answer, he lashed her. The whip whooshed, then it cracked the air, the end licking out and slashing the old woman's delicate skin, leaving muscle exposed to the frosty air. I knew this story. What I didn't know was how this story got into the tea water.

Like I was brought the command to *save her,* from under the owl's wing the night of Tera's would-be kidnapping, like the match flame that sent my warning to Piper that Gareth was raging in her direction, this information was magically passed by an Elemental Witch – but unlike Piper and her raven Socrates, this was a Witch with an affinity for water. There was another Witch in the house. Why would a Witch put this particular story into the tea? And how could they get to the water when it was Cook – who was exceedingly Mundane – who would have prepared the cart?

I took another sip. The soldiers went round and round, each taking their turns, each bringing the leather whip down hard across the crone's body. No one was in the square. No one watched. No one wanted to be anywhere near those soldiers or what was happening. That woman in the middle of the square was Brigid the healer. She was ancient and had probably mid-wifed every single one of the villager's births. She had probably sat beside every single person in their family who was transitioning to the Beyond. Prayed for them. Brought them peace at the end of their lives.

I knew this story that filled my mouth.

I took another sip. Brigid, unconscious was dragged to the stake with the wood stacked high. She was tied in place. The fire lit. I felt tears run down my face. I had this reaction every single time we were shown the story of Brigid and our ancestors' exodus.

Another sip. Brigid, when her hem caught fire, lifted her head and her voice rang out. "Now. The time is now." An arrow flew. It struck her in the heart. The brave man who saved Brigid from unimaginable suffering tore off over the ramparts to hide. Inside the homes all over the village, the Witches gathered their stores and moved to the dock. They left the shores of their homeland.

I let my hair fall in my face as I wiped my tears without Tera seeing.

I exhaled a breath and closed my eyes. This was Haven's creation story. Someone in the house with magical skills knew Haven's creation story.

The implication of their putting this story into water were terrifying.

And confusing.

I looked into my empty cup and asked Tera if I might have a bit more.

She poured, then went back to looking at my books.

The story that I drank in this cup was the same as the first one. There was no second chapter showing how and where the ancestral Witches travelled. Nothing about our island. And here was the baffling thing—

"You know what all this means?" Tera asked.

I startled to her voice. No, I thought, looking into my cup, as a matter of fact I have no idea what all this meant.

She tapped a picture.

"Oh, yes. We learned that in first year, that's rather basic."

Tera popped her eyebrows and went back to looking at the illustrations.

There were a lot of confusing things here – but the biggest one was that all the Witches of Haven accepted the Incantation of Silence. Before we were allowed to leave the island, before we were even given our rings with a gemstone selected for us individually by the Council, a spell was cast. This spell bound us irrevocably to a sworn oath and the accepted consequences of our breaking it. If we ever tried to speak the creation story or anything about Haven aloud, if we tried to write it, or sign it, or even do an interpretive dance about it, our memories would be wiped clean. All of it. Not just the story of our ancestors' exodus, but our whole time on the Isle of

Haven. If we could not remember our time on Haven, we would not be able to remember anything we learned. We would, in effect, have our magical powers stripped from us.

No Witch from Haven could pass this story to the water. And yet the water knew. And that thrust not only the safety of Haven into danger, but by extrapolation the possibility that all of humanity could be destroyed as well. For, when the Witches ceased to hold ritual, humans would be removed from the Earth.

How had this come to be that the water carried the exodus story?

What should I do about it?

This was what fear felt like. It was paralyzing and cold.

Maybe I'd discovered the reason why I was sent to save Tera, so I could be here in this home and do something about this – whatever *this* was.

Chapter Sixteen

Cook made us a light meal. The servants seemed jumpy as the wind and thunder came in bursts then receded. The Nobles seemed at ease. Though, at ease didn't seem quite the right word... Tera had a headache that could be seen beating at her temples. Crispin was outwardly gracious, but his energy tasted of sardines – slick and salty and crowded together. Those sardine feelings seemed to be pointed toward Noble Sr.

I scooped up a spoonful of soup, afraid of the story that would fill my mouth, but all I got was the rich taste of bone broth. The water that had been used to make this soup had nothing to tell me.

I had hoped that a candle would be lit on the table and that I would be able to sit in the dining room alone with it, perhaps over a cup of tea. But no such luck. They had stored power. The light was on.

My thumb played with my naked ring finger. Crispin hadn't brought me back my ring. I felt vulnerable without it. And this mission, moving into the nest with the viper, watched and judged, already had enough vulnerability to it.

Here I was without any outward tools.

If I got my ring back, I could tie it to a strand of my hair and use it as a pendulum. And there was a connectivity to it that I felt though it was never explained to me. I imagined it as a kind of beacon helping the Council members–the Elders who orchestrated and aided our missions–to find and stay in tune with us.

In the Range, there were things that I missed having at my disposal–a proper tarot deck, though I could use a regular deck of cards. A Grimoire–my book of spells and magical knowledge which, of course, needed to stay back on Haven. There were times when I thought there were better spells, specialized tried-and-true spells, that would help me in my work. Some of the spell work I did from memory, but most of my spells were seat-of-the-pants. I think the energy of need gave them the oomph they required. So far so good, I was still alive.

I missed my Sword of Fire. It was given to me when my affinity was discovered. Rightly named, I was always meant to be a warrior for our cause. When my sword was presented to me in ritual, I was too small and frail to lift it. It took years of training, but mastering that sword gave me the skills I needed when magic wasn't enough—when I needed to use my hands, and feet, and even my teeth to fight for what I knew to be right. In my graduation ceremony that brought me full-fledged into the Haven Coven, before leaving on the ship for the outside world, my sword was archived.

When my boat arrived on the shore of the Range the first day of my Offling Years, I was bid to remove my clothing. Every last stitch. New garments were provided, and I walked over the planks to the wharf. The only thing we could bring with us from the Isle was our rings. They were unique and specially crafted to look Mundane in every sense of the word, but each was deeply magical. They represented the oaths we took to Earth and Sky, to God and Goddess, to the Fates. My ring held a fire opal. My vow, to be the flame. That they had taken my ring from my finger was an affront. And I would not leave without it.

"Ember, you had asked me about your ring," Crispin said.

My head jerked toward him, it was almost as though he'd read my thoughts.

"When patients are sedated, to protect their items from theft, they are removed and put into a vault. The defender who guards that vault was busy with the aftermath of the tornado when I went to get your ring back for you. I'll send one of my men to retrieve it in the morning when the station is open again."

It was interesting to me, something to be noted, that while I was perfectly fine with Crispin retrieving my ring, the idea of his enforcer touching my ring brought anger to the surface of my skin. I had to duck my head to hide my eyes. I swallowed a spoonful of broth and pushed down some of my wrath before I said, "That's very kind. Thank you." I knew that much of the fluctuations and extremes of my emotions were caused by the icy shards that continued to stab at my heart. I was getting desperate for a fire and my cleansing ritual. I crossed my fingers in my lap and hoped that Piper had understood my cryptic message and had sent me some kind of flame, that that was what Socrates had dropped into the water fountain.

Of course, what he dropped could have something to do with the message, "Help Kael."

I had already decided that I needed to go throw a ball in the parking circle with Tera and that I'd let it land in the top basin and that would be my means for getting the gift out. But when I asked if Tera had a ball, she had said no, girls in the Realm don't play with balls, and she'd laughed as if the idea was absurd. Okay. That was okay. I just needed to come up with another plan.

The conversation at the dinner table stilled.

I looked up and all eyes were on me.

"I'm sorry?" I asked, hoping someone would catch me up on what I had missed while my mind wandered.

"I asked where you gained your skills, Miss McGraw," Noble Sr. said.

"Ember, please. Which skills?"

"You are a trained fighter. The men you killed were obviously enforcers. It is improbable that a little slip of a girl like you could spring onto the scene and kill them both."

They must have told Tara more about the accident now that she seemed solidly back on her feet. They probably presented it as a cautionary tale.

A little slip of a girl like me.

I disliked being called a girl. I hadn't been a girl since my thirteenth birthday when I'd taken my oath and become a personification of Fire. But fine, keep thinking I'm weak and silly. "I think that surprise had as much to do with it as anything. And dumb luck. They thought they were alone. But yes, I didn't walk into the brawl unequipped. My father was a defender, and my mother a musician—a harpist, and singer. I, sadly, inherited none of my mom's talent, and my exuberance was a bit too much for her. She preferred I played near my father. I was an only child and—ha!—but I'm rambling." I gave a bashful laugh. "I'm sorry." I lifted slow lashes to focus on Crispin's eyes, I sent warmth. "I do that when I'm nervous…talk too much, that is." Slow soft smile. I focused back on his father. "My dad taught me to fight, a leg up if I wanted to become a defender and follow in his footsteps. I know the defenders in the Realm are men. But in the Range both sexes are represented in the corps. You just have to be able to meet the standards."

"And you're sub-standard and failed to qualify?"

"I was trained to fight, but I never tested. I would willingly join the ranks, sir. But I was accepted to the university."

"A new member of the Intelligencia. Smart, beautiful, and lethal." He turned and stared at his son until his son's gaze found his. "The triumvirate. Formidable. With the possibility of being *devastating*."

He must be referring to Seraphina. From what I'd gathered, she fit that description. Hmm maybe not the lethal part unless he meant that figuratively. Was he warning his son that bad things lay in my future? Was he waving Crispin off, letting him know that getting too attached to me would only cause him pain?

Crispin swirled his wine around his glass and said with studied evenness. "You're thinking of Mother. She was indeed smart, beautiful, and iron-willed when it came to protecting her family. Her death devastated us all." Crispin glanced over at me. "You seem to be pulling up her image for both Father and me. You have the same kind of fire in your spirit, I think."

Fire. He saw fire in my spirit. That was unnerving. But then again, fire as a personality feature to a Mundane was very different than that of a Witch, and he was using it in the common use of the word, not the magical one. I sent him a smile and took another spoonful of soup.

"Speaking of fires, Tera said that you were over at the fire circle and that you had laid the wood. If it weren't so stormy, I'd suggest we light it after dinner. I enjoy a roaring fire. I guess I get that from my mom, she said they inspired her work and brought her peace."

"I would very much like that, perhaps tomorrow the weather will be calmer." I noticed he hadn't mentioned Seraphina and the fire circle. "What was her name, your mother?"

"Enya Noble," Tera replied.

"She had a twin, Aiden, who was equally enraptured by fires. Bit of a pyromaniac, actually." Crispin laughed.

I bet Enya Noble liked to be outside when her husband was around, I'd bet a soft breeze could pull the angry harsh energy away, dissipating it to a point where it was bearable. Even a Mundane must find him prickly to be around. "Tera told me that your mother died. I'm so sorry for your loss."

"Thank you, like many others, she was killed in the storms."

"And your Uncle Aiden, is he around?"

"No, he—"

Tera put her spoon down, "Father, I can't eat. My head is pounding. May I be excused?"

"Do you need Nurse?" Noble Sr. asked, not sounding particularly concerned.

"No, thank you."

He brushed a hand through the air, shooing her along.

"I'll just see that you're tucked comfortably in bed," I said, putting my napkin beside my bowl.

"But your dinner," Crispin interjected, standing politely as I pushed to my feet.

"I'm afraid the medicines are still in my system, and they've left me little appetite. I'll see that Tera is comfortable. And if you don't mind, I'll go to bed as well."

With my hand on her back, I guided Tera to her room. I was glad that I had slipped away from the interrogation I was sure that Noble Sr. had planned.

Hopefully, I could contrive some way to get out of the house and to the fountain while everyone was asleep. I pressed a fist into my chest to try to relieve the pain. *Come storm, I need your cover.*

The minutes ticked by, then the hours and still the lights were on. I expanded my aura to see if there was anyone awake or if the waste of electricity was a show of wealth. On the edge of my energetic reach, I felt the gates open.

I slid out of my bed, and on bare feet moved to the door. *Open silently, my friend.* I slowly turned the knob to crack the door. I let my energy snake around the hall. I picked up no heat stamps from anyone around. I decided I could slip out of my room and if caught, I would simply say I was heading to the kitchen for a bite to eat.

I moved to the railing overlooking the vestibule.

There stood a man, dressed in a long black wool coat, charcoal grey slacks, and highly polished, black leather shoes. He carried a satchel with an insignia of the Noble family large enough that I could see it even from this distance. I wondered how he was connected to Noble Sr. and Crispin. This man didn't have the same genetic makeup as Crispin. This man had almond shaped eyes and silky black hair. He was short and slight, with a feel of calculation and menace, though he tried to gentle that over with a demi-smile.

He was a Noble.

I wondered at the connection, since it was obviously not familial.

It didn't take the same DNA to have qualified for the Noble family designation when it was created, though now it was passed generation to generation. At the time, those who possessed the most wealth and prestige simply claimed the title and decided amongst themselves who would get to use the name. It wasn't that terribly long ago. Noble Sr. probably was a young man when he claimed the status. It was the same time when the barricades went up and the Realm was set separate and apart from the rest of the society. Though the designation of Proprietors versus Poductors and the caste system had become law generations before. It happened at the time when Father Sky said enough was enough and began reprimanding us humans in a sustained way.

I crouched beside the balustrade and cast a glamour, so I could watch.

Crispin walked into the hall, and his energy bristled. "Leopold, it's late in the night for you to be here. Is anything wrong?"

"I'm waiting for your father," he said, dismissively.

Crispin wasn't so easily put off. "And yet, you've come to my home while my family and guest are sleeping. Surely, you wouldn't disturb us for less than an emergency."

Suddenly the atmosphere was painted in fear. It wasn't from the vestibule.

I sent my aura wider. There was a struggle to the left of the door. That was all the information I could gather. Crispin continued to pry at the visitor, trying to gather news.

I slid upward, until I could crouch walk back to Tera's bedroom. My hand on her doorknob I twirled my finger deosil, to the right, in the air.

Sleep Tera sleep,
This spell pulls you deep,
Into your dreams so sweet,
You fly

Rouse not awake,
Your awareness will not break
For your safety's sake
Don't cry.

Energy swirled from my finger and enveloped Tera in happy dreams, making it possible for me to slip into her room and pull the curtain to the side.

It was black as pitch. They'd turned off the outdoor lights. That was good, I'd try to get out and over to the fountain.

The energy of tumult circled in the air.

I opened my auric field to take in what I could. The night tasted of habanero peppers, painfully biting. No relief. I licked my arm trying to rid myself of the sensation. The door to the side of the house opened. The interior light cast a small globe out onto the paved drive. A car was there. The back hood was up. They were dragging a man from the trunk.

What?

As the man was wrestled toward the door, he turned. His face was lit, and I saw that they had Kael. *They had Kael!* Kael was Mundane, but it seemed to me that he knew I was there watching. It seemed to me that he wanted me to see his face, so I would know to help him. If Piper told him I was at Crispin Noble's house, how would Kael even know where he had been taken? No, he couldn't know I was here. He was just searching the windows looking for an escape.

An owl swooped into the courtyard and hooted. The sound echoed off the stone enclosure. It was the same owl who had sent me the message, *Save her.* An owl connected to enchantment. I thought of my tea with the exodus story. A frisson of fear painted over me. Magic was afoot, but I knew not how or from where.

The owl swooped in again, beating his mighty wings, extending his sharp talons. The enforcers lifted their elbows to protect their faces, and Kael took advantage of the moment. He kicked one of the guard's knees. As the enforcer fell off balance, Kael was able to wrench his arm from the man's grip and torque his

187

body slamming his elbow across the other man's jaw with the full force of his weight and speed. That enforcer released Kael as he fell back, and Kael sprinted for the gate.

I desperately searched for right action—I wasn't sure what I could or should do in this situation. While Piper had asked me to help Kael, my mission was to save Tera. Right now, all I could do was watch and wait for an opportunity.

Running full speed toward the barricade, Kael planted his foot on the metal door and leapt upward somehow grasping the top of the five-meter gate with his fingertips. He scrambled his legs trying to get a toe hold on the slippery surface as he hoisted himself up. His waist resting across the top, he repositioned his hands. I was clutching my fists and sending him power, sending him strength. But he wasn't quick enough. A man bolted from the house and leapt up to grab his dangling foot and yanked him back to the ground.

There was a sickening thwack as Kael's body hit the pavement.

The newly arrived enforcer grabbed Kael's collar and dragged him inside. The door swung shut. All was still and black again.

Chapter Seventeen

I slipped out of Tera's room. As I quietly shut her door, I twirled my finger widdershins,

My spell is broken,

you are awoken,

when and how you wish.

I moved back to my place on the stairs as Noble Sr. walked into the foyer.

"Leopold, thank you for coming though it's so late." He reached out and shook the man's hand and at the same time Leopold offered the briefcase with his left hand.

"Can you stay for a brandy?" Noble Sr. asked.

"I must be going but thank you."

I watched Noble Sr. raise his eyebrows asking a surreptitious question and watched Leopold Noble give the slightest of nods.

The moment Leopold left, Crispin turned on his father. "I must insist this never happen again. This is my home, and I'm dressed for bed. I don't receive guests at this hour. I'll be surprised if that didn't wake both Tera and Ember. They need to sleep and heal."

"Ember is quite the concern of yours. Is she sleeping in her bed tonight or yours?"

"I can't see how her sleeping arrangements are any of your business."

Not a "no, she's in her own room." Maybe he had hopes that I'd end up in his bed. *Good.*

"You're my son and that makes it my business."

"No, Dad, it doesn't, not even in the slightest. You are a guest in my house. Please be courteous of my norms and of Ember."

Before his father could reply, Crispin moved to his office.

Noble Sr. stood snarling at the door that was shut in his face, and I knew that he blamed me for his son's outburst. I couldn't have cared less in this moment. I needed to find a way to get to Kael. How was he captured? Why would they want him? Was it possible that his ties to the Resistance were discovered? Could it be anything else?

I moved toward the kitchen where Tera had pointed out the steps that led downstairs, but Cook was busily fixing a tray. I tried to fathom another way to get to Kael besides just walking out the front door, past the two enforcers who stood by the gate door and down the same steps that they had dragged him.

Cook stood at the sink now, washing out his pot. I sunk into a crouch, my head low, my fingers brushing the floor for stability. I quick-footed my way to the massive butcher block table that stood in the middle of the room. I paused there, my head beneath the top, as he shut off the water. The door was right there. Right there.

Well… there was the old gag that we used to use on our friends back on Haven. It was juvenile, but that might work.

Cook, the water made you see
That right this moment you need to pee.
Haste! Haste! Speed is key.

To the lavatory you must run,
It takes some time until you're done.
This weakened bladder spell is spun.

Okay, I wasn't proud of myself, but sometimes a situation called for base magic instead of elegant. Cook hopped from one foot to the other as he reached desperately to turn off all the stove burners before he squeezed his knees together and swiveled his lower legs to propel himself toward his bedroom.

Keeping low lest someone see me through the window, I made my way to the basement door and found it locked. Fates, I don't have time for this!

Hello, I've come as a friend
There is no need to defend
Open, open, open for me,

So I speak it, so mote it be.

I turned the door handle, checking the lock to make sure I could get back up this way—somehow—and slithered down the dark, steep stairwell. I heard the men's muttered words. The scrape of furniture across cement floor. The odd echoing against the stone surfaces.

The door above me banged open.

I squirmed into a recess and held very still, using my mind to paint a glamour over me. I heard feet in hard soles take the stairs with a little dance in the step, just as Gareth had done as we were leaving the apartment building yesterday morning—when this whole misadventure started. I was horrified that this might be Gareth coming to interrogate Kael. I couldn't move to look. I daren't even flutter a lash, so I stood with eyes shut.

Once the sound tapped past me, I lifted my lids and saw Noble Sr. swaggering to the back of the basement. I followed his course with my eyes. When he rounded a corner, I tip-toed to follow him.

I slid against the wall, watching what was happening through the reflection in the mirror that leaned against the wall, half draped in a grey motheaten blanket.

Noble Sr, pointed his finger at Kael. "Get him up."

Two enforcers rounded to either side and lifted Kael's unconscious body.

I stretched my aura to check on him, hoping he was faking it. He was a good fighter. A great fighter. Lethal kicks, amazing speed. Between the two of us, I felt sure we could easily take down both enforcers and Noble. But no, this was not faking. That bar that the man in the door wielded must have cracked down over Kael's head with a vengeance. Being passed out for so long was a very bad sign.

Noble Sr, slapped at Kael's face as I pulled together a spell.

Afraid to uncover my position, hiding behind the glamour, I used my imagination to draw a pentagram of increase, the invoking pentagram of Fire. I started at the top point and with each stanza I crafted, I drew the imaginary lines down to the right, over to the left hand, across to the right, down to the left, and back up to the center point.

By the North, the South, East and West
I call the powers as ye know best
How to follow Fates lead.

With etheric light I bind Kael's wounds,
I bring Fates power to these rooms,
Survival, I plant your seed.

With strength and speed of fire's roar,
Protect this soldier of holy war,
That evil may not feed.

After my third pentagram, I closed the spell – short and to the point. Kael was rousing under the smacks to his cheeks.

By the power of three times three,
So I speak it, so mote it be.
This soldier, I will not cede.

They lifted and dragged Kael to a chair and ran a rope around his arms and torso as much to hold him in place as to bind him to the spot.

"Well, hey there young man," Noble Sr. said. "Look at you, handsome." He squeezed Kael's bicep then shook his hand as if he was burned. "Strong too." Noble Sr. chuckled as if this was the way he was best amused.

"What are you doing? Why have you brought me here? I have no business with you. I haven't done anything," Kael lisped past a swollen lip.

Noble Sr. pressed forward until he was almost nose to nose with Kael. The enforcers leaned against the wall. I could see Edgar standing in the mix, casually resting his crossed arms over his chest enjoying what was unfolding, knowing he had no role at the moment. I tasted the air and what I got back was surprisingly rich and buttery. I wondered at it until I realized that both of the enforcers expected an abundant reward for bringing Kael to Noble Sr.

"Let me tell you a truth," Noble Sr. said. "You will die very soon. There is nothing you can do to stop your death." His tone was so matter of fact I questioned whether I was hearing this properly. "Of course, before you die, you will tell me everything it is that I want to know." He stood back up and took a step backward so he could tower over Kael, but Kael could still see the conviction in his face. "Oh, you're going to want to die long before I let you." He popped his eyebrows for emphasis. "You'll beg me for mercy. You'll pray for death. You'll reach for that proverbial white light and want nothing more than to cross over to it, and peace. But the peace will only come when I allow it. Yeah?"

Kael sat stoically. I didn't know if his head was clanging still from the impact of the strike or whether he was just a cool warrior playing a role. None of my instincts could tell the difference. I was a sweating, adrenaline-addled mess. He was central to the Resistance. He knew every name, including mine. He was a leader. And important to our work. He was my friend. And important to me.

I hated this.

I was a warrior of the Fire Sword. Flames licked through my system begging for action. Action made me in sync with my calling and the universe. Hiding behind this glamour was everything I was not and took immense training and fortitude to maintain. If I went against my instinct and spun into the room to destroy the enemies one and all, it would not solve the problem at hand. Someone meant to harm Tera. Tera was part of some bigger picture that I didn't understand. Until I understood, the best I could do was try to spring Kael from this trap without getting us both killed and giving myself away.

And too, while I was a good fighter and a better Witch, I was not impervious to death. I was as likely as anyone to die, my witchcraft notwithstanding. There was a lot of brawn and weapons in that room with Kael. Pragmatism and strategy were as important as any other fighting skill, I reminded myself.

But, when Noble Sr. moved over to a tool box and pulled out a hammer, I knew he wasn't playing psychological games. This was happening. If I ran to get Crispin, I might not make it up the stairs. If Crispin was able to intercede, I would very likely lose my place in the house and my ability to save Tera, my mission. Nothing could interrupt my mission.

There must be another way, a non-violent way. A way that… and I got it in a flash of inspiration.

Moving my hand anticlockwise, I formed the pentagram with my index finger.

In my imagination, Tera slept soundly in her bed. Her dark hair spread over the white pillowcase, exactly the way I left her just a moment ago when I was looking out her window. I reached out the image of my athame, a knife given to me in ceremony to be used for the Fate's ends. I cut into her aura until there was an opening, and into it I let this spell's smoky tendrils seep:

Into a trance of doom your spirit flew
Watch the cauldron of horror brew.
Everything you loathe and fear
Is coming fast, is drawing near
To eat you

Tera, the screams within you grow
Forcefully blast, shrill frightening show
Continue their course they don't abate
The cries to save your life. The flames of Fate,
They heat you.

Tera, your monsters come ever close.
You fight for life. You desire most,
To get away, to dive and flee.
To draw your helpers now you scream.
I beseech you.

And as my spell filled her mind, a horrible shriek severed the air. It was the hair-raising call of one who knew they were about to die. Goose pimples raised on my arm as the note hit a pitch high and strong, desperate, frantic. A gasp for air, another shriek.

The men in the room stilled in the shock of it. The desperation of it. The life and death of it. And when their brains unfroze, all of accord, they took off running, to save Tera.

Harming none, my spell is wound,
Continue thus until unbound.
By the power of three times three
So I speak it, so mote it be.

I'm so sorry and so grateful, Tera, thank you. Stay asleep and continue to scream.

As soon as the last man rounded the corner, I sprinted toward Kael. Awake now, his eyes wide in horror, I was sure he thought that the screaming was coming from someone else who was destined to die that night and was past the begging part of the torture and had succumbed to the death spiral part of pain.

I untied his ropes and still he sat there unmoving.

Now, it was my turn to smack at the poor guy's cheek. "Snap out of it! We don't have time for this. You have to function. It's me, Ember."

My name did the trick. I saw his eyes shift back to his intelligent, courageous self, ready for do-or-die action. He leapt to his feet. "Who is that? We need to help them."

That was Kael, alright. He'd already forgotten that he was the one at danger's door.

"That's a mirage, no one is imperiled. I needed to get the enforcers out of the room, so Tera is upstairs feigning a nightmare." I couldn't tell Kael she was under my spell; he was Mundane. "Come on. I need to hide you away until I can get you out of here."

With Kael leaning heavily on my shoulders, we stumbled up the stairs to the door that led outside. I snaked my aura out in front of us spreading it around the courtyard, checking for enforcer energy especially around the gate. I found no heat from any bodies anywhere nearby. I hoped they had all run to Tera's aid.

Her screams had not abated. If possible, they sounded even more horrific. A wash of guilt moved through me. *I'll fix it later*, I promised her.

I sent a lick of fire her way to keep the energy up, as her voice was growing scratchy. Hauling Kael outside under the full moon, only partially masked with dark clouds, we lurched to the enforcer shed. There, I found tools. I handed Kael an oversized wrench as a weapon, then grabbed up an emergency first aid box, and an electric torch. I searched but could find no key or fob to open the gate. "I'll have to hide you out here until I can formulate a plan. They'll start looking for me soon. I should be in Tera's room by now."

Kael nodded and licked his lips.

Thunder roared overhead. Bad plan, it said to me. "The weather's growing harsher and the temperatures are dropping.

You'll freeze to death out here." My gaze scanned for inspiration. "They'll be looking for you." I tried to juice my brain to come up with a viable plan. Turning three-sixty, I noticed a line of light at the front door, it hadn't shut properly when the outside enforcers ran toward the screams.

I leaned Kael against the wall and took the chance to run to the fountains and retrieved two objects larger than I thought they'd be. I didn't even stop to identify what they were, I just kept sprinting until I had Kael under the arm and was propelling us in the direction of the doorway.

Right into the lion's den.

Coming into the foyer, I pushed him toward the lavatory. I shut and locked the door, flipping on the light and the water faucet. When Tera had given me my tour, yesterday, she had noted that the linens were stored here. I opened the double cabinet doors to find it lined in cedar and filled with stacks of sheets and comforters. At the bottom there were large woven baskets with blankets. I pulled them out and thought there would be plenty of room for Kael to slide in the back. They wouldn't think to look there, because alone, it would be impossible to both slide the baskets in place and shut the doors. If they brought in dogs, the cedar would throw off the scent.

I helped Kael get situated then handed him the supplies that he could take care of his wounds. I was thankful to find there were three bottles of water in the kit.

"It may be a long time before I can get you out. I'm working on a plan."

"Thank you," he said gruffly as I shut the doors.

I checked the mirror to reassure myself that I didn't have any dirt or blood or other tell-tale signs of my rescue efforts. And now I had to go save Tera, ingratiating myself with the Noble family a little more.

Wrapping myself in a glamour, I hugged the stairs and slid toward Tera's room. Her bedroom light was on, and still she screamed. The men stood uneasily shifting from foot to foot, not sure of what role they played here with no danger to destroy. They didn't have a directive for combatting nightmares, but still it wouldn't do for them to go back to their torture task at hand, while Tera was in this state.

I untwirled the glamour and pushed into the room. Noble Sr. was glaring at the end of the bed. Crispin was trying to hold Tera down as she thrashed against him, kicking her sheets until they knotted around her legs.

I lay my hand on Crispin's shoulder, and he startled. I tightened my clasp and looked him dead in the eye. *Let me.* I sent him the thought, my words wouldn't be heard, so loud were Tera's screams coming now in hoarse rasps and gasps for air.

When he stood, I slid into his place and wrapped my arms around her. Her trance was deep. That in itself was interesting. I'd have to revisit how deeply she'd succumbed to my spell, but at another time. I drew the pentagram in the inverse on her back and whispered in her ear.

The time has come, the monsters fade,
The play at hand, has now been made.
From the trance you come anew
But remember not what chased after you.
You've done your part to save the day,
Your voice restored this I pray.

Harming none,
This work is done.

Great hiccupping breaths were drawn between Tera's trembling lips. I simply held her as she moved back from her tranced state. I rubbed her arms, her back, her hair, helping her to remember her body and come fully home. I painted her with red light for grounding and a sense of safety. Then I gave her context. Gave it loudly enough that all the men could hear. "It's Ember. You're safe. The accident is in the past. I pulled you from the car. You're safe now." I rocked her and stroked her hair. "The accident is in the past. You're safe. You're home in your bed." I crooned like a mother comforting her infant. "You're safe."

Tera pushed herself up, her breath coming much more normally. "Oh, Ember," she croaked then cleared her voice.

I painted her throat with green light for healing.

She looked around her bedroom—light on, father's impassive glare, her brother white as a sheet. Four enforcers crowding the door, looking physically capable of fighting a tiger; and yet incapable of handling this situation with a dream-tormented girl.

Everyone seemed relieved when I gave them a reason for her night-terror. She had been in an accident. They knew she had traumatic amnesia, as is typical, and they also knew her subconscious took in all of it. The chase, the fights, the deaths, the attempt to kidnap her.

"You're alright now," Noble Sr. said. "Your tough. You'll shake this off. It's over." The way he said it was less soothing and more a pronouncement. The kidnapping attempt was a done deal. You survived, move on. His words were warm enough, but the sentiment was cold.

Crispin turned exasperated eyes on his father. "Dad—"

Before he could reproof his father in front of the enforcers, his father turned and made a shooing gesture. Another point of interest; those men were loyal to Noble Sr. and not Crispin. Noble Sr. probably brought them along when he moved in.

As he exited, the last thing Noble Sr. did was send me a hard look that told me he absolutely thought I was an intruder and had no business sitting in that room, holding his daughter.

I wanted to listen as Noble Sr and the enforcers quietly conferred. I felt uneasy about pulling their conversation toward me since Crispin's focus was on me. I imagined what they were saying, though. Let's get downstairs and beat the information out of our hostage.

I hoped against hope that my absence from the scream-scene for so long wasn't remarked of. And I sent a glamour to cover Kael. It was the best I could do in that moment.

"Are you okay, sweetheart?" Crispin was asking Tera.

"I'm perfectly fine. I don't even remember dreaming." She swallowed. "Though my throat is sore. I must have been screaming my head off." She offered a self-conscious laugh.

"We all have bad dreams. Everyone came running because we were worried about you. All's well." I combed my fingers through her hair. "Do you think you can tuck back down and gets some rest?" I sent warmth down my hands, sleepy pink warmth.

She slid down her bed, and I stood to untangle her covers and get them rearranged and smoothed.

Her eyelids were drooping, as if she struggled to stay awake.

"Go ahead, let your eyes close. Sleep deeply. Heal. The morning will bring another day." I had my hand on her head and was painting my thumb back and forth over the worry line between her brows, smoothing, soothing, charming her into a deep and restful sleep.

When I stood, Crispin ran a hand down my arm and stepped very close. "You're magical with her." he said.

I worked at not bristling. He meant those words the way a Mundane uses them. He didn't recognize me as a Witch. If he had, he'd be calling for the enforcers and not bending down to lay a soft kiss on my lips.

Chapter Eighteen

Noble Sr. stood in the foyer conferring with his men.

"Stop. Go to bed," Crispin said. "You're disrupting the house with all this activity." He crossed his arms across his chest and his father seethed, knowing that this looked like he lacked authority. He was the patriarch, but this was Crispin's home. They were at loggerheads. This felt like new energy. Like Crispin had not acted this way toward his father before and his father had not factored this into his decision making.

Interesting.

I wondered what changed.

Noble Sr. patted his son on the arm, like he was dealing with a wayward child. It was a show for his enforcers. He walked over to the men who stood at attention waiting for their orders.

I reached out and pinched the air and drew the conversation to me.

Noble Sr, snagged one of the men's sleeves. "Tell Driver that I need to see Leopold, now."

The man went out the door and the exhausted-looking servant closed it behind them.

Kael was safe for the moment.

Noble Sr. sent a scathing look Crispin's way then moved to his office.

Crispin uncrossed his arms and stalked toward the stairs.

I scuttled back to my bed.

The door to Tera's room opened and after a moment it closed again. Then, a light tap sounded at my door. As it swung open I turned toward the hall light feigning half-asleep confusion, pushing the long strands of hair from my face.

Crispin crouched by my bed. "Don't wake up. I'm just checking that you're alright." He smoothed his hand over my hair, then stood, bent, and kissed my head. "Thank you for everything. You're like a miracle, coming here. I'm so grateful." He walked quietly out. Closing the door behind him.

The light went out in the hall, and I waited.

I waited for about as long as I could stand to. I sent my aura out to its far reaches. There was a pool of warm pink light where Tera slept. Another pool of light red, yellow, and indigo where Crispin lay. His consciousness hovered in the space between awake and asleep. His mind jumbled. It was a thought-provoking combination, those colors.

Red energy lived at the base of the spine, and I expected to see that color. Crispin seemed like a grounded soul. Beyond that, red energy had to do with physical survival, and he had just experienced his sister's attack and ensuing nightmare. His survival instincts would be primed, ready for fight or flight. Though Crispin seemed like he was always ready and willing to fight. He was a big man – tall with broad shoulders and hard muscles.

The yellow was also not unexpected. The way he kissed me was gentlemanly and filled with kindness and concern. If the energy was orange, I would think he expected a roll in the hay. But that wasn't the case, I felt the warmth of a bourgeoning relationship in that yellow. I stayed with that color, using my clairvoyant skills to help me interpret it. Yellow was indicative of emotional life, and as much as my picture was there with positive feelings, this yellow held other emotions, as well. Exerting personal power. Ambition. The ability to achieve. And anger. There was a lot of anger, frustration, and even victimization.

That made sense to me, too.

The events that had put me in Crispin's path were things that would bring up Seraphina for him. I bet he imagined that what had almost happened to his sister was similar to what had happened to his fiancée. I bet that the feelings that even Tera felt between Crispin and me were also a point of fear. My background mirrored Seraphina's in many ways. A budding member of the intelligencia, a connection to Gareth…

The energetic color that I wasn't expecting to burn so bright was the indigo. That was the color of connection. It was indicative of a spiritual nature. Of intuition and wisdom. It was a color that I had seen associated with few Mundane. Gareth, for example. But typically, this color was associated with people with psychic skills and a relationship with Sky and Earth. Gareth had developed intuition as a survival technique. Many did, when they faced repeated life or death situations. But here? A Noble? It made me very curious about Crispin's life up to this point.

I pulled my aura back from him. Fishing in my pocket, I pulled out an emergency long-burn candle and a small lighter. Poor Socrates. This must have been a heavy burden for him to carry. I'd have to get him a special thank you treat when I got home. *If* I got home.

Could I attempt to light the candle?

The sound of an engine's roar as it climbed the steep hill, approaching the front gate told me that the person Noble Sr. had sent for, had arrived. Crispin didn't hear his father and didn't know of this new person in his home. I could magically wake him. Make him hungry and send him down to the kitchen. But something inside told me that Crispin's intrusion would be punished.

Punished by whom? How? Why? I asked, but I got nothing by way of reply. I guessed I'd have to discover what was going on for myself.

In bare feet, with my back pressed to the wall, I slid toward the stairs.

From where I held my position, I could see the downstairs lavatory door. I wondered how Kael was doing bunched as he was behind the baskets in the closet. If it were me, I'd be freaking out. That small space with torture and death on the other side pulled up images of me in a similarly desperate situation, back in the cave with the salt water over my face. Just the thought and my palms sweated. I didn't even want to send Kael any kind of helping charm. I was afraid that my own fears would ride along the energetic flow and pull him into a bad place, emotionally. I hoped that tomorrow I could find a secondary egress, some other way to get him out of this fortified estate.

The door opened and there he was again, the man who had brought Kael and dropped him off to be tortured. My lip lifted in a snarl.

I pulled the air from their words close enough that I could hear. With the house so quiet, it was easily done, even as they spoke under their breath.

"Of course, he's upset," Leopold said. "Crispin lost a good man. His driver was a war hero. I told you we should let him in on the scheme. We could have paid the driver a little money, and he would have handed the girl over to us instead of speeding up and rolling the car."

"He's Crispin's man, not mine. He'd never have gone for it."

There was the slick of glass against glass, then liquid trickled, I imagined Noble Sr. swirling a sniffer of brandy.

"The driver did his best to save her. Crispin hired a commendable man. Too bad, we could use someone who knows the value of loyalty."

"Save his own skin is more like it," Noble Sr. said.

"We'll never know."

More liquid poured into glass.

"Thank you," Leopold said.

"We need something else." Noble Sr. announced then paused. "We can't use Tera any more. She wasn't supposed to be hurt. Captured, drugged, held for a few days. Amnesia effects and put right back in the cottage to be found safe and sound."

That thought was met by a grunt from Leopold.

"They found the sedative in your guy's pocket. Any way that can be traced back to us?" Noble Sr. asked.

"None, I assure you."

I slunk down the stairs, I wanted to see the men's faces as they spoke. I wanted to pull everything I could from this conversation. If I wasn't mistaken, it was Daddy Noble who had endangered his daughter's life with a kidnapping or a fake kidnapping, or a...*Something.*

"Imagine what else they found in your dead enforcer's pocket," Noble Sr. asked.

I had made my way to a spot where I could see the scene reflected in the window. It was always safest to look at a reflection rather than a person themselves. Humans, even the Mundane, held over the ability to tell when they were being watched. Watching through another resource lessened the chance that the intuition would raise its hackles and spin the person's gaze in my direction.

"They have the note?"

"Yeah, the note. The one declaring Crispin should exchange Dr. Brighton's research and the good professor himself for Tera."

"As a safety tactic, the ploy still might work. The speculation that we had taken Dr. Brighton won't have credence now that the defenders think there was a kidnapping attempt. It almost works in our favor. Nobody else needs to disappear. That little student, Ember – what's her name, stepped in and did the killing for us."

As I was processing, Leopold was lamenting the situation. "So at least your name has been taken off the short list of people who might have kidnapped the good doctor. But that's a small issue. Dr. Brighton is no longer our guest. Someone got to him."

"Was an inquiry made? Did anyone see anything?" Noble Sr. asked.

"An ambulance showed up and took off. That's all anyone said." Leopold shook his head in disgust. "If we don't get him back, this could be very bad. If Brighton's experiments become publicly known, if energy gets to the people of the Range, then everything we've built in the way of power will be dissipated."

"Exactly."

Leopold slammed his drink and held out his tumbler for more. Noble Sr. obliged him. Leopold drained that one as well, then banged the glass onto the credenza. "Did Gareth have any information on who might have taken him? Does the Resistance have him? What if it was someone from the Northern Realm?" He stopped. "The Northern Realm having the energy source and not us, that's just as bad as the people of the Range getting hold of this resource. With the advantage of consistent and unrestricted energy to consume…with their numbers? They could quickly eclipse us and make a power grab. One that we couldn't thwart." The man was pacing and waving his arms about maniacally. "Are there any clues? Any possibilities that we could get Dr. Brighton back?"

"It turns out that the good doctor wasn't just a researcher but also part of the Resistance. His initial interrogation gave us some names to work with. Kael Boswell, the man you brought up for me, he was top of the list. We'll be looking for the others. Someone knows where Brighton is hidden."

I'd have to get that information back to the Resistance immediately. They'd need to find out from Dr. Brighton which names he'd shared so we could protect those whom he had named. Everyone knew the score. Torture was torture, and everyone had their breaking point. If Dr. Brighton wouldn't share or couldn't remember, I'd use my fire opal as a pendulum to try to figure it out. I hoped Crispin would get it back for me soon.

"And he's being interrogated this Kael Boswell? Where is he now?" Leopold asked.

A slow smile slid across Noble Sr.'s face. It was the happiest I'd ever seen him. "In the basement. Shall we go and have a visit?"

Chapter Nineteen

I was curled under my covers, feigning sleep as the falderal began downstairs.

I pulled the voice of Noble Sr. closer. "Search the grounds. It's all but impossible that he'd get in to the main house. All the doors were bolted."

I sent appreciation to the Fates that I had bolted the front door when I came in. It had been a gamble – leave it open the way it was? Then, Kael could be inside. Lock it and no one own up to throwing the latch? They'd know Kael was in the house. But it looked like the ploy worked.

My door opened and closed.

Tera's door opened and closed.

Crispin moved down the stairs. "Honestly, Dad. Tera and Ember are trying to sleep. You saw the state Tera was in. I think her subconscious is trying to remember. Two men almost kidnapped her. Almost got to her. You have to let her sleep."

"The enforcers say someone has breached your walls," Leopold said.

"Impossible," Crispin's was unswerving.

"Improbable, perhaps, but not impossible. We're going to look. But I'll tell the team to keep their noise as quiet as possible. You've checked on Ember, have you? She's in her bed and asleep now?"

"I did, and she is, why do you ask?"

"I'm wondering if the intruder has something to do with the Intelligencia-student your harboring."

"Harboring is not what I'm doing. I'm allowing her to heal after saving Tera." Crispin said between clenched teeth. "And there is no intruder. The walls weren't breached."

***

I waited for the house to settle, then moved to the little lavatory off my room. There were no windows in here. The doors were made of metal, and they slid across the doorframe rather than being pulled open and pushed closed. I assumed this was a safety feature, and when I opened the cabinet and found blankets and food stores, I knew that was exactly what it was. A place to run to and hide should the weather get so fierce that windows were breaking, though I saw that all the windows had workable shutters. This must be in place in case the house was collapsing around one's ears.

It felt like just such a thing was happening, that things were collapsing all around me and I was pushing hard trying to hold everything up. There were so many spokes on this mission. I needed to sort it all out and find the answer.

The most pressing was my task to save Tera.

Was I saving Tera from her father? He seemed to think that boat had sailed—that Tera had fulfilled her use in throwing off the scent from the defenders' investigation into Dr. Brighton's disappearance.

I pulled my gifts from Piper and Socrates from the pocket of my robe. It was a lighter and an emergency candle, the kind that could burn for over a day. It should give me enough communication time to get help from outside the compound. It wasn't, unfortunately, enough flame to bring me respite from the death energies I'd absorbed. I'd have to wait for the balefire for that. At least Crispin had seemed open to the possibility tomorrow. If Father Sky would just allow it.

I grounded myself and prepared a sacred circle in my mind's eye. I set protection by both the lavatory door and my bedroom door, so I would be left alone.

When everything was ready, I reached my mind out to Giselle, the Wise Woman who had been my mentor as I learned to wield the Sword of Fire. My priority was to know why I was so tasked, and how to proceed.

"Merry meet," she said.

"Merry meet, Giselle, I come to you in haste. Time is both short and of the essence."

"I am here for you, child."

I quickly unfolded the story from the point where things went awry, when Gareth's men chased me until now.

"Who?" Giselle was asking me. "Who told you to save her."

"An owl brought the instructions."

"It had to be an acolyte of Athena or the owl would not have done the bidding twice that way. Bringing you the message and then giving Kael a moment to attempt his escape. That will make it easier for me to figure out who sent you the command. It didn't come from the Council as a whole."

"Have I done something wrong?" I could see Giselle tapping her chin as her face flickered in the candle's flame.

"I imagine what happened was that an Elder saw a problem and saw a solution and acted. I have been on the far side of Haven, visiting some of our far-flung villages. Full Council has not been in session, but the Petite Council is always at hand to help the witches in their Offling Years to navigate the outside world. I will cut my journey short and return home. I'll look into this further, but it will take a while to cover the distance. Do you have access to a fire?"

"Possibly. Hopefully. Right now, I have this candle from Piper and Socrates."

"Well, my dear," said Giselle. "Whoever called on you to intervene had a great deal of faith in your abilities. And beyond that you are now well placed to help the Resistance as they face this new and quite concerning issue. Whoever has access to Dr. Brighton's work weilds a great deal of power in every sense of that word. It

220

should be the people. But greed is an insidious drug. And the Noble family has a history of clawing for what others have."

"I understood that the family is new to their designation." I offered. "Perhaps their roots weren't deep. Perhaps their alliance networks weren't impossible to evade."

"New, yes, however, ruthless and determined are also adjectives. Do not think that because they haven't worn their mantle long that this makes them less formidable. Remember, the young rattlesnake is the most dangerous, as they haven't learned when a strike is required for survival, and they simply attack any movement that is unexpected." She paused for a long moment. "You are unexpected. A puzzle piece that does not fit. I have looked and the path forward is not clear to me. There is potential. There is also great danger."

"I believe that to be true," I said.

"And the men involved—"

"Noble Sr. and Leopold?"

"No, my dear, I speak of Gareth and Crispin. Your heart stutters."

I sat silently.

"They are both useful. And both dangerous for their own reasons—and I don't mean that either are malicious or evil, but simply that working in concert with either or both can place you amongst the black-hearted."

The flame flickered, and her face came and went and came again as she contemplated my situation. When she finally spoke she said, "They are handsome, powerful, intelligent men. Of course, there is attraction and feelings…"

"I know my duty."

"Duty can become distorted."

"Don't doubt me. I'm stronger than that."

"See that you are. In the meantime, your pain is palpable. You haven't done a cleansing ritual."

"I tried, but this flame isn't strong enough."

"Yes, well, six deaths in one day is a burden for any Witch to carry. I'm sure that candle light wouldn't do the trick. Are there no wood burning stoves or fireplaces where you are?"

"There's a fire circle. I've already laid a magical balefire, but Father Sky wasn't cooperating."

"There's a reason, I'm sure, since you said that Sky came to your aid to help Tera."

"And I already know the reason why. They had captured one of the Mundane resistors, Kael Boswell. He was part of my mission yesterday morning to save Dr. Brighton. Had I been at the fire, I wouldn't have known he was brought to the house. They meant to torture him for information. I saw and was able to hide him away. It's a cramped spot where he can't get out on his own."

"Even as you say that I can feel the fear at your throat. Some people find small spaces lovely, they find them secure. Surely, being

222

hidden in a small space is better than being in the hands of torturers. Not everyone has your phobia, don't put that energy out there, it will only make it harder for your friend." Her face wavered with the dance of the flame. "You have two missions now. Helping Kael escape and saving Tera. The last one is the hardest since you don't know the enemy. I promise to get you those answers."

"Giselle," I whispered. "There's magic afoot."

She pushed her face closer to the flame when she heard the seriousness of my whisper. "How do you mean?"

I took a moment to tell Giselle about the metal that protected Tera in the car. About the strange communication that tried to come to me while I was under the razor wire fence that sounded as if it were a foreign language. About the depth of the trance in which I'd found Tera, when my incantation shouldn't have placed her that deeply under my spell. And then I told her about the exodus story that I'd sipped from my tea cup.

Giselle's face hardened into the Fire warrior that she was. Fierce. Intense. Aggressive. It was the face she wore to battle. Her words though were those of a general and showed her thoughtfulness and control. "This is very concerning. I've never heard of such a thing before. Surely, if someone was delivering a message to you they'd make themselves known in a less cryptic way. But even that makes no sense at all. If a Witch was sharing that story they would deny themselves the memories of Haven here after and lose their skills as a Witch."

"Exactly. I've been rolling it over in my brain ever since I drank the tea, and I can't understand how this could be."

"My dear, take no offense, but is it possible that you imagined or conjured this yourself? You had been through a series of traumatic events. And you still carry the energy of the deaths with you."

"Giselle, please. I've been through much worse. You know that. This wasn't my imagination. Perhaps that's why I was sent here, to discover some great risk to Haven. But if that were the case, why would I be asked to save Tera?"

Chapter Twenty

Breakfast was a silent affair. Crispin had eaten early and was now in his office in a closed-door meeting. I pulled the words through the keyhole, and they were talking about a holding wall near a project he had under way, so nothing that I needed to keep my awareness on.

Tera fiddled with her food. Her face didn't have the same warm color it had when we were at the hospital. Nor did she have the bouncy puppy energy about her. I wondered if that was residue from last night's spell, or if eating at the same table with her father put her off her meal.

Noble Sr. hid his thoughts and actions behind his newspaper. Only on rare occasions did the people of the Range get hold of a newspaper, and then it was usually too old to have useful information for us. Gareth let me read the news if all the drapes were drawn in his bedroom. To me it was a bunch of propaganda. Still I was glad to know how the powers that be wanted the people to perceive the world about them.

I built an energetic illusion in front of me to mask my actions as I pulled together all the food I dared to and hid it in my pockets to give to Kael. I hadn't talked to him yet this morning. I didn't know how extensive his injuries were.

The nurse came in and asked Tera if she'd finished, because it was time for her bath and massage. Tera gave me a half-hearted smile, wiped her mouth and followed dutifully along behind the older woman.

I took the opportunity to excuse myself and leave the table.

Noble Sr.'s paper never even wavered. It was as if I were just smoke to be ignored.

Fine by me.

I went to the downstairs lavatory and turned on the faucet. I whispered into my hand, "It's me, Ember, I brought you some breakfast." Then, I inched the door open and released my words inside, so I wouldn't frighten Kael into defensive action when I opened the door.

I got the baskets out and reached in to help Kael. He was stiff from his cramped position. I used warmth from my hands and brisk rubbing to get his limbs functioning again. I stood with my back to the room, so he could use the toilet and get washed. After helping him with fresh bandages, he sat and ate, as I filled his water bottles and stored them away.

Time was ticking. I was anxious that being here so long would raise suspicion. I checked outside of the door and felt no energy focused in our direction. That was good, still I didn't want to push. I whispered in his ear that he had been picked up because his name had been compromised during Dr. Brighton's stay at the torture hotel.

Kael nodded.

"When I get you out, you need to get Brighton to tell us what other names he shared from the Resistance. We need to get them and their families into protection."

He nodded again.

"I'm doing my best to find a way out, but you have to be prepared. This is the safest place I can find to hide you right now. I'm sorry. How are you holding up?"

"I'm holding as best I can," he said.

"Gareth is coming to give me my tests. He should be here tomorrow. I'm hoping to find a way to get you out with him. Right now, it's all I can figure. I'll look for another exit point today. But I think in someone's car is the only way that gives you any chance."

Kael gripped my arm and sent a steely gaze my way. "I'm not going with him. Gareth would hand me back over–you can't trust him." His eyes searched mine. "Do you think you can trust him?"

"No," I said on an exhale. "I know I can't. Look, I'll do my best to find an alternative–but I wasn't thinking of putting you in the seat next to him I was thinking about the trunk."

"The driver, the enforcers."

"I didn't say it would be easy. I just said I'd do my best." I pulled my arm from his grip and stood, lifting my chin toward the closet. And he crawled back in.

***

That night, there was candle light on the table. I noticed they were using limited electricity and wondered if their batteries were growing low.

Sky was grey all day, blanketing the sun's glow. And now that it was night, the moon was hidden as well. But after I sent pictures and desire to Tera, she had convinced Crispin that we should all go down to the fire circle after dinner.

I wasn't sure that was going to happen.

Noble Sr. had been conferencing with the enforcers about where Kael had gone. They had the dogs out searching for him, but my understanding was that they didn't have a good scent item for the dogs to work from. An enforcer was dispatched to the Range to take one from his house. Curfew had come, and the man wasn't back. The defenders would shoot anyone they saw on sight — no questions asked, no papers or badges or explanations accepted. He was, thank the fates, not coming back tonight. I had until the curfew lifted at dawn before dogs and scents became a worry again.

Tera still didn't seem as well as she had been the first night.

Even Crispin was off in a way that I couldn't quite fathom.

As I spooned up my cream of garlic soup, I thanked the flame for its warmth and said my nightly dinner prayers, changing the words ever so slightly to make them fit the situation.

Fire, Water, Air and Earth,
fill this home with health and mirth.
Bless my mission, find its heart,
Hestia's blessings to impart.

Peace and safety, love and light,
Respite, solace, compassion bright,
Warmth of family, Steadfast and true,
Laughter of friendships, old and New,

Gentleness, kindness, glowing flame,
Hestia, Hestia I call your name!
Heat of flame and three times three,
So I speak it, so mote it be.

It was more out of habit than actual conviction that magic this simple could work to make this home a happy place. Imagine my surprise when Crispin pushed back and said to the room, "We've been boxed up inside for too long." He leaned back in his chair. "Cook," he called and waited for the man to run in, his face red from the heat of the stove and alarm in his eyes. "We'll eat around the fire in the field."

Tera jumped up and clapped her hands.

"No," Noble Sr. growled. He sent daggers toward his son. "And you know why. No one's been found."

"Because there's no one to find, Dad." Exasperation painted his words. "No one can get in or out of these walls without giving us ample knowledge. The only place that isn't alarmed and on cameras is the front gate. Stop. Now. Truly, you'll frighten the ladies."

I looked over at Tera, he must mean us. She was twelve and I had never thought of myself as a lady before. I was a warrior of the fire sword, *not* a lady. But that was indeed interesting information. There was no sneaking Kael out in any other direction. He'd have to go out the front gate.

Tera took me into the library, so we could pick a book for after our picnic. I chose a collection of Shakespeare's plays. I wanted to read over the speech of St. Crispin's day to search out the reason why Crispin's mother chose his name. As I stood there leafing through the pages, Crispin came over to me and lifted my hand, looking me in the eye, I felt him slide a ring on my finger. It buzzed its relief to be back with me. Without even looking, I knew he'd brought me my fire opal.

"Thank you," I said, as he lifted my hand to his lips.

"What's going on in here?" Noble Sr.'s enmity washed over me. I flung up a protection spell to shield both Crispin and me, keeping Noble Sr.'s loathing from adhering to us. I needed Crispin to be my ally. I couldn't let the energy get clouded by his father's animus.

Crispin didn't answer, he merely took my hand, and we walked out the door. Tera trailed after us as we made our way down to the fire circle.

I had to admit, I was conflicted. I wanted desperately to get to the flame where I had left the healing spell in play. It would start its work as soon as the fire burned bright, and I was watching the flickers of light. But the walk there was nice. I liked holding Crispin's hand. I had to admit to myself I had, in this short span of time, found myself not just comfortable with Crispin, not just intrigued by him, but genuinely liking him. Genuinely attracted to him. Thinking about him. Wondering about him. And there was no doubt that I felt the strong physical attraction that he seemed to feel as well.

And this was all wrong.

In my role with the Resistance, falling for a Mundane– especially a Mundane in the Realm, especially a Noble—was not a smart move. It was in fact dangerous.

Gareth was right, I had to play the Crispin hand to have safety and capacity in this situation–though Gareth had no idea I was on a mission. But there lay a danger here. As I sent out energy, as I convinced Crispin that there was something special between us, as the energy swirled around us, there was the danger that I would fall for him, too.

Dangers of the heart were just as treacherous as any danger I faced in a fight.

"Are you okay, Ember?" Crispin asked. "You're very quiet. But I can almost hear your mind hashing through something."

"Oh," I laughed softly. "I was thinking about my exams. Your runner brought word that Gareth was coming tomorrow to have me sit for my first test."

"Exam anxiety. I still wake up from nightmares that I forgot to show up in class all term, or that I missed my test and failed the class. I don't know that it will ever go away." He lightly squeezed my hand. "Hopefully the weather will hold, so he can come tomorrow, and you can get it out of the way. Are you ready?"

"Yes, I shouldn't be worried about it. But…" I let the phrase fade as I approached the circle.

"I have faith in you," Crispin gestured toward a lounge, and I took a seat. With a lift of his chin the groundskeep lit the fire.

A heavy sigh released from my lungs. I couldn't help it. Relief was on its way. There was a little guilt there too. I had brought more food to Kael and let him use the toilet. But being cramped in the cupboard that way was lousy. I needed to come up with a plan to get him in Gareth's car tomorrow.

Crispin was tucking an extra blanket around Tera.

He had faith in me.

This was getting complicated, and I couldn't let it. Staying here too long was a hazard. I was looking forward to getting more information. As the flames lashed against the night air, I sat back and waited for all of the death pain to leave, then I'd try to contact Giselle.

Chapter Twenty-One

I had opened the book of Shakespeare's plays on my lap to Henry V. I set up a do not disturb spell, so Crispin and Tera would both forget I was around. If they looked, they'd see me reading and if all went according to plan, they would feel no need or desire to engage me.

Doing a ritual in front of others was part of our training, but it was advanced magic. Connecting on the spiritual and mundane planes at the same time took experience and was never the preferred method. It was a last resort.

I drew my circle and put up my protections, I called to the Fates to help me, my higher self, my guides. I called to Giselle. I had to get a handle on my mission. I needed to enact whatever it was that I was called to do, then I needed to get out of here. Being with Crispin endangered me as much, though differently, as Noble Sr. and his goon squad did. No wonder the pendulum I asked in the hospital had swung deosil–he was not a force against me, I was almost perfectly sure of that. That didn't mean he wasn't a problem.

"Giselle, I call to you," I said in my demi-trance.

"Merry meet, Ember."

"Merry meet."

"I won't be back to the village for a few more hours yet. I've stopped for the moment, but only have this candle. I need to make this brief."

I waited. In my mind's eye, I was under a tree along the roadway, sitting across from Giselle, and there in the atmosphere we could talk freely.

"I've asked for research to be done on the family you're with. This is all from Mundane archives mind you. I have nothing magical for you yet. I will before dawn. I'll wake you, and you can go to the lavatory with your candle."

"Alright, thank you. What did you find out?" I turned the page of my book. Staying both lightly present in the mundane world and working in the ether was a challenge of huge proportions. As the ether pulled at me, and I grappled to keep an awareness inside the fire ring, the sensation of push and pull lit my nerves on fire. I felt like I had to escape—that I was trapped in a limbo that was airless. Like I had been under water too deep and for too long. It felt a little bit like the tidal cave. And I hated it.

"Noble Sr. is Ruthberg Noble. He was a general in the war between the enclaves. His nickname was Ruthless and was known for his proclivity for torture. He worked the political side as well as the military side. This is how he amassed his wealth. Extortion and blackmail are tools in his bag of tricks. He accumulated enough wealth that he was on par with the Elite. His eldest son was his right hand—a child born outside of a marriage bond when Ruthburg was a teen—and was equally depraved. But he got as good as he gave. Just before the signing of the peace treaty, his son was found murdered and mutilated."

"But he's a Noble. How would that come about? And Crispin said there were only two children. I don't understand."

"Ruthberg is now a Noble. His last name was Steele before the wars."

"A tradesman, then."

"After the war, he was elevated, and his last name reassigned. He married a woman from an elite family anchoring himself to the most powerful dynasty in the South. She died before they had any children. Ruthberg's second wife, Enya, was from the Productors and had passed her Diploma Intelligencia, an artist who became a fashion designer for the elite. At that time, she worked for the Resistance. She used her time with the elite—designing and fitting their gowns—to gather information and pass it on to us. That is a grey area. I have no more information on her except that it was this second wife who gave birth to Crispin and Terabithia. She later died at the time the fever swept through the South. Terabithia, Tera, was still a toddler."

"The children survived. Do we know who raised them?"

"I don't, but I'm curious as well. We know they were sent to the coastal islands for a time. We're looking into that. You're right though, those formative years away from the Enclave, away from their father… they might have a perspective which would benefit us."

That probably explained why Tera and Crispin were so different from the other Mundane I had met from the Enclave. "I need to know why I'm here." I turned a page and let my gaze settle on the top line. "My mission?"

"I don't have any answers for you, yet. I will once I'm back at the Council. In the meantime, I've searched Crispin's heart. He has been open to and accepting of your warmth."

"Yes," I said.

"And while that connection is problematic because of Gareth, I believe that deepening your relationship with Crispin will serve you best as you work to complete the mission."

"Are you asking me to be his lover?"

Even through the dim etheric link from Giselle's candle flame to my blazing balefire, I could see that knowing smile spread across her face. She was my mentor because we had a similar calling. We were of the same affinity, both called to be fighters in the Resistance. There were no new stories in this world. She had been where I was. She knew the risks to playing with this kind of fire.

"It's always your choice. That is not something we ever ask of you. I'm merely pointing out the obvious energies swirling between the two of you. You are human even if you are aligned with the divine. The Goddess wants you to enjoy your body. Sexuality is a gift for you to experience as you wish, you know this. I said a deepening relationship. It's telling that your thoughts jumped to sex." She cocked her head to the side. "Having said that, I looked at your vibration around this, I find you have an affection for Crispin. If you follow through, I expect you to remember the role you play at the house and keep your emotions in check."

I turned the page in my book and looked over at Crispin. He raised his eyes to meet mine. He sent me a smile across the flame. I held that gaze while I swirled my finger behind the spread pages then flicked the symbol in his direction guiding the fire's warmth toward his heart. I could see the effect, and I lowered my eyelashes shyly, leaving the shadow of a smile on my lips.

"See?" Giselle asked. "That felt quite natural didn't it?"

I let my heavy lids close. Let myself fade farther behind the Veil. *He's the enemy*, I reminded myself–even if he doesn't feel like one. "When I leave, he'll be hurt," I told Giselle in the ether.

"This is war."

"Understood. A hurt Noble can be a dangerous Noble. I'm piling up enemies with this mission. Gareth is very jealous. And that will make him a problem."

Giselle seemed to mull that over. "Gareth understands now that you Resist. And on days when it suits him, he resists, as well."

"And on days when it doesn't suit him, he stands for the enemy. Gareth told me to do what was necessary with Crispin to forge a connection to stay safe. But I'm not sure if he saw it play out if he would put up with it for long."

"Don't overestimate your place in his heart. In the end, Gareth will always look out for Gareth."

"Meaning?"

Before I could get that answer, a hand brushed my hair over my shoulder. A kiss pressed to my forehead. I quickly closed the circle with the absolute minimum of words and gestures to disconnect. I worked to bring myself back to the here and now, to ground after my time in the flames. And then, I blinked my eyes open.

Crispin knelt beside my chair and lowered his forehead to touch mine. With a chuckle he said, "Ember, you're falling asleep behind your book. Come, let me take you to bed."

Chapter Twenty-Two

We moved back through the terrace doors together. Tera gave us a wave and skipped up to her room. Her door shut with a snap.

Crispin and I walked to the staircase. I stood at the bottom looking up, my hand resting on the rounded newel post. The distance to the top seemed so much farther than I remembered. I breathed in to give myself a little gumption to make it all the way to the top but struggled to lift my foot to the first tread.

Exhaustion was only a part of the problem. Up all night last night, I was going on my third day without any sleep. That was dangerous. A mind without sleep couldn't be counted on to think clearly. Without the pain medication, my injuries were brightly sharp with a low note of sustained ache. I wished I were back on Haven, where our Healers would use tinctures and chants that would bring me back quickly. And too, the way I'd had to close my circle, left me a little woozy and out of my body.

"Here, let me help you." Crispin reached around me, tucking me under his arm.

We took each step as if I were an enfeebled elder. A glimmer of something swirled the air and snagged at my attention. It was the second time in less than twenty-four hours that I could hear information, but it sounded like a foreign language. I got no pictures, nothing that let me know from whom this message came. Nothing but buzzing vowels and consonants even let me know a message was out there. As Crispin and I made our way down the hall, I focused on the sounds, and reached for any possible meaning. Or even an emotional vibration. Pleasure? Anger? Was I receiving a warning? I came up with no definition or explanation. It made me feel uneasy not being able to identify the energy that eddied around us.

In front of my bedroom door, Crispin took my hands in his, and kissed them. It was an old-fashioned gesture that read like gallantry. I thought his mother had chosen an apt name for her son.

"Are you alright, Ember?" he asked. "You don't seem alright." He gave a small chuckle that I read as self-awareness. He didn't know me well enough to know what 'alright' felt like around me.

I searched out his eyes as I took a step forward pressing against him, sending warmth from my solar plexus into his. I offered up a sweet closed-lip smile.

Parvati,
Warm his heart, my goal to meet.
Lace the air with sex and heat.
Rouse his lust, my ends fulfill,

I shall do as the Fates doth will,
A path forward, I seek a key,
So I speak it, so mote it be.

I tipped my head back, so I could better watch how he'd respond. "It's strange. When we're together, when you touch me...it's something I haven't felt before, and I'm trying to give these sensations context. I'm at a loss," I said in all earnestness. Why not just lay it out there and see if Crispin didn't have a better handle on the confusing energy circling around him.

"I feel it too." His smile was full of discovery and expectation. He had released my hands, reaching down to my hips to pull me tighter against him. "When I'm near you, I think of springtime. Warmth." He reached up to touch a strand of hair that had fallen across my forehead. A kiss hovered on his lips. "I think of the Sun's rays." His smile softened to something sentimental. "New beginnings." He stopped and cleared his throat.

Those images and sensations he'd just described weren't the truth. They were simply my spell, and not what I was talking about at all. I was disappointed. Something about him... I just couldn't place it.

He pushed on. "When we're together there's an emotion that's so familiar. I want to say a belonging, but I believe a word like that might frighten you."

Yes, that one. That was the emotion that I wanted to understand. Why did I feel a belonging? I pushed the heat between us up another notch.

"Maybe a good fit is a better choice of words. Or comfort." The smile dropped from his lips. "I don't normally sound like a stammering schoolboy."

"No. I...A belonging." I tried those words aloud. Again, I thought he was right; that seemed right somehow. But not in a loving, coupling way, which, if I was tasting Crispin's words correctly—like hot buttered bread—was his interpretation. No, it was more in a...huh, interesting. "Somehow that seems the right word. Isn't that curious?" I asked. "Confusing?" I let my voice grow soft and introspective.

"You're tired." Crispin dropped his hand to the knob and twisted it, pushing my bedroom door open. "You need to sleep to recover from everything."

I turned my head toward the bed. Giselle wanted me to deepen my relationship with Crispin. Taking him to my bed wouldn't be a hardship. He was an intelligent and gentle man—in this guise anyway. I'd just need to remind myself, continually that, despite his demeaner, he was the enemy, a Noble of the Southern Realm. I turned back to Crispin. He was a handsome man, too. Giselle was right when she checked my emotions. I did find myself wanting him. I sent him a frown and with a quavering voice said, "Can I tell you a secret?"

Crispin tipped his head.

"I'm afraid to go in there. I think that as soon as I'm alone, I'll end up reliving everything that's happened like I did last night."

His expression changed. The muscles around his eyes stiffened, and he stopped blinking. I could see his thoughts racing, and they needed a direction.

I tightened my grip on his hand. "I don't want to be alone."

He held perfectly still as the wave of energy I'd sent out, pushed through his unprotected auric field. His eyes grew dark, and a pulse of lust blazed up. Crispin lowered his head, his lips hovering just above mine. He paused and held, his movements asking if he had permission to kiss me. My esteem for this man increased dramatically. He was holding back despite my invoking Parvati. That was admirable. Typically, this was the moment when my targets started clawing my clothes off. I closed my eyes and pressed my lips against his, gently discovering the warmth, the softness—I stepped backwards into my room.

Crispin reached around my waist, splaying his hand on my back to pull me flush with him. And I opened my mouth, letting his tongue slick in and entwine with mine. I held him tight as I took another step back, stalling as Crispin's hand sought behind him. He snagged the door and pushed it shut. There was a click as the lock tumbled into place.

The decision is made.

The thing I had to do know was make him believe that this was deep, and good, and true. The only way to accomplish that, I'd found, was to be vulnerable. Vulnerability was my hardest hurdle, I didn't like it, though I understood its power.

Gently, carefully, Crispin pulled my shirt up over my torso. I lifted my arms and tried not to wince, but he caught the pain moving across my face. "I'm so sorry," he said, tossing my shirt to the side. He took my chin between his fingers and tipped my face up so my gaze met his in the dim lamplight of the room.

I popped the top closure on my pants. And he covered my hand with his. "Is this too soon? Too much? I don't want to hurt you."

I slid into his arms and lifted my lips. His fingers spread across the back of my head, cradling me as he kissed me back. It was getting harder, in this moment, to remember he was the enemy, the bad guy, and I was here on a mission. As I tasted his hesitation and concern both sweet and sour it was harder to think of him as my target.

I'd have to report this to council.

But for now, I was willing to lose myself in his kiss. I pulled his hand around to cup my breast. His thumb slid back and forth across my nipple until it hardened under his touch. "Make me forget," I whispered.

Ah, those were the right words. He was no longer taking advantage of me. He was my hero; he was coming to my aid. Our making love would be balm to my turbulent spirit. Crispin undressed with a level of immodesty and grace that told me he had had many lovers, and he was confident in his skills. A wave of heat washed over me and out. I could see it hit him hard as I let it cascade his way. His gaze gained a wolfishness that he reined in. Watching that sent a thrill through me that I hadn't felt in a long time. Not since I was on Haven with lovers that I chose to take to my bed for fun, instead of the power it gave me here on the mainland.

I undid the closure then wiggled my pants over my hips. When I bent to shove them lower, I came to a sudden stop. Whew, the pain in my ribs was a sharp knifepoint that held. I gasped, at the brightness of it. Crispin touched my hand to release the cloth, stroking his thumb along my shoulder. "Let me."

Standing, my breath came easier.

Crispin was on a knee, gently gliding my pants, then my panties, down my legs. I stepped, so he could drag them over my ankles and toss them to the side. He turned his face toward my abdomen. His fingers brushed over each bruise that colored my ribs. He winced, as if he could feel them too. "Oh," he said and shook his head. "Oh, Ember." He turned my body, so he could see my back. His gentle caress traced beside the lines of slices, not too deep, but angry like a thousand little paper cuts. He rested his forehead against my lower back and held my hips firmly in place. "How will I ever be able to pay you back for what you did for my sister? For me?" The words were little puffs of air on my flesh. I wasn't meant to hear them. I only grasped them as I put index finger to thumb and pulled the strand of air closer to my ears. Giselle would be pleased. To be honest, it pleased me, too. This feeling of reverence. This feeling of being held as precious. It was heady stuff that swirled around me and made me moan with a level of desire that shocked me. Truly shocked me.

I began to tremble. I began to think it was me who had fallen under a spell.

Crispin stood and pulled me against him as if he could provide a buffer. "I'm so sorry." He chanted between kisses that he sprinkled across my face. "I'm so sorry. So grateful." He bent his knees and gathered me up to cradle me in his arms and moved me to the bed, where he lay me down. He hovered above me. "I'm scared I'm going to hurt you."

"Please," I whispered, worrying that he'd refuse to make love to me, and bring me relief from this growing sexual tension.

"Yes, yes, it's just that… you'll have to help me find a way." He crawled onto the bed next to me, stroking his fingertips lightly over my arms, down my legs, waking my flesh. Cupping my breast, he licked over my nipples, lightly biting, sucking at them until I arched my back.

He stopped to smile at me. His smile was one of discovery and delight. His fingers slipped between my legs and as he found me slick and wanting. He licked his fingers and the wolfishness lit his eyes again. "Ember…" he whispered, lifting my knee and moving it to the side to make space for himself between my legs.

My fingers gripped at the bedsheets as he kissed and licked my inner thighs, making me writhe. Making me pant. Heating me.

His tongue licked up toward the top of my leg. "Yes?" he asked.

"Yes," I hummed, squeezing my eyes closed, pressure bubbling in my veins, hoping he wouldn't change his mind and think me too fragile. I tried to hold back the moans, though when he swirled his tongue, the groan he elicited was deeply animal in my arousal. He chuckled knowingly, and swirled again. And again.

It felt... mmm... beyond lovely. Waves lapped through my system, and I floated on them. But soon the sensations became a tumult. He was good at this, very good, but it wasn't what I needed. He was too far away. I wanted his weight. I wanted my arms around him. "Please stop," I gasped out.

And he did.

Instantly.

Pushing himself forward, kissing my quivering stomach, he moved up to see my face, his torso hovering over mine, posting his weight on his elbows.

"It's too much. And not enough." *Well that was clear,* I admonished myself. I reached up and grabbed handfuls of my hair, holding my fists against my head. I tried again. I laughed. "I felt too exposed. I'm feeling...please."

Worry creased between his brow. "What do you need?"

I reached out my arms to him. "Would you hold me? Can I just feel you moving inside me?"

He stalled. "I wasn't going to do that. I'll make your injuries worse. We should wait until you've healed more."

He'd planned to give me an orgasm and not follow through with our coupling? I appreciated the thought, well, no I didn't, I wanted him inside me. I wanted him to help me release all the energies I'd battled today. I pushed my head back into the pillow. I slid my hands over my eyes and panted. I just needed relief.

"I get it. I've got this," he said. He laid between my legs and slid inside me, rocking back and forth, in a slow steady cadence.

"Yes," I moaned. "Yes." I bit back the thank you. I didn't want it to sound like I was groveling, supplicating myself. I was still on a mission, and it was me who needed to bend him to my will. "Thank you" gave him too much of the wrong kind of power. What we both needed right now was our bodies responding easily and naturally together. He needed to feel at home inside me, to feel like this was a place he'd like to stay.

And it did feel that way.

Good.

Right.

As he pumped himself in and out, his skin heated and slicked with sweat. His breathing became ragged. I let the energies build in me, gathering the warmth of friendship then letting those waves develop a froth of a passionate heat. I closed my eyes and let it all crash through my system and out to include Crispin. His body stiffened with his orgasm. Then he crushed and bruised my lips with kisses, finally rolling to the side and pulling me with him until my head lay on his heaving chest.

"Incredible," he whispered as he caught his breath. "That was…astonishing." He laughed into my hair. "*You* are astonishing."

I lifted my head to look at him and gasped at the sight. Shimmering in the darkened room, his aura was vivid with etheric power. This was the energy I recognized from my lovers back on Haven after we'd coupled. Crispin's orgasm had lit him up.

Now, I could see.

Crispin was a Witch.

"Did I hurt you, Ember?" His euphoria shifted to concern.

I blinked back the shock. I worked to push those thoughts to the side. I'd take the time to adjust in a minute. Mundane Crispin needed an answer.

"Are you okay?" His alarm was growing.

I forced myself to think like an operative for the Resistance, the other information had to wait. My mind raced forward. In any other situation I knew that I could give him only a little. It was good for a target to think maybe they needed to try a little harder to prove their sexual prowess. And he was still a target, and would remain so until I had more information about my mission. Feigning dissatisfaction meant most men wanted another shot to demonstrate their skills. But that wasn't going to work here. Crispin's concern wasn't about my orgasm so much as my wounds. And guilt would not serve me in the same way as a faltering ego. "I feel much better, sleepy, though." I let my lips curl with the shadow of a smile, and I closed my heavy lids as I lay my head on his shoulder and slid to his side, leaving one leg draped over his hips, anchoring him in place. "Please stay. I feel safe with you here."

"Of course, I will. Of course, you're safe." He tucked me tight. And again, I had to pull the air closer to my ear to hear the words he barely whispered. "I won't let anything bad happen to you."

Chapter Twenty-Three

"*H*e's a *Witch*!" I was kneeling on the lavatory floor glaring into the flame of my emergency candle.

Giselle raised an admonishing eyebrow. "I know that, Ember. You need to calm yourself."

"That means Tera is a Witch as well."

"Yes."

I was so confused by the revelation that I had been hard pressed to keep from twitching about in my bed and rousing Crispin. After I painted him with a sleeping charm, I locked myself in the lavatory. My bedroom door was locked as well. I should be safe.

"Are you ready for some information?" Giselle asked.

I pursed my lips hard to keep myself quiet.

"Enya, Crispin and Tera's mother and their father Aiden were Witches who were trained on Haven."

"Ahh, no. That can't be right. Aiden was Enya's twin."

"That was the story they told, so they could be together. They were both Fire Witches working for the Resistance."

"Did Enya die fighting?"

"She was killed by Noble Sr. when he realized she was informing the Resistance. He'd laid a trap to test her, and she fell into it. Aiden escaped. He's still with the Resistance but works closer to the Northern Realm."

"Alright, moving on, Tera and Crispin aren't trained, I would know them if they were. I'd recognize them from Haven. We aren't that far apart in age."

"Exactly. Hush now and listen, we don't have all night. You can't rouse any suspicions."

I sat back on my heels and crossed my arms over my chest.

"Enya was a Fire Sword in the Resistance sent to gather information. She thought that people were growing suspicious, so she entangled Ruthburg Noble. He is not the children's father. Enya was merely married to him. Noble Sr. was, by spell, incapable of conceiving children with Enya. Tera and Crispin are full-blooded Witches, as is required."

"Fathered by Aiden... Why didn't their children go to Haven?"

"Enya couldn't get Crispin out of the Realm. She acted as if she tried – but looking back at the events clairvoyantly, I see that she really wanted to keep Crispin with her. His presence kept her safe from Ruthburg's wrath, and she simply couldn't bring herself to let Crispin go. Enya was killed before it was time for Tera to leave. Both siblings have very strong magic about them. I'd wager that if you ask in the morning, you will find that Tera made the tea for you.

I believe that in her dreams she connects with her ancestors. And perhaps she was telling about her dream while she prepared the tea, telling the water. Her affinity is water."

"Cripsin's affinity is metal," I said. "I'm thinking back to the car that held Tera the night of the crash. I could imagine that at some point that Crispin had put Tera in the car, patted the hood, and said, 'Keep her safe.' He had no idea whatsoever that he had instructed the metal and cast a spell."

"Exactly," Giselle said.

"That's not supportable. Tera cannot be left to dream and share."

"Agreed. Your job is to put her on a ship and send her to Haven. She's only just twelve now, perhaps we can catch her up."

"If she refuses?"

"We don't offer the choice. She *will* be brought to Haven. And if that proves impossible then she will not be allowed to live. Everything depends on the secrecy of our island. Everyone's survival."

Ice painted over my body. "You want me to kill her?"

"That's a last possible resort. Every single Witch is required to fight for the equilibrium to be restored. Our numbers are growing fewer as the genocide of Witches continues."

"Alright. I understand that part of the mission. But who sent me my orders to save her?"

"A Witch named Seraphina. She is not as dexterous as one would hope. She simply called to Athena and asked for help and did no spell work to accompany the plea. She had no idea what she was putting into motion. She's a Fire Witch with a pale flame of magic, I'm afraid. She did have other qualities that helped the Resistance, she has a keen mind. She was Crispin's—"

"Fiancée. Yes, I'm aware. But then she disappeared."

Giselle nodded. "She developed an architectural medium—"

"And she was working with Crispin to design housing for those in the Range, inexpensive and solid against the weather."

"See how much you've learned in such a short time? Did you also learn that this project would make Noble Sr. very angry? The best way to handle it was to burn her construction formulas, her designs, and her in a fire."

"You can't burn a Fire Witch," I said, starting to form a picture of how this all unfolded.

"She escaped the flame. It would have been good if people had thought she'd died in the fire, but she was spotted by too many. So she just disappeared."

"To Haven. Let me guess, she uses the flame to check on Crispin and Tera."

"True, but how would you know that?"

"Tera says Crispin can feel her. He's struggling to find her on the mainland. He's tormented by it. Can Crispin come to Haven with Tera?"

"The Council will meet. This is a very concerning turn of events. We, of course, knew that Crispin and Tera existed and were in the Mundane world. The Elders who were tasked to watch them chose Seraphina as having the personality who would best be able to forge a relationship with Crispin, so she could send back information about them. They waited until Crispin was of an age that he would want to find his soul's mate. It was only in this way that the Elders felt they would understand how Crispin and Tera, raised to be Mundane, would interact with their natural magic. To see if well enough could be left alone. I told you her flame was weak. She didn't pick up on any of the energies that you have reported. Certainly, if it is, as I suppose, Tera who laced the tea with the Exodus story, there must have been other times that something similar had happened. Seraphina picked up on none of this. She said that Crispin and Tera had no sign of latent skills. Had we known, we would have taken proactive steps years ago."

"Well Seraphina was certainly wrong. Are you sure that she wasn't just holding the information to herself? That she had some other calculus in play?"

"I asked the same. We looked. That doesn't seem to be the case. While the Elders chose correctly—a Witch who would elicit a loving relationship with Crispin—they chose poorly in that the energies she would be trying to find were subtle. It is as it is."

"Does Seraphina want to be with Crispin?" I searched myself for signs of jealousy that would interfere in my decision making and found none. My attachment to him had not yet gotten out of hand, and I was glad to know that.

"Seraphina married an Earth Witch whom she loves very much and is with child."

"And yet she still scries Crispin? What am I going to do about all of this? This is incredibly volatile. All of it. *All of it*."

"Go and get some sleep. You know more now than you had before our talk. Though I am duly impressed by what you've been able to gather. I will think on this and search the Grimoires and histories, talk to the Council. We'll have more tomorrow. Do you need another candle?"

"Not yet. Besides, it would be hard for Socrates to bring me another. I can't have anything happening that might bring attention to me."

"Merry meet, and merry part, and merry meet again."

"Blessed be, Giselle." And I blew out my candle.

***

Crispin slipped quietly from the bed and dressed. I kept my eyes shut, pretending to sleep. He bent over me, pulling the covers under my chin. "Ember?" he whispered into my ear.

"Hmmm?"

"Don't wake up. I just wanted you to know I'm going back to my rooms to clean up. I have a meeting this morning. You're to stay in bed as long as you can. Your body needs time to heal."

I opened my eyes part way, and Crispin smiled at me, brushing my hair from my face. "Sleep," He whispered as he kissed my forehead.

He padded softly across my room and let himself silently out, shutting the door behind him. The level of quiet caught my attention. He didn't want people to know he'd slept with me.

I went to the lavatory and emptied my bladder with a sense of relief. I thought as I moved to the sink to wash my hands, that it would be easier to have water as my element. Water was much more accessible in terms of sharing information than fire. But then my school mates who excelled with water didn't have my ability to shift the temperature and the emotions of others around them the way I could. Well, that was probably why the Fates had placed me here instead of a Water Witch.

I dressed and slipped out of my room to go and check on Kael. Yesterday, I had wrapped him in a trance spell. I thought still and unaware was the absolute best way to pass the time. I needed to get him out of here. He was a major complication. The enforcers wouldn't stop looking until they'd found him. If they got to Kael, they'd eventually get to me.

Today was the day that Gareth was coming. I needed a plan but could think of nothing that wouldn't directly involve Gareth's knowledge. If we were caught—with or without his knowledge of the situation—well, then Gareth would take the fall along with Kael and me. I couldn't imagine Gareth being willing to do that. Magic only got one so far. Spell work worked best when a mind was primed to absorb the spell. To go against someone's will was black magic and not something that I was willing to work with. No Witch should ever play with the dark side of magic. *Ever.*

As I walked down the hall, I sent out my aura to find anyone else who was up and about. I didn't want them to find me slipping into the downstairs lavatory.

There in the hall in front of the library stood Noble Sr. *At this hour?*

I painted a glamour over myself before I slinked forward until I could see. Noble Sr. shot Crispin a look of disgust.

I swirled the air and pulled their words toward me. Their undertones were distorted and elongated but understandable, nonetheless.

"Get rid of her."

Crispin's brow furrowed. "Whom? Ember? No."

"She's not worthy of mixing with this family. I can smell sex on you. You slept with her. I hope you were smart enough to use protection."

Well, that was disgusting. Who says things like that?

"Our relationship is none of your business. And why exactly are you saying she's not worthy? She's brilliant. You know how few students are accepted to the university. She's brave. Clever. Look what she needed to devise to save Tera. Can't you just be grateful? Do you always have to be this paranoid and guarded? Tera would be somewhere being tortured if it weren't for Ember's extraordinary capacity and empathy." He paused to return his father's glare. "Have you been wondering why Tera was targeted? I have been. The only thing I can think of is that your enemies want to punish you. The only thing that stopped those goblins from touching Tera is Ember. Treat Ember like the gift she is."

"You don't think that was quite the happenstance? What was Ember's story? She was out jogging to deal with pre-exam stress and not paying attention when she realized the late hour and location? Just happened to be at the fence and wiggle herself under, facing death if caught, because she wanted to check on a noise?"

"Not a noise, Dad, a scream. Tera was screaming in fear and pain. Look, what are you proposing? That Ember staged herself beside the fence? That she waited for the men to attack Tera's car? That she decided to wear a coat too thin to protect her, so she could shred her skin to show – what?" He threw his hands in the air, and now that I knew to look for magic, I could see energy flying from his fingertips. "I don't know why someone would do that to themselves for a stranger. I'm not sure at all that I would. I could practically guarantee you that *neither* of us would. Then in this scheme you've cooked up to make Ember the enemy, she what? Killed the two men who were on her team? Couldn't they have just run away? Those men wore the brands of enforcers. They were from inside the Realm not from the Range. How, Dad? How would any of that make sense?"

"I don't know. But I trust my gut. We need to get her out of here. You watch, she's up to something, even if it's just to try to wriggle her way into a life in the Realm amongst the Significants."

"She'll be here of her own capacity after next semester. She doesn't need me to bring her to a better life. She's done it for herself."

"I want her out."

"And I want her to stay. And while she stays, I want her treated cordially."

I vibrated with energy. Someone wanted to talk to me. I turned on my heels and made my way back to my lavatory, locking the doors as I went. I cast a protection spell to dissuade anyone from disturbing me. I hoped Giselle had a plan.

I lit the candle and found a stranger in my flame.

"Seraphina?" I asked.

"I…"

"You weren't expecting me."

"No, I…"

"You were scrying to check on Crispin. I felt you and decided to answer the call. You do this a lot don't you?"

She looked around her but not into the flame, not into my eyes.

"I'd guess daily. Don't you?" I insisted.

"I needed to make sure he's okay. He seems better since you've arrived. He seems very much attached to you in a very short time." She attempted to turn the energetic focus of this confrontation from her to me.

"I'm told that you've had a handfasting ceremony with an Earth Witch, and you're expecting a child. It seems odd to me that you are still invested in Crispin's wellbeing all these many years later."

"Is that jealousy I hear in your words?" she asked, finally able to settle her eyes on me.

"Let me be clear, I like Crispin very much. I feel comfortable around him. I enjoyed him in my bed. But I'm not here to fill the void you left. I am here because I was directed by the Fates, after you called to Athena, to save Tera, pure and simple. Are you planning to come back and explain yourself to him? He deserves the truth. You ran away in the dark of night to fulfill your destiny and left him to mourn for you, to fear for you, to fight for you. Every. Single. Day."

"Ember your fire is showing," she admonished me.

That was both fuel and spark. I exploded. "Of course, it is! You're manipulating a good man with dark arts."

"*You* are manipulating a good man. You've done spells and influenced energy around him since the moment you opened your eyes in the hospital."

"His spirit has the right to reject the energy I offer him. He chooses not to. I don't impose my will on him. The guidance I offer is not visible from a conscious point of view, but I don't mask or hide anything from his subconscious. Seraphina, you were trained from childhood in the importance of white magic vs. black magic, but surely the Elders need to explain once again to you that there are two places of energy: the direction of increase and the direction of decrease. Increase is white magic. We on Haven embrace the light and work toward the greatest good. And on the other side there is black magic. The Seers here in the Realm play with black magic, though they're not trained in the proper use and aren't born to power. What they do is contrive to use their Mundane skills to manipulate through fear and oppression. You are emulating the Seers."

"I'm not! How dare you." Fire to fire our sparks flared.

"I dare because the light is not afraid of the darkness, and I see the results of your black magic."

"Fine," she crossed her arms over her chest and glared. "Let's pretend for a moment that you're right. Pray tell, exactly what magic do I shape that could possibly be called black?"

"You're reaching out to him energetically. You know that he's from our ancestry and though untrained, he was born with magical affinity. One of the abilities he has is to be open and aware of your energy because he loved you. He wanted to marry you and have a life with you."

"Still, how is that black? Make your point."

"My point is that when he feels you, you remain a focus. He senses you're alive; it drives him to search for you to save you. You don't need saving. You're tormenting him for your own ego. You like that he suffers. You like that you were so loved. You tell yourself that you're concerned, and yet, you've done no spell to sever the relationship and allow him peace. You have not sent word, as well you could on the Mundane level, that you felt endangered and have sought refuge elsewhere and that you are perfectly fine. Better than fine, you're thriving and have moved into a new pledge with a different man. Crispin thinks you're captive and tortured, hungry and cold, and hurt. Release him from his bond. Give him the peace he deserves." I had to work very hard to keep my voice down, but I was sure that even as I whispered and hissed my words that she felt their heat. I meant to scorch her.

"We were never bound," she stammered.

"But you were. He's of Haven ancestry. His word was magically binding when he swore to love you for the rest of your lives. That was a covenant. He is bound to protect you, to keep you safe. And you tease at him every day, looking, tickling his conscious, serving your vanity at his expense. You are performing black magic and the Council will hear of this with my next flame."

"I... I...You're angry." She decided to try to shift the focus to me, again. "I can understand that you don't want Crispin hurt. I see your attachment to him."

"I'm not angry. I am *enflamed* at the very idea that a Haven Witch would use her powers for black magic. It's unconscionable. Yes, I care for Crispin. But any feelings I have for him are of little importance. I have taken vows to serve. I am a warrior at war. My focus is singularly on my mission to save Tera. That you saw the danger, that you set the Fates in motion, for that I thank you. But now, you must extinguish the fire that you have been feeding since the day you escaped on the ship and headed to Haven. He is already tormented with his untrained potential. He is already terrified that he sees Tera's affinity to magic. He realizes what she's going through and tries to tame it. You must give him respite. You *must* do a ritual unbinding, to release him on the subconscious level."

She said nothing.

I tried again. "Do the ritual and release him from that binding spell. Knowing he is of the metal element, can you imagine how this must wreak havoc in him?"

"Stop. I have it. I understand. I'll do the ritual now. I'll seek Giselle's counsel for how it's best done. I thought it was love," Seraphina said. "Now I know different. I'm imagining it's the same for Crispin. He felt kinship, not bonding love. You know you've sparked that in him. I can feel it when I scry him."

"You won't scry him anymore, or my wrath will hold no bounds."

"I promise, not unless I have Giselle's permission, and it's for a bigger purpose. But you just focused on me and not the message I am giving you. His feelings for you began when he paced your room while the doctors worked on you. You never needed to use your magic on him. He was already in step."

"Of course he was, or my magic would not have worked. There must be a spark of truth before a flame can build into a fire. When I leave and there is no more kindling, those feelings will be extinguished."

"I disagree. That's not what I see."

"Let's be clear, Crispin is not my fate. My path is to serve. My mission is to save Tera."

She paused and looked over her shoulder.

"I'm called to the Council. A plan is being formulated. More soon."

"Tell Giselle I'm searching for a path to get Tera on the next ship. Something needs to change. Right now, Tera and I are prisoners of Noble Sr. We cannot move an inch without his enforcers knowing."

"Yes," she said.

And poof, I found myself kneeling on the lavatory floor, staring into the candle, feeling deprived of satisfaction and dumfounded by this situation. What was I going to do?

Chapter Twenty-Four

$\mathcal{K}$ael ate, stretched, was refolded and hidden behind his baskets. He easily slid back under his trance. He must be glad for the respite from reality.

Gareth was in the foyer removing his overcoat; a satchel with my exams rested at his feet.

Tera and I waited for him in the salon, the tea cart beside her. This morning the tea filled my mouth with visions of the maypole dance performed each Beltane on the Isle of Haven. The maypole dance was ordained strictly unlawful by the Mundane here on the mainland, punishable by death. There was really no way that Tera could ever have seen the women with their pastel dresses dance with the ribbons attached to the top of a tall pole – the phallus. It was a dance of fertility, performed on May first, each year. And true to Giselle's conjecture, Tera said she made the tea herself with herbs from a garden she liked to tend just outside the kitchen door.

This was indeed a danger. Tera couldn't stay here.

How could Seraphina not have tasted Haven's secrets in Tera's tea? How could she not have recognized power when Crispin orgasmed and sent out the etheric glow? Was Seraphina telling the truth when she reported that there was nothing there? Was her magic that poor? I hoped the Council would examine the situation carefully. It could well be that Seraphina liked the life Crispin held out for her – being married to a Noble was a far easier task than the deprivation and danger that the Resistance bore each day living and fighting from the Range. Perhaps she'd planned to follow through and marry him and live life in the Enclave, passing information from time to time to the Resistance the way Enya had, knowing her children would be full-Witches as was required to maintain the hereditary powers. Perhaps this had been the plan until Noble Sr. decided that she needed to be disposed of and then her only escape was to return to Haven…

Yes, that could well be the scenario. Seraphina was indeed willing to practice dark magic. I'd make sure an inquiry happened. But first, this knot of a mission needed to be untied.

Gareth walked into the salon, rousing me from my introspection. I didn't want to take the exams. I'd pass easily, but the thought of sitting still under Gareth's scrutiny didn't make me happy. I wasn't in the mood to sit still for anyone.

Gareth waved me toward him. "You ready to have your brain squeezed for facts?" He stalled; his eye on the window. "What the…"

It was like a wall. It was like a monster. It had a hunger to it, I thought as Tera and I moved closer to the window to see the greyness creeping.

"Is that smoke?" Tera asked wide eyed, hands pressed against the glass.

Gareth opened the door and walked out onto the mosaic terrace and inhaled. "Fog," he said.

Fog?

I sidled up beside him. The grey was opaque in its density; as if, with athame in hand, I could carve into it. It sped toward us, engulfing us. It was so thick I could imagine getting turned around and stepping in the wrong direction, losing the mansion and wandering forward until I hit the security walls. I groped out for Gareth and Tera and didn't move until I touched them both.

Curling my fingers into Gareth's clothing, I pulled him toward me. I sent out my aura, searching out the metal on the terrace door. I fixed my focus there as I moved the three of us toward it. The fog had curled into the salon. Even inside, I couldn't make anything out. I slammed the door against the incursion. I could see nothing but grey. As soon as we were through the door, Tera moved off on her own. I tightened my hold of Gareth as I put my back to the door. I knew if I walked in a straight line that I'd reach the foyer. If the fog got that far inside, there would be respite upstairs with the doors shut. Maybe.

Was this magically sent? Did the Council conjure the fog to help me somehow or was this Father Sky tormenting the humans?

Either way, it was serendipitous. Could there be a better cover to get Kael out of the house and into Gareth's trunk? I just needed to get away from Gareth long enough to get to Kael.

There was a thud and a mewl from Tera.

"Stay still, Tera. I'm coming to you. I just need you to keep calling to me," I said, my vision filled with grey.

"Here. I'm here," Tera cried out. "This is crazy!"

Tera's voice was to my right. I pulled Gareth to my left-hand side. He hadn't said a word. "Keep calling, Tera." I slid a foot out and around, searching for anything in my path that would trip me. I stopped when I hit Gareth's foot. "Are you okay?" I asked him.

"You seem to have a plan. I'll follow your lead."

I let go of his sleeve, sliding my fingers down his arm to grab his hand. "Coming, Tera." I stepped forward. Then with my right toe I made the arc. Stepped again. "Keep calling, Tera." My right foot swirled. Her voice was just over there. I closed my eyes and reached for her heat signature with my senses. I was surprised to find so many in the room. "Tera?" I asked my hand groping toward the heat closest to me.

"Yes, that's me."

I couldn't ask who belonged to the others. They'd wonder how I knew there was anyone else there. "We're heading for the stairs," I said.

"I'm at the doorway," Crispin called. "Come toward my voice."

Ah, okay that was the other heat, but there was one more here who had not called out. I reached out to the person who hid in the shadows of the fog. That energy was angry to have been thwarted in its intentions. It was a cold kind of heat – merely an energy that produced a temperature rise but had no emotional warmth. It tasted of moldy cheese. Daddy Noble. He came in here with malevolent intent. Had he thought he could hurt me under the cover of fog? Made it look like an accident? There was a vibration of truth to that thought, and I pulled both Gareth and Tera closer to me. I stepped forward with a keen awareness of where Daddy Noble stood, so if need be, I could catch an attack before it landed.

Hands slipped around my waist. "Got you," Crispin said. "It's clear in the library, let's go there."

I felt a buzz of energy around me. I needed to get to my candle. "Crispin, here take Tera." I slid her hand into Crispin's "I forgot to take my pain pill this morning."

"I thought you were off those," Gareth said.

"I'm trying to be. But I need one now."

"Can you make it okay?" Crispin asked. "Shall I go up with you?"

"I'll be fine, thank you. I think I'll just lie down for a minute while I'm waiting for the medication to start working. I'll be down soon," I responded.

I waited for the three to move off. I stood at the bottom of the steps, making sure that Noble Sr. wasn't coming after me. Instead, he headed out the front door. I pounded my way up the stairs and locked and charmed the doors before I knelt and lit the candle.

I set a circle and called to the forces. I made the magical connections and found myself before full Council.

"Merry meet," I said, addressing the Council Empress. Giselle was to her left in the seat of Justice. The Elders who held the seats of High Priestess and Temperance sat close enough that I could see them as well. Our High Council being framed as the Tarot's Major Arcana, had twenty-two seats held by the Wise Men and Wise Women on the island.

"Not so very merry," the Empress replied. "Decisions have been made. We have talked to Seraphina to gather more information."

"Seraphina…" I exhaled. I didn't want to work off of any information that had been shared by her. I just didn't fully trust her and there was too much at stake.

"We understand your concerns," the High Priestess said. "Giselle voiced them as well. But the circumstances are thus: Crispin is doing magic unwittingly, and Tera is cellularly aware of her ancestral secrets without taking the vows. Neither can be allowed to remain as is. They will either be brought to Haven, or they will be otherwise dealt with."

"It is the will of the Council that I assassinate two Witches? Am I understanding you correctly? I have never heard of such a thing in all of our history," I said.

"This is not your normal assignment, Ember. Your task is not to take down an enemy but to facilitate their rescue. Crispin and Ember will be brought to Haven," Giselle said. "Either voluntarily or bound." She cast her gaze around the other Elders who sat on the High Council.

"Their deaths would be an extreme and rash decision and one that is our very last resort," the Temperance Elder said. "Such would be antithetical to our ways. And too, such would not be lost on Father Sky. The Fates are watching."

That, at least, was good news. I had taken vows to serve the Fates and I had taken vows to defend and protect my fellow Witches. I didn't want to have to unweave these two aspects to find the right vow to follow. The goal was to save both Crispin and Tera – whether they wanted to be saved, or even thought they needed to be saved, or not.

From the moment when I heard my mission's call to "save her," and until it was over, it was dangerous. All the more so for Noble Sr. and his willingness to kill not only his wife, Enya, but Seraphina. "Have you a plan?"

"Speed, for one. The ship will go out with the morning tide. Other than that, they will need to be kept hidden away for two more months' time. They will not be allowed to stay as they are."

"Only a few hours." Whew! Now that was going to be a feat. The boat dock was a good distance once I had moved everyone out of the Realm.

"We have decided that Tera will be moved by her brother's wishes," Giselle said. She waited for my nod before she added. "We have decided to tell Crispin the truth. You must be ready for any eventuality."

"I will do as bid," I said.

"You will contrive to take him, now during the fog, to the fire ring and light the—"

"He's coming through your doors now," The High Priestess interrupted. "Let him find you before the flame. We can see his response and we will—"

A knock sounded at my lavatory door.

"Ember? Are you okay? Do you need anything? I could help…or Nurse?"

I had locked my bedroom door. I couldn't imagine him using a key to open it.

The tap sounded again. Then I saw the lock slowly turn, then the handle. The door cracked. "Ember?"

I swallowed. *Do or die.* "Come in, please."

Crispin stilled with his hand on the knob looking down where I knelt; the candle burning in front of me. "You opened the doors without a key?" I asked.

His face turned pink. His eyes widened. It wasn't for me and the candle; it was my pointing out to him what he knew he could do but had kept secret.

"You're gifted with metal magic," I said.

He stood there, stunned that I knew.

"As is Tera gifted, though her affinity is with water," I said, not shifting from my spot, giving him time to process. If he tried to move, either against me or away, the full power of the Council would be used to block him.

"As was Seraphina," I continued, "with fire."

He blinked.

"As was your mother Enya and your father." I didn't add the name Aiden, I thought that was too much to absorb in this moment but did stipulate. "Who is *not* Ruthburg Noble."

He swallowed visibly, audibly.

"I was sent to you because you and Tera are in danger. I want to get you answers that you can trust. Would you like answers, Crispin?"

I waited. He stood, staring wide-eyed, his hand on the knob. If I was a trap, he could be burned at the stake. If I had answers, then he might find relief. What should he do?

"I know where Seraphina is. I know what happened to her."

That was the phrase that shook him, quite literally, out of his stupor. He was at my side his hands gripping my shoulders, lifting me to my feet. I glanced down at the flame. "He's not hurting me." I told them.

He looked down, too, and saw nothing but the flickering wick of an emergency candle.

I wouldn't help him here. I'd wait to open his third eye when we were down at the balefire where there was more energy, and everything would be clearer.

"What do you know of Seraphina?" he asked.

"The answers can be found in the balefire. Will you go with me to the fire ring?"

"In this fog?"

"Tera's in danger. We haven't a moment to spare."

Chapter Twenty-Five

"I'm at a loss," Crispin gripped my fingers tightly as he watched Giselle in the flames telling him of his lineage, explaining the how of the situation, as well as the why—why he and Tera were left in the Realm untrained and unclaimed.

I sat beside him on the lounge. The fire blazed in front of us, burning off the fog in the fire ring, leaving the view clear. I couldn't imagine how painful this would be to hear. How disorienting. I pulled up vague memories of my mother hiding my skills and proclivity from the world when I was a very young child. Vividly though, I remembered the relief I felt after I landed on the Isle of Haven where I could publicly use all my senses and say whatever I wanted about the energies I perceived. No wonder Tera told the tea water her experiences.

"Your situation is a rarity." Giselle's voice painted a soothing balm over the prickling emotions that Crispin wore like a haircloth cloak. "Elders were assigned to your well-being after your mother's death. They sent Seraphina to get close to you when you were old enough that you might share your intimate self with someone. Her job was to measure how you were handling yourself—if you were having trouble with your magical inheritance. She reported that you weren't aware of your gifts."

"She was wrong. I've been fighting a battle with them my entire life," he muttered under his breath. There was a lot less bitterness in his words than I might have expressed. Sadness and fatigue were his overriding emotions in this moment.

"This is a lot to take in," I said, rubbing my hand over his back, reminding him to be in his body and grounded. Crispin needed to be on my side completely trusting me if I were make this work. Other than that, I'd have to make other decisions. Decisions that would be much more rash and difficult. I needed to know one hundred percent how he would function in this escape–if he even understood why he needed to abruptly—and possibly permanently—leave the life he'd been living. It was a shift of seismic proportions, and it needed to happen now. "I think that Crispin needs to understand that we are speaking the truth, and this isn't an illusion or fictional story we're handing him. After all," I chuckled, "it isn't every day one attends a meeting through the flames. Perhaps if Crispin can talk to Seraphina, she could share a story that only they would know…"

"She's there? She's alright?" Crispin was shaking. He fought against his emotions.

I wrapped my arms around him and felt Crispin absorbing the warmth I sent to him.

From the flame Seraphina's image emerged.

She didn't look him in the eye. Instead, she focused on her knotted fingers in her lap. "Hi, Crispin," she muttered.

"Seraphina," he breathed out, leaning forward as if he wanted to crawl into the fire with her.

"This is a shock, I'm sure. All of this." She lifted her eyes and spread her arms.

"You're a Witch?" he asked.

She nodded. "Same as you."

They stared at each other. I felt emotions shifting through Crispin; they landed on betrayal. "This is a spell. You're trying to compromise me," he said. "This can't be true."

"Locks have never kept you out of anything that you wished to enter," I reminded him. And I felt the truth of that sift through his system.

"It's not Seraphina. This woman has on a wedding band, and she's obviously with child."

"Crispin, it's been many years since I left..." Seraphina's voice conveyed her shame.

She should be ashamed for not breaking the bond and for not letting Crispin know in a mundane way that she was safe and living a life of her choosing, I thought. "Perhaps if Seraphina tells you a story from your life. One that only the two of you would know."

Crispin looked up expectantly.

"Let me start at the beginning. How I even came to be part of your life." Seraphina explained how he was her target in a mission for the Resistance and commanded by the Elders to investigate him. She emphasized that the emotions they shared had been real. Then she described how Noble Sr. had tried to kill her.

"Kill you? Burn you?" Crispin looked at the ground and nodded as he found some sentiment in his own heart that read that as true. "How did you survive the inferno?" Crispin asked finding her gaze again.

"A Fire Witch cannot be burned unless it is ordered by the law. I can't burn my finger in a candle flame, but my power to protect myself is stripped if I were to be tried and found guilty of witchcraft, tied to a balefire, and burned for my ancestry. That's olde magic. Magic that cannot be unwrought. I was able to walk through the flames of the burning building. I knew your father would try again to kill me. I left the mainland to return here to the home of my ancestors and wait for the Fates to determine my path."

"You're safe? You've been safe all this time? All these years?" He exhaled hard, coming to grips with the end of the long journey of trying to find and save her. "That's an enormous unbelievable relief." He turned to me and shook his head, trying to find stability when his paradigms were shifting so violently. Though I sensed he was still fighting his senses, still trying to make this event into an illusion or a break with sanity.

"Seraphina, this is a lot to take in. Crispin needs affirmation that what he's now hearing is truthful and not spell-wrought. I need you to think of a moment that Crispin will remember vividly, a moment that no one else shared, and tell him that story."

"Tell me how we became engaged," Crispin said, his body stiffening in my arms.

"Of course," Seraphina began. "The day we were engaged, as it turned out, was the day before your birthday. October twenty-fourth, St. Crispin's Eve. We were scouting for a place for you to build the home that I was to design for you. A storm blew up out of nowhere. It was fierce and terrifying. Hurricane force winds bent the trees. Your car was at a far distance, not that we would be safe in your car, but it was the only shelter we knew. It was impossible to see though. The sheer speed of the winds made the rain fly sideways. I was panicking, sure that I was about to die. We moved from tree to tree. I pointed to the sky and thought a spell of necessity, asking for illumination for a place to shelter. And just like that, lightning struck beside that massive redwood. You remember it?" She waited for Crispin to nod. "You dragged me toward it. It was hollow which is dangerous in the wind, but debris was hitting us, and we took the chance. You pushed me inside, and then came in behind me, acting as my shield. We clung to each other as the storm continued to rage.

"When it was over, you were bruised and cut. You needed stitches. At the hospital, I sat on your bed with my hand resting on your bandage and recited the lines from Shakespeare:

And rouse him at the name of Crispian.

283

He that shall see this day, and live old age,

Will yearly on the vigil feast his neighbors,

And say, "Tomorrow is Saint Crispian."

Then will he strip his sleeve and show his scars,

And say, "These wounds I had on Crispin's day."

"You turned to me and kissed the tips of my fingers, then pulled my hand to hold it against your heart. Remember?"

Crispin nodded.

"You said, 'Together. Together we will live old age. Together, we will remember this day. Marry me and be my wife, so I can always protect you and keep you safe from life's storms.' It was so perfect. Romantic. Wonderful. And I was in love with the idea of being in love. In love with the idea of being safe. I was not built to fight in the Resistance where every day I lay my life on the line. I just wanted rest. And peace."

Crispin's brow furrowed. "And that's what you loved about me, the protection I could afford you?"

"I care for you Crispin. I always have and always will. But it is a kindred affection. I'm married."

"Got it." Crispin rubbed his hands up and down his thighs as if he were about to jump up and leave.

Giselle put a stop to that. With a commanding voice she said, "Decisions have been made about your immediate future."

"I'm not okay with decisions being made without my input," Crispin said, the full authority of his place as a Noble in the Southern Realm inflected his tone.

"You are always at choice; but in this case, your choices have limits. You will either cooperate or you will be impelled to cooperate."

His muscles grew tighter, primed for a fight. Though what was he going to do, throw a fist at the flames? I recognized this energy; it was what I pulled up before I went into a battle.

"What does that mean?" he demanded.

"We are offering you a means for understanding and using your gifts. You will have an opportunity to see what paths are predestined for you in this lifetime. You may take vows, and you will be allowed to follow your fate. If you then wish to return to the Realm, so mote it be."

"Tera?"

"The same. Of course. Until you have a better grasp on your gifts, we cannot allow you to proceed as you are. This is for your safety as well as ours."

"A win-win," Crispin snarled.

"Which is far better than a lose-lose. Tera will not be able to hide her nature after her thirteenth birthday when the power comes at full force. Do you remember turning thirteen?" Giselle waited, watched.

Something profoundly awful happened for him. The energy of it swirled around him. It tasted bitter and oily like an orange peel.

I was trying to imagine what that would be like, to turn thirteen, to have the powers come to him without guidance, without explanation, to be alone and trying to hide the gifts given through heredity. It must have been awful. Terrifying. Devastating. I bet he woke up every day fighting the power that needed to be grounded and released. This explained the energies I had felt when we were at the hospital. He was a man of incredible fortitude to have made it through with his sanity intact. My heart burned with empathy for the boy becoming a Witch on his own amongst those who would burn him at the stake. It made me weep for his younger self. And rage that the Elders had allowed that to happen.

"Ember, you will suppress that fire," Giselle commanded. "Crispin, you know what a thirteenth birthday can be. We have a single boat that leaves the mainland before that happens to Tera. Don't you want her amongst those who can best direct those energies and help her make the transition one of joy and expanse? Think about what that would have meant in your life."

Crispin's muscles tightened down like bands of iron and steel.

"She doesn't have your capacities for dealing with the energies that will engulf her," Giselle said, "This is so dangerous while existing amongst the Mundane."

"Mundane?" Crispin asked, a warrior gathering information for a battle he thought he must fight.

"That's the term we use for those born outside of magic," I whispered.

He nodded. "Alright. I get that. I had no idea that Witches followed a hereditary line. I just thought—"

"That some people were cursed with the ability," Giselle said.

"Exactly," he replied. While his tone was thoughtful and controlled, I knew I held a Metal Witch in my arms. That first impression—Hammer to the North, Viking energy—I was right. I was right about the closely held anger, too.

"I have to get her out of here, or she'll be burned at the stake," he said. "How do we get to you?" he asked Giselle.

"Ember will guide you."

"I haven't got a car. It was destroyed in the accident. My driver, killed. There's no one I trust… Do we go on foot?"

"Gareth is here," I reminded him.

"Is he a Witch? Can he be trusted?"

"No," I said. "Neither." I reached for his hands. They were steady and warm; it told me he was dealing okay with this sudden turn in events—shocking as it must all be for him. Or maybe not. Perhaps he always knew.

His eyes filled with the thoughts he was processing. "It'll take me a few days to get things arranged."

I shook my head. "You haven't got that kind of time. Your window for escape is down to a few hours."

"This fog, you've created it?" Crispin asked the fire. "It would help us to get out of the compound, but it would make progress very difficult. Could you lift it once we're down the road out of sight?"

There was a general murmur of laughter.

Crispin turned to look at me.

"Father Sky creates the weather. We have no power there. Be it fog, or tornado, or ice storm, we'll have to press forward."

"Alright, a plan then—"

"We have a complication," I interjected. "Do you know the name Dr. Brighton?"

Seraphina stepped forward, pushing toward the etheric demarcation. From this side, it looked like her face licked out with a burst of flame. "I introduced you before I ran away. He was developing the energy source for our Range building project."

"Yes, alright, I know him."

I took a moment to explain his kidnapping, his rescue, and the fact that Noble Sr. was chasing him down. And to that end, they'd kidnapped and planned to torture Kael to death.

"Kael was going to be tortured in my home?" The color drained from Crispin's face. "By my father?"

I nodded.

"He escaped? That's who the enforcers were searching for last night?"

"He's hidden in your house. We need to get him out as well. But we can't depend on Gareth. I have a plan."

Chapter Twenty-Six

*T*he fog was lifting as Crispin and I slid through the terrace doors. It had cleared from the house. I perched on the edge of the settee and gripped my head as if I were in pain. Crispin went off to check on Tera, or so he said.

Gareth walked into the room and looked at me. "Are you actually in pain or are you trying to stretch out your time here at Castle Noble by avoiding the exam? It might be a good choice. It's hard to tell; you're going to have to go with your gut."

I looked up.

"Noble Sr. is distracted by something else. Your being here so far is running just under the radar. I haven't figured out how to get you out. I'm sure his orders have already been issued."

I frowned at him. "Gareth, I need to get up to my room. Will you help me?"

"Seriously? You can't make it on your own? Were you that hurt saving Tera?"

I glared at him. "I wasn't hurt saving Tera except for the razor wire. I was hurt saving you."

I saw his back teeth clenching, making his jaw bulge and pop. He owed me. He was ethical enough to know it. I didn't want to hurt him. I hoped this worked, and he'd come out of this mission okay.

He pushed himself up and came to my side. "Should I carry you? Should I put an arm around you? What do you need?"

"Let's start by getting me up." I reached my hands out. "Just let me use your arm as a bar to pull against." I grunted as I hauled myself up and thought I did a fine job of acting this out.

Gareth took hold of my hand and wrapped his other arm around my waist. "I'll find some way to pay you back. I promise," he whispered.

Maybe he would forgive me for what I was about to do, and we could call it even.

We moved up the stairs and into my bedroom. I lifted my chin toward the lavatory. "Can you help me get in there? I'm having trouble bending to get my pants down."

Gareth chuckled as we moved toward the closed door. "Kind of kinky. I'd never have guessed. But alright."

I used my free hand to pseudo punch him and grimaced from the effort. I pushed the door open, and we moved in.

When I closed the door, Gareth jerked. "Crispin, excuse me. Ember asked for my help getting upstairs. I…"

Crispin reached out and touched the knob and the lock audibly tumbled.

"What's going on? You could have just told me we were going to have a secret meeting, Ember. You didn't need to play act for me."

"For you, no. But when I asked you to take me upstairs Noble Sr. had moved into the foyer, listening."

Frown lines crisscrossed Gareth's forehead. "How?—"

I put my finger to my lips, and Gareth fell instantly silent.

"There's a problem. There are actually several big problems and the solution will set Noble Sr. and the Elites of the Realm at odds with my wishes," I said.

"Your wishes. You mean leaving the Southern Realm."

"Yes. I need to take your car. To keep you safe, I need to make it seem as though I stole your car."

"But my driver. And… wait a minute how are you going to take my car and make it look like I know nothing about it? They'll interrogate me, and I'll tell, and then I'll be punished for lying to protect you."

"You won't spill. I'll make sure that you can't."

Gareth stared at me hard.

"You've figured it out," I said simply.

"You're a Witch. You fight for the Resistance." He combed his fingers through his thick black hair and left his hand on his forehead. He leaned back with a groan and then leaned forward, hands on knees, breathing heavily like he'd just finished his morning run. "Skies above. So much makes sense now. Of course, that's what you are. Why didn't I figure it out before?" he asked, coming to his full height. "Because I was spellbound."

"I charmed you. You found me charming." I sent him a smile and a flip of my long red hair.

"I'm not in the mood for your teasing, Ember." Gareth glared, obviously displeased that I'd gotten one over on him for so long. He turned to Crispin. Their eyes met and held. Gareth realized he wasn't going to be given an option on the conscious level. As far as my ethics went he'd always be given a chance on the subconscious level to make a helpful decision.

"Tell me how this is going to go down. Are you going to cast a spell on the castle and put everyone to sleep?"

"This isn't a fairy tale, Gareth. Witches don't have that kind of power. The plan is this. You will stay the night at Crispin's invitation. Tonight, when we retire to our rooms, you will come with me here. Crispin and I will tie you up and gag you."

Gareth was shaking his head and muttering, "oh no, no, no," under his breath.

"I will wrap you in spell work, so you are comfortably unconscious until they find and rouse you."

"They'll *interrogate* me,"

"When they ask what happened, you will tell them that you were attacked by a man name Kael. This is what he looks like." I flicked my finger and an image of Kael floated like a hologram in the room. Both Gareth and Crispin jumped.

"Ember," Gareth spat out. "You have to warn me before you pull stunts like that."

"Sorry, okay. So Kael is the one who attacked you and stole your car. Kael had Crispin, Tera, and me tied up. Tera was at knife point." I let the hologram of that scene play for him. "He ties you up, makes you take my pills, you passed out. That's all you know."

"Until they *interrogate* me."

"They won't interrogate you because your brain is going to work on this scenario." I moved my hand in front of his face forming the symbols that I needed to effect this spell.

Gareth swatted at me. "What are you doing? Stop!"

"This story you will tell. You will tell it with emotion and conviction. If ever you are tempted to tell the truth, the truth will slip sideways, and you will not know it's there until it slips back into place again. You will never ever be able to tell, or write, or draw, or in any other way share this story." I didn't use magical language as I never share any part of my Witchcraft with a Mundane.

"But why not just take the story away from me?"

"Because Gareth, someday I will need you to remember. I'm not taking your memories. I'm simply making it impossible for you to share them. Your conviction about the scene with Kael will be so vivid and real to those who ask, that you will not be held responsible in any way."

"I don't believe you. That's not what's going to happen. You're putting too much trust in me. What if I went downstairs and told Noble Sr. that tonight you meant to escape."

"To be clear, Gareth, I don't put *any* trust in you at all. I was trying to be the kindest I possibly could be to you, given our circumstances. But let's say you did want to carry this tale to Noble Sr. What exactly would you tell him?" I crossed my arms over my chest and quirked my head to the side.

"I'd tell him that... I..." He stilled. "That's crazy! I'd say... Ember McGraw was..." His eyebrows were in his hairline. "I'm not able to. I can't hold the thought. It just *poof* vanishes."

I smiled knowingly.

"I hate that you can just take my memories like that. Have you taken others? Have you done this to me before?"

"No, that would be black magic. I only did what you allowed me to do right now. Had you not allowed me to work my magic then other choices about the circumstance would have been made – other actions taken."

He stilled. He looked over to Crispin and then back to me. "You were prepared to kill me."

"Always," I said. "This isn't play time. This is a war for survival. You know that better than most."

He nodded, visibly shaken. "So Kael took you. I was bound, drugged, and left unconscious. What of my driver?"

"Can you tell him to sleep in the employee bunks?" Crispin asked.

"Sure. Yes. I'll do that. So that's the plan, you and Crispin and Tera will all leave together. I'm sure there's a good reason for that. I can't fathom it, and I'm not going to ask because I don't want to know."

Chapter Twenty-Seven

*T*era, wrapped in a stupefying charm, was cradled gently in Crispin's arms as he descended the precarious stairway.

I had using a lot of spells which had me packaging people in deep layers of insulation. This was not my go-to means of dealing with issues. I was sent in when a direct approach was needed. Out of my comfort zone here in the Realm, I pulled from my memory the kind of magic, which was more in the affinity of Earth and Air. I knew just enough to get by, fate be willing.

Crispin's task was getting Tera into the car, while I went to rouse Kael.

It was harder than I thought it would be. Except for getting my friend out to eat and use the toilet twice a day, he'd been enfolded in his trance.

Kael lay on the lavatory floor, and I rubbed warmth into his muscles. Quick jerky movements of desperation, mumbling incantations under my breath. "This is our best chance. We're going to move you out now," I whispered.

"What's the plan?" Kael rotated his shoulders, moved his jaw back and forth to get himself back to functional.

"Crispin is going to drive you out."

Kael grabbed my arms in a vice grip. "You told Crispin *Noble* I was here?" He shook me hard enough that my head flung back and forth. "Are you crazy?"

"Yes," I said, plastering a blur of confidence across my face, sending him a reassuring smile. "Crispin has reason to leave as well. He's going to take you to the city." I pulled him to his feet. "You'll have to hunker down along the barricade and hide until curfew lifts, then you need to make your way to a safehouse." I held his eye to make sure he heard me clearly. "Don't go home. They'll find you. You'll end up here, again."

"The plan is walk out of here, jump in the car, and drive to the city. Why does that sound too easy?"

"Because in your mind we'd have to fight an epic battle to get you out of here." I kept my tone light and my smile fixed and warm, but beneath the blur spell a cold fear streamed through my system. It *was* too easy.

As I peered out the crack in the front door, I found there was little in the way of fog left. Father Sky had settled into a cloudy night. At least that masked the light of the waning gibbous moon. Intermittent thunder rolled across the width of the sky, vibrating the air. I turned back and stood on my toes to whisper in Kael's ear.

"Crispin is taking his sister out of the Realm. They're already in the car. Are you ready?" I asked.

Kael jumped up and down, getting his blood flowing. He took a few jabs at a shadow, then gave me a nod.

With too bright of a click, I extinguished the foyer light. Holding just long enough for my eyes to adjust to the dark. I slid the door a little wider. Through the crack in the door, I sent my aura wide. I sensed the heat of four people. Crispin and Tara, and now moving toward them in great haste, two very large forms that must be enforcers.

We waited for Crispin to give them orders. A trail of red energy lit Crispin's murmurs as he told his guards that he was taking Tera back to the hospital. His powers were growing stronger or maybe he just wasn't masking them anymore. "No," he said. "I'll take care of this. An ambulance isn't required." He lifted his chin toward the side of the house, the door where they had brought Kael into the basement. "Is someone patrolling in the storage level? I heard noises down there. You two, go and check."

The heat signatures dashed toward the basement door.

The night had an inky slickness to it. The air was still wet from the fog. I carefully placed my feet as I emerged onto the front steps, Kael's hand resting on my shoulder, letting me decide the speed and direction.

Crispin ran over to me. "He was hiding in the house. I only half-believed you." He held out his hand to shake with Kael, and I slapped his hand away.

"Get in the car," I hissed. "Move. We'll get the gate and meet you on the other side. No lights."

Crispin turned on his heel and pushed off toward the car. In the silence of the night, the clap of the door shutting rang too loud to my ears. The motor purred. He was ready.

Kael and I ran for the front gate and lifted the safety beam. Before Kael could push it open, the outdoor lights blinked on, bright as day, I was momentarily blinded.

"There he is," a man shouted.

Socrates fluttered protectively down to my shoulder. "Fly," I told Socrates, quickly forming a new plan. My mind moved at the speed of a wild fire. Crispin could still leave. But he had no idea where to go.

Gareth and his story was a disaster. They'd kill him.

But the most pressing issue was Tera. She was my mission. If Crispin didn't get her out now, there would be an inquiry and a tribunal, Crispin and Tara would be burned at the stake. "Socrates," I whispered. "Tell Piper to meet the car at the Bay Bridge to direct them to the ship. Fly now." Socrates curled his talons into my shoulder as he pressed off, his wings spread carrying my words with him as he soared into the sky. I threw a spell toward the car.

Metal, my friend, I ask a block,
Keep Crispin and Tera under lock,
Until safely gone, this is my plea
By the power, three by three
To do my will, and bring no harm,
I set in place this magic charm.

With satisfaction, I heard the locking mechanism snap into place.

And that's when I was pulled off my feet. The man who wrapped me in a bear hug, holding down my arms, spun around so he could see what was happening in the driving circle. In swarmed the enforcers holding knives and bludgeoning weapons.

Goddess Athena,

I need your help, so I call.
I do your biding, survive or fall,
Aid my mission is my plea,
So you wish it, so mote it be!

Kael was surrounded, hands in the air, legs bent, I couldn't tell if he was dropping to his knees in slow surrender or if he were getting ready to pounce.

Surrender wasn't an option.

"Bring them to me!" Ruthberg Noble stood sentinel at the front door. "Guard the gate," he bellowed. "No one leaves!"

The car door lock popped. I spun my attention away from Noble Sr. toward the sound, momentarily confused that my magic was thwarted. I remembered too late, Crispin was a Metal Witch and no lock could hold him.

Before he could pull the handle and open the door, I extended my hand, despite the grizzly bear hold on my arms –

Metal, hear me! Help me! I sent heat down my arm and threw it toward the car. I knew that Crispin had some skill with metal, but without training, I was sure that my magic would supersede his.

I call to fire, within me burn,
The doors don't open; the locks don't turn,
Power now blaze within me.
Trapped in the car they must be!
Until with Witches they find release,
Rest inside and be at peace.

Peace is not what they were. I heard Crispin yell out when he was burned on the hot metal. His frustration and anxiety rose in a wave. But right now, my focus had to turn to surviving the fight and getting the gate opened.

The owl who had brought me my mission, *Save her,* flew into the circle of enforcers beating his heavy wings in their faces,

302

scratching and pulling with his talons. Owl reached for the enforcer who had hold of me and grabbed at his head, sinking his sharp claws into the man's bald pate. The enforcer screamed in pain. I dropped to the ground as the man swung his arms high to protect his eyes.

Owl flew off into the night.

As soon as my feet hit the pavement, I leaned forward and threw a spinning hook kick, landing my heel right in the man's temple. He fell to the ground, posting a fist on the rock. I pulled my knee in to my chest and thrust it outward, foot bent up to clear my toes. My heel smashed his nose with all my might, sending him flying backward. The sound of his skull hitting the rocks echoed.

One down.

As my foot touched the ground, I lifted onto my toes and pivoted. Kael was in the fight of his life. He had taken advantage of the owl's intervention, and one guy was crawling away, his leg trailing behind, bent at an improbable angle. That was the last of my clear visuals. Now everything was a whirl.

I spun and kicked, punched and clawed. I bit and bellowed, stabbed and slashed. The full force of Fire blazed through me. I roared. I consumed. I was the inferno.

The number of enforcers who had swarmed the area seemed unending. Every time I extinguished one assailant, another sometimes two or three others—burst up in his place.

Somehow, Crispin had used his magical skills to escape the car. I realized this as I pulled my punch just in time. I nearly crushed his trachea beneath my knuckles. He pushed me behind him and took a solid blow to the chin.

The enforcers were fighting the master of the castle.

Daddy Noble was attacking his own son with his henchmen.

Why didn't Crispin stay in the car?

Now, I couldn't just fight. I had to protect Crispin. He was the only one who had the capacity to drive out of the Realm and get Tera to the boat on time. No matter what else happened, I was still on my mission. *Save her.* Not save them. Just her. Tera. I had to save Tera.

Crispin was a formidable fighter. His arm powerful. His strikes vicious. With each punch we threw, with each kick, and dive, and sweep, hope rose.

I took a run toward the man who just flew over Crispin's shoulder, tossed like a ragdoll onto the pavement. I dropped and slid to grab the knife he was pulling from his sleeve. Twisting his arm, I forced the blade into his own throat.

Rolling to get to my back to leap up, I held in a crouch, legs wide, back hunched, arms ready to block or strike with the blade. My gaze swung about the courtyard. Kael lay on the ground, posted on one elbow, looking up at the sky, gulping at the air. Crispin, was on one knee, fist to the ground, his head drooping as he caught his breath.

I chambered my arm, pulling it back into position ready to thrust out in any necessary direction. There was no one left to fight.

Up until the point where Crispin intervened, the cover story held. The servants who were off duty, including Gareth's driver, were far from the main house in the servants' quarters. The distance and the thunder would have kept them unaware. The moment Crispin dove into the fray to help us, the end was painted a different color. No one could be allowed to live to tell the tale. No one could know it was Crispin who was involved, or so said the owl who chose this moment to return.

"Yes, Athena," I said, through my exhaustion. I bent, checking the status of each enforcer, following my orders to extinguish any existing flame of life.

"Stop! Ember! What are you doing?" Crispin demanded. "Just tie them up."

"It's not my choice. I'm a soldier of the Fire Sword, and I follow my orders." Luckily, there had been only two that needed dispatching. I wasn't sure that Crispin would have allowed me to continue. He had been ensconced in the Realm and didn't understand yet. But as his understanding of his role in this world grew, he'd know what an important and daunting task we Witches were called upon to perform. "Get the car started. I'll help Kael."

Crispin stumbled up and toward the car.

"Skies above, Ember," Kael said as I lifted him to his feet. "I knew you were a good fighter, but that was like watching a tornado taking down a village."

"A tornado is wind," I said. "Hush now." I took his weight onto my shoulder as he dragged his leg. "Get in, Crispin, and start the engine. We have to get out of here!" I hoisted Kael into the back seat where Tara lay, oblivious. "I'm going to open the gate." I shut the door and jogged to the entry.

Sudden rain pelted down again, distorting my view. The cold sting had me tucking my arms against my chest as I jogged forward. At the gate, I reached out to lift the heavy beam, pushing it out of the way. I grabbed the handle and shoved the right side wide.

The car inched forward. The swipe, swipe, swipe of the windshield wipers—rubber scraping glass—formed a note like a high soprano's. The wind held a lower pitch-a bow being pulled across the strings, accented by the timpani of thunder.

My hand wrapped the edge of the second gate when a knife point pricked the skin at my throat. Before the blade could slice through my windpipe, I grasped the wrist that held it, and I whirled out of the way.

My foot slipped out, and I went down, the man on top of me. My arms were trapped under the weight of his legs. He gripped at me with his thigh muscles as I squirmed to get free. When he'd leapt on top of me, he'd ensnared me in the wrestler's hold, we yearlings on Haven were told never to allow ourselves to fall into.

Athena couldn't help me this time. Any owls she would send, any raven friends from Socrates, were thwarted by the rain. The car with Kael and Crispin were too many seconds away and that was what I had—a nanosecond of time. I watched as the blade arched high into the air, so the wielder could bring it down full force.

The beam of the car's light now caught his face.

Noble Sr.

And that's when I knew my decision had been made. I couldn't allow him to live. "Fates! Now!" I screamed with my last breath of air.

FLASH!

With the call that required lives to be on the line. A bolt of lightning like a long finger flicked down from the heavens through the night sky and struck Ruthburg Noble in the chest. He arched back as it sizzled and burned through his system and then mine and drove down into the ground.

Everything went black.

"Is she breathing?" Those were Kael's words.

How was I hearing Kael's voice?

Two stings on my right cheek, two stings on my left.

"Yes." That was Crispin, his cheek rested on my chest. "I can hear her heart beat."

Again, the stings to my right then my left cheeks.

"Ember? Come on, Ember, open your eyes." Another set of stings. Crispin was slapping my cheeks.

I blinked my eyes open.

The rain had stopped. I turned my head and saw in the light of the car headlights that Noble Sr. lay black and burned in a puddle of water. "By the Fates," my voice held the incredulity that I felt. "I'm still alive." I tried to push myself up, but Crispin and Kael held me back.

"Give it a second," Crispin said.

My mind raced around trying to understand why I hadn't been killed in the lightning strike, and the only thing I could land on was that, outside of decree in a court of law, a Fire Witch cannot be burned. My hands patted over my body. Not only had I not been burned but neither had my clothing. Well, there was a revelation.

Not that I wanted to ever repeat that experience.

Ever.

It still took me a few deep breaths before I remembered that I was on a mission. "We're on the clock. We haven't time. We have to get out of here."

"But—"

"The servants will discover what happened in the morning. And they'll find Gareth tied up in my lavatory and wake him. His story will hold given this destruction. It's the perfect cover for your disappearance. We'll let Kael drive on Gareth's credentials once we get to the gate. You and Tera will hide under a blanket. No one will know what happened."

"Why would that matter?"

"Someday," I said. "You may want to return."

***

On the dock Crispin stood in shock. The boat was filled with small children, the next generation of Witches heading to Haven to be trained into the warriors of the Resistance. Tera had been taken to a bunk and was sleeping – still under my spell, as she would remain, at Crispin's request, until they had reached their destination.

I smiled at him. "The fates are at hand. Trust."

"What will happen to you?" he asked.

"I'll figure something out." I smiled up at him. "I always do."

He nodded and reached for my hands, lacing our fingers. We stood pressed together. I sent him warmth, and this time he recognized it for what it was – magic.

"I hate to leave you here. I hate *this*," he said, his eyes dark and brooding. "I feel like we're cutting the bud from a rose when I anticipated such a heady, beautiful bloom."

I smiled. "That was a poetic image."

"You don't agree." A statement not a question.

"I don't *disagree*," I said. "But you have to understand, I walk the path of the Fire Sword. I've taken vows and live those vows. Anything that would make me stop or even hesitate–I just can't allow."

He rolled his lips in and nodded his head. "You've completed your mission."

"Yes." It was as simple as that. All that thought and pain and action, but once the boat moved away from its moorings, I was done until the Fates called me into action again. The sailors gave me a nod to indicate it was time to set sail, then bent to untie the planks. "You have to go."

"Ember..."

I felt it too. We'd started something. The kindling was lit. But fire took fuel and oxygen. "I don't know how to make this work. We can communicate through the fires, but you have an enormous learning curve ahead of you."

"And you have to save the world."

I smiled at that.

His eyes searched mine for more. I wanted to give him that *more*, but I couldn't fathom how.

He reached into his shirt and pulled a golden chain; from it hung a ring. I recognized it immediately. It was a fire opal. "My mother's," he said. "She left it under my pillow the night she died. I've worn it ever since, a sentimental gesture if anyone asked, but I always thought of it as a talisman. It's given me a modicum of peace, a sense of connection. It caught at me when you said your ring was missing and that it was a family heirloom. Funny how I didn't put the two together. In my mind, I recognized the importance of having that family link because that's what this ring meant to me." He held the delicate gold ring with the small oval stone. He kissed it. "Will you wear my ring and remember me until I can come back to you?"

"Crispin, I… it's your mother's ring. If I were to be killed—" I stopped instantly as pain washed over his face. I was used to the dangers, they were part of my everyday world. He was not. "What are you asking from me with this ring? My missions cannot be restricted by a bond. It's a magical ring; if I take it, I am in agreement. A spell will be cast."

"First, you would agree that there is no covenant between us that would make your missions more difficult or dangerous because of me. Second, you will know that the place of belonging that I tried unartfully to explain to you is my truth, and if you agree and the Fates will allow, I would like our relationship to grow. And third—I need a third, don't I? Some kind of power belongs to the number three?"

I nodded.

"Third, I would ask that you know that every day I'm working hard to get back to you and fight by your side. And I ask in return you do everything in your power to stay safe for my return."

I pulled my ring from my hand. "I ask in return that you find and follow your path, knowing that I will understand if or when you ask for your ring back."

His body jerked, and he shook his head.

I lifted my brow to still him, so I could finish. "That you will train very hard and come back as quickly as possible so that we can fight side by side. And thirdly, that you will know that I meant my words, too, when I said that a "belonging" felt like the right word."

He silently slid his mother's ring onto my finger. I wasn't surprised at all that it fit perfectly. I slid my ring onto his chain and stood on my tiptoes, leaning into him as I fastened the clasp around his neck, kissed my ring, and tucked it next to his heart.

My lips found his, and we kissed goodbye, only to be interrupted by the ah-hem of the sailor. "We have to push off now, ma'am."

Crispin walked up the planks onto the deck. He stood at the railing, his hand raised in salute.

"We'll meet in the ether." My heart squeezed down. I wasn't sure I'd ever see him again in the flesh, but I called out hopefully, "I'll see you in the flames."

This is not THE END

Look for the next book in the Elemental Witch Series

Readers, I hope you enjoyed getting to know Ember McGraw. If you had fun reading Resistance, I'd appreciate it if you'd help others enjoy it too.

Recommend it: Just a few words to your friends, your book groups, and your social networks would be wonderful.

Review it: Please tell your fellow readers what you liked about my book by reviewing Resistance on Amazon and Goodreads. If you do write a review, please send me a note at FionaQuinnBooks@outlook.com so I can thank you with a personal e-mail. Or stop by my website FionaQuinnBooks.com to keep up with my news and chat through my contact form.

Let's stay in touch!

For new release notifications, free offers, gifts, and sneak peeks for members only, please sign up for our Fiona Quinn mailing list. We don't want to leave you out of the fun!

Join Fiona Quinn's newsletter at FionaQuinnBooks.com

Also:

@FionaQuinnBooks on Twitter

Fiona Quinn Books on Facebook

Join my Fiona Quinn's Street Force on Facebook – a street team and ARC team.

Fiona Quinn Books on Pinterest

USA Today Bestselling Author, Fiona Quinn is now rooted in the Old Dominion outside of DC. There, she pops chocolates, devours books, and taps continuously on her laptop.

Copyright

Fiona Angelica Quinn

Fiona Angelica Quinn

www.ingramcontent.com/pod-product-compliance
Lightning Source LLC
Chambersburg PA
CBHW032241010726
47494CB00002B/573